Passionate Pursuit

Dangerous Desires

Tina Donahue

LYRICAL PRESS
Kensington Publishing Corp.
www.kensingtonbooks.com

Lyrical Press books are published by
Kensington Publishing Corp. 119 West 40th Street New York, NY 10018

First Electronic Edition: August 2016
eISBN-13: 978-1-60183-591-8
eISBN-10: 1-60183-591-4

First Print Edition: August 2016
ISBN-13: 978-1-60183-592-5
ISBN-10: 1-60183-592-2

Printed in the United States of America

To the wonderful authors at Sweet 'n Sexy Divas.

Author's Foreword

The moment I was old enough to realize there was a difference between males and females, I've been an avowed feminist. As I was growing up, my most frequent question to my parents was – "How come he gets to do that and I can't?" I was speaking of my older brother.

Researching women's lives in fifteenth century Spain was a revelation. Although women of that period had few rights, many amazing ladies challenged authority and changed the world. Beatriz's story shows how spirited a woman can be in the most adverse situations. Tomás proves that a real man wants a strong woman who can stand beside him.

Is their passion strong enough to break her chains?

Andalucía Spain, 1489: Innocent Beatriz is desperate to escape the threat of a miserable marriage to a cruel Marquis. Forced into the betrothal by her ruthless merchant papá, her only hope is to conceal her identity and become a servant in a nearby castle—a life drastically different from her comfortable upbringing.

Tomás doesn't know what to make of his well-spoken new servant girl. Her beauty and charm captivates the military hero; her mysterious nature intrigues him. And the desire she ignites burns brighter with each glance, as does his longing to claim her for his own.

Beatriz can't resist Tomás' passion nor deny the heat of her own. But neither the lush countryside nor the walls of the opulent Moorish castle can entirely protect her—and if he were to discover her secret, she could be torn away from him forever. Yet how can she sustain his love if she's living a lie?

Visit us at www.kensingtonbooks.com

Books by Tina Donahue

Dangerous Desires Series
Loving Lies
Wicked Whispers
Passionate Pursuit

Published by Kensington Publishing Corporation

Acknowledgements

To Penny Barber for her wise and always accurate suggestions.

Chapter 1

Andalucía, Spain—1489
The castle of Tomás de Zayas

The siege had begun. Not from bloodthirsty Moors. Oh, no. Tomás de Zayas would have welcomed such a prospect. He'd fought Spain's enemies with ruthless determination during his service to the Crown. Those battles were frequently grisly, but the conflicts had always ended. What he'd face in the coming hours however...

Two carriages approached his estate. The first of many, less than half a league apart, wheels kicking up dust clouds within the heavily vegetated land. Inside each conveyance was a scheming mamá and daughter with naught but marriage on their minds with him the unwilling suitor.

His gut churned. He refused to budge from the parapet until dragged away.

If only he could fly from his castle as jackdaws were doing, their wings outstretched on the mild breeze, sweet scents beckoning. Several birds dipped to spring flowers and lush vegetation shaded from the heavy sun. He longed to ride past the scene, laughing, loving...with the right woman.

The dark-haired beauty he craved was hopelessly out of reach.

He gripped the stone, despising circumstances, dreading the arriving females.

He'd held them off for months, declining invitations to countless gatherings. The mamás had persisted with endless requests to visit his estate, claiming they and their daughters wanted to see how he was doing after his brush with death.

He was hearty as ever and wanted to enjoy life again, though not with them. The woman he desired was already here.

Heat, unbidden and insistent, rushed through him.

"Here you are," Nuncio said.

Just what he didn't need. His manservant. An ancient fellow who'd been with the de Zayas family well before Tomás's birth. Despite Nuncio's sixty years, the man held himself as erect as a Spanish knight. While his bearing and white hair gave him a courtly appearance, his casual manner was more intrusive uncle than groveling servant.

Nuncio arched a bushy white eyebrow at Tomás's goblet.

Gleefully, he finished his wine, wanting more to fortify himself against the coming hours.

Clattering horse hooves and wheels quieted.

The first carriage had arrived. Mother and daughter left their conveyance, chattering endlessly. Their voices rang with excitement. Their silly giggles grated.

According to his brother, Enrique, and sister-in-law, Sancha, this was Tomás's proper future, with someone from his own world. His wayward passion for a woman not of his station couldn't amount to anything, ever, except trouble and heartache.

He slumped against the railing.

"Are you planning to throw yourself off?" Nuncio sighed tiredly. "Should I be alarmed?"

He would be when Tomás tossed him off the side. "You should do your duty and see to my desires." He held out his goblet. "I need more wine."

Nuncio remained planted to the spot, wrinkled hands folded in front, striking a lord of the manor pose. "Your guests might believe otherwise."

The carriage and footmen were off to the side, the women nowhere in sight. Presumably, mother and daughter were within the castle, waiting for what they believed would be a private visit with him.

Pity that.

He offered a pleased smile. "As they have no regard for my feelings, I hardly care what they think. If you remember, I politely declined their requests to come here, until you hounded me about my indifference to their marriage plans with me as their grudging victim. Now, I have a chance to tell the mamás I have no intention of wedding any of their daughters."

"By gathering all of them here at the same time."

"Clever, no?"

"Some might say reckless, considering their families are your political allies, though they may not be after today."

Tomás waved away Nuncio's comment. "Better to get this over with at one time rather than dragging the matter out through countless visits. Besides, my public declaration will keep gossip to a minimum. None of the women will be able to say I rejected any señorita because of her shrill laugh, slow wit, poor shape, or dull converse. They were all equally lacking."

Nuncio looked heavenward. He might have even started to pray.

Tomás gritted his teeth. "Equally lacking in my desire for them. Never fear, I shall be unfailingly polite and let each lady know how wonderful she is. More beautiful than stars sparkling in the night sky, more promising than the hint of spring after a brutal winter, more—"

"Forgive me for interrupting, but one would hope they would still be listening at that point." He squared his narrow shoulders. "Cook prepared a feast for your guests. If any of them have an appetite after your pretty speech, I propose we hide the knives. For your safety, of course."

"I can take care of myself. And I refuse to settle for less than what Enrique and Fernando have."

"You mean the families they started."

Not entirely. However, Isabella had given birth to her and Fernando's first child, a daughter. They named her Juana after Isabella's late mother. Sancha hadn't yet delivered. Given what Enrique had repeatedly said, he didn't care whether she bore him a son or a daughter. He simply wanted her and the child's health and happiness.

Nuncio cleared his throat delicately. "If I may be so bold…"

"You will be, anyway. Get on with it."

"Very well. If you seek children, I advise you wed first as your brothers had."

"They fought for the women they wanted. Neither let convention get in his way."

"Your brothers wed women from their own backgrounds."

"They fell in love with them first and overcame numerous obstacles to be at their sides even though none were originally meant to be together. Have you forgotten Fernando's betrothal to Sancha was long before she married Enrique instead? What about Isabella pretending to be Sancha and wedding Fernando before he knew the difference between the two sisters? Despite such chaos, all are blissfully happy now."

"Miracles do happen, though in your case you best not hope for one."

Tomás shoved his hair back from where the wind had blown it. "As the youngest son, who I end up with, or if I end up with anyone, is of no consequence. Enrique inherits everything from Papá. Building upon the family dynasty is his duty. I can do as I please."

Nuncio looked off into the distance, his expression suddenly a mask, though the lines in his face seemed to have deepened. "Is this about Beatriz?"

Tomás's heart slammed into his chest. Lightheaded, he gripped the stone for support and pretended to drink from his empty goblet, since he was unable and unwilling to answer. Above, a jackdaw cried out. Below, wheels rattled against stone, announcing more guests. Three carriages drew near.

He wanted to run. His legs were too leaden to work properly. "Where is she?"

Nuncio shook his head.

Frustration oiled Tomás's limbs, allowing him movement. Fist clenched, he approached, prepared to thrash Nuncio to get an answer.

He stood his ground and kept his tongue.

Tomás crowded him further. "Answer me. Where is she?"

"Seeing to her tasks as the other servants are doing."

And would most likely finish her work before Nuncio offered anything more than he had. "Inform my guests I shall be delayed slightly."

"You plan to clean up a bit? Excellent. I suggest your dark green robe and doublet. The blue you have on hardly does you justice. As to your hose, one in peach, the other in white will work far better than the striped ones you chose. You should also have a shave."

Tomás slapped his goblet into Nuncio's palm and hurried down the steps, his shoes ringing on the stone. On the next level, he rushed through the castle once owned by a Moor, the same as Fernando's castle had been. Their service to the Crown had won them the reconquered estates. Although Tomás's new home was far smaller than Fernando's and certainly Enrique's, he still had to search numerous halls and countless rooms for Beatriz.

He wanted to see her. No. He needed to. A compulsion he couldn't seem to resist despite her being a servant. A matter important to Nuncio, Enrique, and Sancha, with them advising Tomás not to take advantage of his position and Beatriz, since a dalliance between them could lead nowhere.

He was well aware of the perils and hadn't done anything except watch her whenever he could.

She was remarkably different from his other servants, her air, manner, and speech refined. Intelligence shone in her eyes. She even seemed able to read. Weeks ago, he'd come upon her tidying his study. She'd regarded the book spines at length, the way one would when considering titles. Surprising and odd. If she were educated, he couldn't imagine why she'd willingly spend her days here in endless drudgery.

When he'd asked his housekeeper about her, Señora Cisneros said Beatriz came from one of the many villages Tomás owned and that she needed work to support her ailing mother. He hadn't bothered to check out the story, sensing Beatriz might have an ill parent, which drove her to seek work here. As to the other part of her background... Deep inside, he sensed she hadn't come from any village.

Not that he cared whether he was right or not.

Seeing her again, settling his overwhelming desire was his only goal. Today, he could compare Beatriz to the other women and determine if his desire for her was only a passing whim. Once he'd had another look at her, he might be able to dismiss his feelings as mere fantasy and have peace at last.

Where had she gone?

He strode toward the first hall and the bedchambers, this area open and airy, his face warmed by sun spilling through arched windows that stretched from floor to ceiling. Rays glinted off intricate Moorish mosaics, flashing blue, yellow, green, and red, turning the stone columns and floors milky and bright. He squinted.

Upon reaching the chambers, he checked room after room, each filled with rich wall hangings and Spanish furniture, the dark wood and leather carved with ornate designs. Every chamber was spotless and duly aired to smell quite fresh. Also empty. With only two more rooms to go, he sensed Beatriz might be elsewhere in the castle, tending to those rooms.

No matter. He'd run her down in time.

After a quick check of the remaining chambers, he turned.

Beatriz stood across the hall, holding linens heaped in a basket.

His mouth went dry.

Despite her red gown, white tunic, and linen cap, the same livery his other female servants wore, she might as well have been a queen.

She was certainly beautiful enough. Her skin was paler than most, the color of a fine pearl, features delicate, light brown eyes lushly lashed and softened with what appeared to be need.

His chest tightened, breathing became difficult, the air too thick suddenly.

Her plush lips, pink as an Andalucían dawn, parted in what seemed to be an invitation.

Everything grew quiet. Colors and the surrounding area faded into the background, leaving nothing except her to feast on. Dewy skin, sensuous mouth, full breasts, lush hips.

His shaft thickened and grew hard, craving her heated sheath damp with her excitement.

His for the taking. He merely had to cross the small space separating them.

The distance seemed wider than the ocean with too many warnings bombarding him. Sancha's advice that he not ruin Beatriz, leaving her few options for marriage to a respectable man. Enrique warning about the child Tomás would eventually sire with her. Nuncio's repeated admonitions about her peasant background that wouldn't allow them a future together no matter how much Tomás may have wanted one.

He shouldn't have sought her out. His plan to dismiss any feelings he'd had failed miserably. He wanted her far more than earlier.

He tipped his head. "*Buenas tardes.*"

Pink bloomed in her cheeks. Her eyes cleared, no longer dreamy or aroused. She stepped back.

The distance between them was already too great. She didn't need to add to it. Although he understood her prudence, he hated that they had to resist their desire.

"Buenas tardes, *Patrón.*" She propped the basket on her hip and retreated two steps.

In another moment, she might bolt.

He prayed not yet. "Are the linens too heavy?" He wanted to help, needed to be near. "Do you want me to carry them?"

She shook her head, dark, silky tendrils dancing near to her cheeks.

He ached to wind the strands around his fingers and ease her closer. "Are you quite certain?"

She gripped the basket hard enough to make her knuckles white. "I can see to my duties. I can work all day and night if necessary."

"Have you ever needed to do so in order to finish?"

"No." Beatriz frowned, then made her face a mask, the kind servants show a master, leaving the poor fool no way to know what they thought. "I finish my tasks quickly. Without problems."

"How wonderful." He stepped in her way before she could get around him. "How is your mother doing? Does she need a potion or poultice?"

She stared, color draining.

Why? He only wanted to help. "Señora Cisneros mentioned your mamá's troubles in passing. How sad I am for you and her. However, I know a physician who may be able to make things better. Tell me the symptoms and I can bring you what she needs."

No matter what ailed the woman, Sancha could prepare a remedy. She was a healer. When Tomás had fallen ill at the *fortaleza*, she'd saved his life. A dangerous matter for her because of the Inquisition, which led to accusations claiming she was a witch. Thankfully, he, Enrique, and their brothers had handled the matter, leaving her free to practice healing in secret.

Beatriz hefted the basket and settled the thing more firmly on her hip.

"Those linens are too heavy for you." He grabbed them.

She held on.

Surely, she didn't think she'd win against him. He was a head taller, nearly twice her weight, and far stronger.

He tugged.

She let go.

He locked his knees to keep from staggering back at the weight. Far too cumbersome for such a delicate flower as her. He'd have to talk with Señora Cisneros about Beatriz's future duties.

Rather than offering a sweet smile for his help, she bit her lip.

Tenderness welled within him, along with unruly desire. "No reason to be afraid. Your position is safe. I merely want to help. Tell me what ails your mamá."

"Nothing at the moment. She recovered fully from her latest illness. I must get back to work." She reached for the linens.

He kept them away. "Is my housekeeper demanding too much even with you willing to work day and night?"

"Señora Cisneros is a lovely woman."

She had a mustache, hairs on her chin, weighed more than two women combined, and owned a high-pitched voice that set his teeth on edge. However, she did keep the castle running smoothly without being too overbearing. "I find her efficient in a slightly masculine way. Is that what you meant?"

Beatriz's mouth curled up, though she didn't allow herself to smile.

Making her laugh meant everything to Tomás without him understanding why. "Do you promise not to tell her I said such a thing?"

She gripped her skirt. "We rarely speak. Work keeps us busy."

"So you do promise. Wonderful." He grinned and lifted the basket to his shoulder, showing off his strength. "Where did you plan to take this? I can bring the linens to whatever room you—"

Loud throat clearing flowed down the hall.

Either Señora Cisneros or Nuncio had just entered from behind. Hard to tell which, since they both made the same noises when displeased with the help. He looked over.

Nuncio.

Beatriz pulled the basket from Tomás with surprising strength, though she did totter.

"Careful." He reached for her.

She twisted away.

Nuncio cleared his throat once more.

Tomás frowned at him. "Did you inform the guests of my delay?"

"Several times. They still await your presence. Every one of them in the same room."

Surely without knives if Nuncio had anything to say. Tomás gentled his mood for Beatriz. "If your mamá should fall ill again, please tell me. I can help."

Her attention remained on Nuncio.

Wanting to speak softly to her, Tomás leaned closer, catching her seductive fragrance, freshly washed clothes and clean skin. He reeled, finding speech difficult. "If Nuncio rails at you for keeping me here, let me know. I shall thrash him soundly."

Laughter bubbled from her, which she quelled without pause.

Her joy, no matter how brief, was a balm for everything wrong with today. How marvelous if they, at least, became friends, speaking freely, laughing, enjoying themselves. An odd notion for any man when faced with such a delectable woman. However, he didn't see many other options at this point.

He strode to Nuncio. "Shall we go?" Halfway down the hall, Tomás spoke. "Make certain the ladies' carriages, drivers, and footmen are ready to depart. I trust no one will be staying long once I give my speech."

"As you wish. Whatever you wish. Whenever you wish."

Tomás rolled his eyes. If wishes were his for the asking, he'd still be speaking to Beatriz, inviting her to ride the grounds with him, having a late supper with her on the hillside overlooking his estate, finally carrying her into his chamber for some much-needed passion with them discovering wondrous things about each other.

He surely wouldn't be facing women who might want to harm him once they understood he had no intention of wedding anyone.

* * * *

Beatriz González y Serrano sat on a guest bed when she shouldn't have. She should bolt from the estate and Tomás.

Her legs wouldn't support her. If she left, she might not be able to secure work at another estate. No one in the villages would hire a house servant to toil in the fields. Even the children would fare better than she at the backbreaking labor. The few merchants in town would do the work themselves or have family to help. Returning to the city was far too dangerous unless she wanted to live out her life imprisoned by a man she loathed who'd use her in the vilest ways possible.

Hopeless, she did the only thing she could, savoring the few moments she'd spent with Tomás. Magical and enticing snatches of time that shouldn't have happened.

She hadn't meant for him to see her, prepared to duck into a room so he'd never know she'd spied on him. His purpose in searching bedchambers hadn't occurred to her. She'd been too taken with his size and promise of the warrior he was, all lean muscle and man. Too many nights she'd dreamed of her lips pressed to his rich mouth, fingers buried in his thick, blond hair, drowning in his heat and strength.

Her nipples tightened, the tips hard enough to sting. The soft folds between her legs were damp and ready for him. A nobleman with countless women who wanted to share his life and bed, each desiring his looks, wealth, and position.

She adored his gentle teasing. How easily he'd made her smile and laugh, despite her caution and lies.

She buried her face in her hands, ashamed at what she'd said about her mamá. When he'd brought up her supposed illness, Beatriz hadn't recalled telling Señora Cisneros about an ailing mother in order to secure a position here.

Tomás seemed to believe her falsehood. Unless he'd pretended with her as she had with him.

Shoes slapped against stone. She pushed to her feet and froze.

Nuncio stood in the doorway, taking in the scene.

Quickly, she smoothed the bright red counterpane where she'd sat. "I was just finishing here."

"You were sitting. I saw you." He closed the door and approached.

Fearing the worst, she backed away. "I can work an extra hour or two to make up for the few seconds I sat on the bed. I can go without food for the rest of the day. I can—"

"Your silence is all I ask. And for you to listen to me. Do you think you can do such a thing?"

She didn't want to hear anything he had to say but nodded readily.

Nuncio folded his hands behind his back and paced, his tapping shoes sounding horribly loud.

"Don Tomás is our master." He stopped and glared. "He never carries linens."

"No. I mean, I agree."

"Then why was he holding your basket?"

"He wanted to help."

"Were you bent over from the weight of the linens? Had you fallen because the basket was too heavy? Could you not breathe? Were you in danger of swooning or dying?"

"No. Of course not." Forgetting herself, she frowned.

Nuncio narrowed his eyes.

She hid her feelings as any intimidated servant would. "I had no trouble with the work. I was merely standing in the hall when he came upon me and offered to assist."

Nuncio inhaled deeply but didn't argue the point as she'd expected. Surely that couldn't mean Tomás was wont to help all servants when seeing them in hallways.

"You should have told him you were busy." He straightened even more. "Then went on your way."

"I tried. He blocked me."

Nuncio frowned hard, making terrible dents in his face.

She wanted them gone. Him too. "Don Tomás merely asked about my mother's health. I told him she recovered. Everything is fine." She grabbed her basket. "I should go back to work."

He approached more quickly than his age should have allowed and stood between her and the door. "You must stay away from our master. If you see him, go in the other direction. If he comes upon you, do not smile sweetly. I know you can as I saw the one you gave him. Forget that. Move to another area in the castle even if you have to leave your work. Never fear, I will have a word with Señora Cisneros, letting her know if you fail to finish your duties, the fault is not yours. Do you understand me?"

All too well. If she'd been in another position than the one she was currently in, she would have laughed in his face and gone after Tomás on her own. Given her precarious situation, she could only agree. "*Sí.*"

"About Rufio."

He was also a house servant, close to her age. His duties took place in the kitchen or dining hall, not the chambers as hers did. "What about him?"

Nuncio observed her carefully. "I see how he is when the two of you are near. Make certain you never encourage him."

She bristled. "I never have or will. I keep my distance from him and all the men."

"Make certain you continue to do so, especially with our master."

"Does Don Tomás behave with the other female servants as he has with me?"

Nuncio remained turned away but did look over. "His habits are not yours to know."

"Did you tell those servants the same?" Did those women obey and stay away from him?

On a loud sigh, Nuncio faced her. "The monarchs granted Don Tomás this land quite recently. Before that, he was away for years fighting the Moors. I have no idea what he did at the fortaleza. This castle is my only concern."

Then Tomás hadn't behaved with the others as he had with her, or Nuncio would have said so, warning her what became of those women. Beatriz's spirits soared until she recalled her and Tomás's impossible situation. Hopeless because of their positions, as long as she remained a servant and never revealed her past. There was also Nuncio's dogged determination to protect Tomás from himself.

Nuncio opened the door.

She joined him. "One last thing."

He regarded her warily and closed the door. "What?"

"Even if I flee every time I see Don Tomás, what do I do if he follows and catches me?"

Nuncio gave her a cold stare. "If he does, your days at the castle are over. I should make you leave this second, seeing the trouble you could cause. However, I know Don Tomás far better than you ever will. If anyone stands in the way of what he believes he wants, he craves it even more, making everyone as miserable as he is. Long ago, I learned to let him reach the proper conclusion on his own, which he always does. Therefore, you may remain here unless you force my hand by making yourself available to him on purpose or accidentally. The burden to avoid any trouble is upon you. No one else."

He left without a backward glance.

Chapter 2

Tomás entered the parlor, prepared to do battle. Ten señoritas, ten mamás rushed him. He backed up. Too late. Despite their silks gowns, cloying perfumes, and sparkling jewels, they surrounded him like hungry beasts in the wild, everyone speaking at once.

"How are you, dear Tomás?"

"Your color is excellent, but perhaps you should sit."

"Here, take my arm. I can lead you to a bench."

"No, take mine."

"Why yours? I asked him first."

He stood between the arguing young women before they came to blows. "Sit. Please. I have something to say once you do."

The mamás hurried to the carved wooden benches and box chairs, tugging their daughters with them. The señoritas were young, most lovely, all educated, and trained to please a husband in every possible manner, to bear his sons willingly and with great frequency as duty demanded. To remain at his side for a lifetime whether he desired that or not.

Sweat trickled down his back. He wanted to flee. "As you know, I battled the Moors for many years."

"How brave you are, dear Tomás."

"No man has an equal."

"You are a warrior among warriors."

A stout countess worked her jeweled fan. "My daughter and I thank you for your kind service to God and Spain. Now, you must see to the rest of your life."

He shifted his weight. "About that. Given my many battles and then my illness, I need to adjust to my role here."

The women exchanged glances.

"I need to relax." He strode to the right, the left, unable to keep still. "Marriage is a huge and sacred undertaking. As dear to everyone as the monarchs' desire to conquer Granada and the Moors. No one should make such life decisions lightly. I cannot and will not. I need time to do things right. Solitude in the coming months, perhaps years, will give me a chance to think, plan, and eventually move forward with my life. Until then, I regret being unavailable."

Finished, he steeled himself for shrieks, perhaps curses. Hopefully, they'd then leave his castle so he could find Beatriz again to tease and laugh.

The women stared, none railing or departing. Their sniffling soon filled the spacious parlor. More than one dissolved into tears.

They couldn't be that desperate for a union with him. Surely, there were other victims for them to run down.

"You poor man." A viscount's wife pressed her hand between her ample breasts. "How greatly you suffered."

The other mamás nodded and elbowed their daughters. The señoritas raced across the Persian rugs toward him. One touched his arm, the other his shoulder, another his wrist. All daubed their eyes with dainty pieces of linen decorated with lace and embroidered with flowers.

He edged away.

As one, the young women pursued until he ran into a large wall hanging. Trapped, he prayed for escape. The señoritas colorful gowns were too bright, the reds, blues, greens, yellows, making his head ache. Their faces swam before him, their eyes widened in worry, mouths trembling.

Zita glanced around the room. "Someone call a servant."

As a boy, Tomás had run into Zita at numerous gatherings. When her parents and his had stopped keeping an eye on them to enjoy themselves, he and Zita had shared as many steamy kisses as they could.

Ines stroked his thumb.

He eased his hand away. "Why?"

Ines looked at him quizzically. "Why what?"

"Does Zita need a servant?"

"To pull a chair over for you. Unless you would prefer me to lead you to one." Zita offered an indulgent smile. "So you may rest, poor man." She stroked his other thumb and winked.

He cringed inwardly.

The young women chattered without pause about his health and need to rest. Each agreed with everything he'd told them earlier. Curiously, no one mentioned the months or years he'd require before wedding

Tina Donahue

anyone. Their mamás watched closely, smiling or frowning at their daughters' behavior.

A sharp rap on the door interrupted the scene, saving him. He hoped. He shouted above the others, "Come in."

Nuncio slipped inside, his expression neutral, as a servant's should be. His eyes however...

The old devil enjoyed Tomás's pain.

"Forgive me for interrupting."

He didn't sound sorry in the least.

"Refreshments are served." Nuncio threw open the door and gestured to the dining hall.

Inez placed her hand on Tomás's left forearm for him to lead her to their meal. "You must eat well to keep up your strength."

He prayed she wouldn't feed him each bite to make certain he'd had enough.

Zita rested her hand on his right forearm. "Our family cook has many wonderful recipes, hearty dishes to keep a man strong, preparing him for anything." She winked again. "I can share them with you later."

Before he could decline, everyone spoke at once.

Tomás plodded toward the dining hall, a lamb going to slaughter. Trunks lined the castle entrance. Surely, these women hadn't planned to spend the night, or worse, the entire week. Staying until they'd worn him down, much like the monarchs' battle plan against the Moors.

He would have given anything to be in an armed conflict now. Queen Isabella had relocated the Castilian court to Jaen on Granada's border. There she'd wait, while Spain's invading army pushed toward their enemy with a legion of fifteen thousand men on horseback and eighty thousand on foot, the force led by King Ferdinand.

That meet Tomás would readily enjoy.

This though...

Given what Cook had prepared, the meal might never end. Roasted fowl, pork, mutton, and beef filled one table in the cavernous dining hall, capable of accommodating a hundred men and certainly twenty women.

He dragged to his place at the head of the long table designed to seat thirty.

Inez directed a servant to pull out a chair for him, as one would for a man more decrepit than Nuncio.

Tomás wrested the chair from the female servant who was as broad as Señora Cisneros. "I need no assistance."

"Strong men never do." Zita waved away the aged servant she'd called over.

Tomás waited for the ladies to sit.

Galina, a duke's third daughter, and Damaris, a count's fifth child, glared at each other. They'd chosen the same chair, two down from his, with Zita and Ines having claimed those closest to where he would sit.

Before the young woman tore hair or clothing, Tomás gestured to the chair across from them. "Damaris, sit over there."

She scowled. Her mother pinched her arm. Damaris's frown transformed to a sweet smile. "Of course."

She rammed her shoulder into Galina's. The other señoritas knocked elbows and stepped on each other's toes, accidentally or on purpose, while they gained their seats, then daintily allowed the servants to push them toward the table.

Nuncio marched to Tomás side and leaned in. "Is all well?"

"Trunks are in the entrance hall. Why?"

"Many of your guests traveled great distances to be here."

They should have stayed away. Now that they'd arrived, they should leave quickly for their own castles or someone else's before nightfall. "How long will they be here?"

"As long as they wish. Remember, their families are your allies."

Tomás had never experienced such vulnerability or aching loneliness. He sank to his seat and turned at a flash of red.

Beatriz.

No. Another servant, whose name he couldn't recall, her face, form, and manner equally forgettable. He sagged into his chair and gestured for Nuncio to lean down to him.

Nuncio spoke quietly. "Whatever you want me to say to get rid of them, you should reconsider. I am not a good liar. I advise you to stay and face your guests. If you run, they will follow."

He already knew as much. "What servants work in here today?"

"Why?"

Tomás clenched his jaw.

Nuncio sighed. "Those you already see."

He waved Nuncio away. If Beatriz worked in the dining hall, she'd be here daily, during meals. Tomás wouldn't have to hope to run into her while she tended the chambers or wait endlessly until she dusted his study.

A talk with Señora Cisneros about Beatriz's duties would easily change matters.

* * * *

Beatriz dusted a second floor windowsill overlooking an expansive lawn. Mulberry and cork trees bordered the clearing, along with countless flowers in an array of types and colors. White carnations, bluebells, roses, red-and-white striped lilies. Their exquisite scents perfumed the air.

At any other time, she might have smiled at the beauty. Not today.

A gentle breeze carried laughter and converse from the señoritas who surrounded Tomás, each vying for his attention. The one in dark green silk with a matching caul danced around trying to get closer to him. The one in red with a white flower in her hair elbowed past another girl. Those in gold and bright yellow were even less demure, pushing into each other, speaking loudly, far removed from how a lowly servant had to act.

Especially to please Nuncio.

How dare he make her solely responsible for a man's carnal moves? Beatriz had no control over anyone's passion except her own. Thus far, she'd failed miserably at quelling her desires.

Despite what Nuncio had said, she still ached to feel Tomás's heat and strength, to have him imprison and possess her. No threat in the world would change her longing. However, she wasn't foolish enough to act on her attraction. Poor man already had enough trouble.

His broad shoulders were slumped, mouth turned down. She wanted to make him smile. To have him stand as the noble lord he was, magnificent in his dark blue robe and doublet, his hose snug to his sinewy thighs and calves.

Several young women spoke to him at once. A señorita in a bright yellow gown touched his upper arm. The girl next to her, clad in vivid orange silk, touched his jaw.

Jealousy heated Beatriz's face and throat.

Tomás drew back until the young woman groped air, not him. He faced the window, his gaze touching Beatriz, his dark brown eyes flooding with warmth, bronze complexion deepening.

Weak with desire, she leaned against the sill for support.

The señoritas gestured to him, talking endlessly, their words too garbled to understand.

Whatever they said, Tomás ignored them. He studied Beatriz's eyes, then her lips and lingered there. She was smiling without realizing it. He answered with a broad grin and stepped closer.

A young woman gripped his sleeve and tugged him away. He gave her a hard frown.

Beatriz leaned forward to catch what else he'd do, and her hand slid off the polished stone. Startled, she jerked back and dropped her cloth.

The linen drifted on the breeze, coming to rest on a fat bush, marring the area's perfection.

No, no, no, no. She willed the air to blow the cloth behind the vegetation to hide the stupid thing.

The linen stuck there, flapping in the breeze for everyone to see. Particularly Nuncio who might guess she'd spied on Tomás.

The señoritas babbled loudly. Two held his hands, pulling him across the lawn. He looked back at Beatriz several times, his expression yearning.

She would have leaned out the window to keep him in sight but feared falling to the ground. As it was, she needed to wait until he and the others left before risking a trip to retrieve her cloth.

When she could neither see nor hear them any longer, she left the window and froze.

Rufio blocked her. Of average height, he had broad shoulders, powerful arms, and large hands, perfect for hauling heavy trays to the dining hall or meal sacks and animal carcasses to the kitchen. Although he was a handsome young man, she found his attention off-putting. Since she'd arrived at the castle, he'd haunted her every move.

He smiled slyly. "Better not let old Nuncio catch you spying on our betters."

She warned herself not to show any reaction he could use against her. "What are you doing in here?"

"Talking to you." He edged closer, danger in his black eyes, hard lust in his expression.

Her pulse jumped. She couldn't run with naught but the window behind her even though flight was her duty in order to save men from their vile natures. If she didn't accomplish such a worthy goal, Nuncio would toss her out in a second, smiling evilly. She lifted her chin and made certain to show no fear. "Step aside."

"Why?"

"I need to get back to work, the same as you."

"No one will miss me for some time." He glanced at the bed.

Disgusted, she slammed her hands on his chest and pushed.

He flailed his arms to right himself. Once he had, he was still in her way, not giving an inch.

"Stop following me." She spoke quietly to avoid anyone overhearing. "Nuncio is on to you."

"What if he is? Means nothing except we have to be more careful. We can do all sorts of things without him ever knowing. Same as the other servants."

Not her. Never with him. He was too careless with his passion, too crude. He'd made it quite clear she meant nothing to him except as a warm body to ease his lust. The same as the man she'd escaped from. "That will never happen between us."

He glared and crowded her. "You too high and mighty for such things or too good for me?"

His anger alarmed Beatriz more than his base desire. He seemed the sort who'd exact revenge if anyone dared mock him, whether the insult was genuine or only in his mind.

"You misunderstand. I need this work to support my mother. Nuncio has his eye on me already. I have to take care."

"Why would he worry about you? He attends to Don Tomás's affairs, not…" Sudden understanding registered in Rufio's eyes. "He caught you trying to seduce our master."

She forced herself not to react. "Why would Don Tomás ever notice a mere servant? Nuncio caught me sitting in a chamber. I was resting when I had no right. Since then, he hounds me, showing up without warning. I need to watch my step."

Rufio's grin returned. "Not with me."

She wanted to scream. "If anyone finds the cloth I dropped outside, I could be dismissed."

"Let me fetch the thing for you. Once I do—"

"No." She inched past him, praying he wouldn't touch her. "I have no intention of putting you at risk. Please, return to your duties before Señora Cisneros or Nuncio asks where you are."

Beatriz bolted from the room and down the hall.

* * * *

Tomás slumped in his chair. A lone candle barely illuminated his desk, leaving his study in shadows. The hour was late, moon high, silvery rays bleeding around the window screen. His guests were finally in their bedchambers, asleep or devising plans to trap him.

He hardly cared anymore. To have these few seconds without them was a relief, though he didn't want to be alone, and wouldn't be for long if history proved him correct.

He relaxed as much as he could, waiting, wanting.

Light tapping sounded in the hall. Beatriz's footfalls, as he'd expected.

Each workday before retiring, she came to his study to dust and straighten up. At least he supposed that's what she did in here. He'd always waited in another chamber to hear her leave. Once she had, he'd return, hoping to catch her clean scent.

Sometimes he did. Most often, he did not.

Knowing her schedule, he took to straightening up before she arrived, hoping to ease her burden so she could go to bed sooner. Even with his efforts, she often spent close to an hour in here. Perhaps curled up in his chair, napping, because she preferred his study to the servant quarters or she might have simply roamed the room, touching the fine leather, books, and other items she'd never have.

The silver door handle lowered. Tomás sat up. She slipped inside and closed them in, secluded from everyone else on earth.

He held his breath.

Candle and dust cloth in hand, she crossed the space, glanced his way, and stopped abruptly.

He smiled, aching to see her return his greeting the same as she had earlier at the window. What a moment. No riches or position could replace the desire, acceptance, and pure joy he'd seen on her lovely face then.

Gone now. She was back to being a servant, curious or cautious as to why he was in his own study at such an odd hour.

"Forgive me for startling you. I had things to do in here." He wasn't about to explain what they might be.

For him to admit he wanted to be her friend, as he'd considered earlier, would be reckless. She might laugh or think him mad. Best he approached the subject carefully. "Go on, tend to your duties." He lit five more candles so she could see easily. "If you need me to move from my desk, say the word. I shall obey your command immediately."

She lowered her face, though not before he caught her smile. His mood soared.

"I can return later." She pivoted.

He stood. "If you leave, so will I. Do you want to drive me from my work?"

She stopped, but didn't face him. "Never." After putting down her candle, she hurried to the bookcase and swiped at the shelves. "If you want me to stay, I will. Whatever you wish."

Ah, more wishes. Tomás sank back to his chair. If only she knew what he had in mind for them, past friendship, of course. Evenings, afternoons, and every morning filled with the most wanton delights, them naked, laughing, loving.

She looked over.

He grabbed a book from his desk and flipped a page. The moment she resumed her work, he turned the book right side up. He read the first line several times, not understanding a word, and gave up.

She dusted the bookshelf, removed a volume, scanned the other spines, then inserted the book she held in another location.

Where the text should have been from the start.

She'd done so effortlessly, without pause or forethought. The same as him, not an illiterate servant.

He considered the titles he had on the shelves. "You come in here every night you work, no?"

She nodded, her back still to him.

"I seem to have lost one of my volumes." He stated the title. "Have you seen the book in here? I looked earlier, but have yet to find the thing anywhere."

"Here it is." She pulled the edition off the shelf and had nearly reached him when she stopped, her face horrified at what she'd revealed.

Tomás wagged a finger playfully. "You can read. I thought so."

She put the book on his desk and backed away. "Only a few words. Titles mainly."

"Of Spanish history?" He gestured to the volume she'd brought to him. "And agriculture?" He pointed to the book she'd relocated on the shelf. "How odd you learned those things, not merely a few passages from the Bible as most would."

"I must return to my work."

"Wait. I insist."

She faced him but squared her shoulders, her stance surprisingly defiant.

He had no idea why. He wanted to talk to her, hopefully kiss her, not fight. "Who taught you to read? Your secret is safe. I promise never to tell anyone."

She certainly hadn't. At least not in this castle, since he would have heard about her skill from Nuncio in the most negative way possible. Odd that she'd keep such an ability hidden. Not that Tomás intended to question her. With her previous fight gone, she reminded him of a frightened doe, ready to dart away.

"Come." He pulled a box chair over and patted the leather seat. "Sit. Tell me about your teacher."

"I have nothing to tell. My father taught me before he passed."

"Your father from the same village where your mother resides?" All of them supposedly peasants, yet they knew how to read.

She twisted her cloth. "He was a baker with a small amount of money to his name. He loved to read and taught me the skill, even though I have no use for such things."

"Do you read in here after you dust?" Surely, books were what had kept her inside the room so long. "Tell me which volume you like best."

She made a sound somewhere between a whimper and a moan.

"I promise never to tell anyone. Come, sit. Talk to me."

"Will I still have my position here if I do?"

"Of course. Dust never goes away for long as you well know."

She laughed softly and sank into the chair, but remained perched on the edge.

"Go on and lean back." He gestured encouragement.

She remained where she was. "Señor Nuncio would rail at me if he saw this."

"Saw what?"

"Me sitting in one of your chairs."

"Better than the floor, no?"

She worked her mouth trying hard not to smile.

He wished she would. "I have no plans to tell Nuncio anything that might give him another gray hair, wrinkle, or push him closer to the grave. Do you?"

She laughed. "I think not. The volume I enjoy most is *Cantar del Mio Cid*."

Tomás couldn't have been more delighted. The epic poem detailed Rodrigo Díaz de Vivar's exploits during the early days of Spain's Reconquista. "The book is my favorite too. We can share his adventures together. Where did you stop in his tale? Wait. Have you finished the story?"

"Not at all. I was about to begin the part where El Cid plans to conquer Valencia."

"We shall do so together." He fetched the poem and offered the volume to her. "Read to me, please."

She took the book reluctantly. "I can only manage titles."

He laughed at her teasing, liking her ready wit, the way she already treated him as a friend. He brought over two candles to give her enough light. "Pretend every line is a title. Your duty now is to read to me."

"For how long? I still have to dust."

"After we finish with El Cid, I can help."

She laughed throatily.

"You doubt my ability?" He feigned insult. "How can you? I have the combined skill of three dozen servants, the stamina of twenty men, and the dedication of every zealot on earth."

"Someone should write an epic poem about you."

He laughed so hard his belly hurt, tears stinging his eyes. "Go on." He gestured. "Read."

She did, flawlessly, her skill as great as his, a nobleman. Or her father's, the baker.

Tomás had never met one educated in anything other than making bread, cakes, and such, along with having the most elementary knowledge of reading and mathematics to operate a business.

However, since he'd spent most of his days battling Moors, his understanding of those who lived in the villages was limited, even the ones he now owned. In years past, the only time he'd stepped foot in those places was after the Moors had raided them. With the destruction he and his soldiers had faced, there hadn't been time to get to know the people.

He wouldn't make the same mistake with Beatriz.

Her lashes cast shadows on her cheeks from the candlelight, the glow adding a touch of gold to her complexion. Her lips caressed the words she read, the movement bewitching, beckoning him to taste her mouth.

He resisted.

She turned the page. Her hands were lovely and quite pale, despite the work she did here. She bore no healed burns from hot pans in her father's bakeshop, nor had washing pots there left her skin red and raw. Tending a feeble mother hadn't harmed her beauty, either.

With Beatriz here, her mamá had no one to care for her, unless another relative handled the task or Beatriz paid someone. Given her reading skills, she should have gone to one of the large cities, rather than staying in the countryside. In a more populated area, she might have found work as a tutor for a prosperous family, earning far more.

He might never have met her.

She was here now, tending to him, reading a story they both loved, sitting close. He touched her arm.

She stopped reading.

He smiled softly, unable to help himself, his soul and heart bared to her. Although she was one of the loveliest women he'd ever known, he liked her as a person, enjoying her voice and laugh, how she looked at him with wonder and desire, no different than his passion for her.

He cupped her face. The book slipped from her grasp and hit the floor. He brushed his mouth over hers. She inhaled sharply, her hand on his chest.

He slanted his mouth over hers and parted her lips with his tongue, entering her, tasting sweet moisture, reveling in the clean, fresh flavor. The finest food had never been better. He had to have more and angled his mouth for greater penetration, his tongue probing deeper.

Beatriz suckled him.

They tried to get closer to each other, their chair legs scraping the floor. Tomás cupped her breast. She moaned around his tongue and wreathed her arm over his shoulder. Her tunic and gown were frustrating barriers, her erect nipple covered by too much cloth. He ran his thumb over the tightened tip, wanting the garments off, her bared to him.

His kiss grew heated and uncontrolled. He pulled off her cap to little avail. She'd coiled her hair in a braid, the style difficult for him to take down.

He had to try, and fumbled for the first pin.

She pulled her mouth free, desire and shock on her face.

"Beatriz."

On her feet, she backed away, then returned and swiped her cap off the floor. "I have to go."

He stood. "I meant no harm."

"I know." She shoved the cap on her head.

The silly thing was askew. He set about straightening it. She twisted away and grabbed her cloth.

"Wait." He stood between her and the door. "Was our kiss so awful?"

Tears shone in her eyes. "How can you ask such a thing?"

"I want to know if you enjoyed me as much as I did you."

"You know I did." She approached so quickly, he took an instinctive step back. "How could I not?"

He grinned.

She moaned. "I have to go."

"When will I see you again?"

"Like this?" She gestured to the room, her eyes wide and wild. "Never. If Nuncio caught me here, he would make me pay dearly for my indiscretion."

"Our kiss was hardly your indiscretion. It was our shared pleasure. You seem to have forgotten this is my castle, not his. Ignore him. I want to see you again and have you read to me every night."

She frowned. "No. Never ask again."

"Ask? As I said, this is my castle. I give the orders."

"Not to me." She pushed past him, opened the door, and ran down the hall.

Certain he'd catch up, he followed seconds later but was still too late. The next hall branched in two directions, every door within both spaces closed. She'd disappeared like a ghost or had slipped into a room.

He feared opening the doors. A señorita might have wandered into a chamber and would welcome his presence with kisses and a plan to trap him into marriage.

Muttering a curse, he retraced his steps to the study.

A door closed two rooms prior to his.

He stopped, not even considering Beatriz. He would have seen her duck into the space. Had to be another servant tidying this area...or a señorita checking out the fine furnishings and other riches he owned.

Once past the door, he walked backward, waiting for movement.

Nothing.

He turned to his study. Nuncio stood at the end of the hall. The older man regarded Tomás despairingly and left.

Chapter 3

Beatriz hid in the shadowed room, fingers to her mouth. A poor substitute for Tomás's silky lips, his tongue invading, demanding, possessing like the lord he was, his bristly cheeks rasping hers.

His role may have been to give orders, but he hadn't needed to do so with her. She'd surrendered more willingly than a seasoned harlot, experiencing no shame, wanting far more, their carnal adventures surpassing anything El Cid had encountered in his fantastic tales.

She could still smell Tomás's scent, fresh as the morning air, musky with male need. Her incessant longing would surely do her in. At the pace they'd managed tonight, they'd never finish any tale. Nor would mere kissing satisfy for long. She predicted no more than two days, maybe less, before they lost restraint. Already she craved him mounting her with a warrior's right. Having them pretend his forces had invaded her country and now she, the conquered maiden, was his for the taking, to do with as he willed, no matter how shameless.

Footsteps rang in the hall.

Beatriz held her breath. The sounds drew nearer, paused, resumed, then stopped outside the room. Candlelight spilled through the crack beneath the door.

Tomás.

Despite her longing for him, she cowered. Good sense said he should never approach her again. If she conceived, Señora Cisneros and Nuncio would insist she leave immediately with nowhere else to go. No lord would hire an unwed woman who was with child. She'd starve.

If she stayed here, rumors would rage, servants speculating as to the child's father. Nobles might follow suit and wonder if Tomás was responsible. Soon, everyone would gossip about them, which could lead to complete ruin. If Tomás learned what she'd hidden from him and the others here, he'd see her in a different light, never trusting her again.

The door handle moved down. Still wanting him but fearing she'd lose control or that Rufio might be on the other side, she huddled closer to the wall.

Nuncio entered and spotted her immediately despite how she hid. "So here you are." He sounded as if he'd expected to find her on Tomás's lap.

How dare he? She'd done exactly what he'd wanted, stopping Tomás and herself before they went too far. For her stellar behavior, she received Nuncio's ridicule. Outrage hit Beatriz so hard, she shook. "Do you never sleep?"

His wan complexion reddened. He closed the door.

She stormed toward him. "I was reading to the master, nothing more." She kept her voice low so no one else would hear, including Tomás, Rufio, or a señorita who might also be stalking her. "If you must know, the book was *Cantar del Mio Cid*. The part where El Cid conquers Valencia. Care to hear more?"

Nuncio stepped back.

She followed. "No need to be shy. The tale is quite stirring. Even you might enjoy it. If not, perhaps the adventure could put you to sleep once and for all."

"So you know how to read."

Her stomach fell. She kept giving away her secrets too easily.

"How do you have such a skill?"

"You mean as a servant or as a woman?"

"Either will do."

How casually he'd insulted her. At another time and place, she would have made him pay. Not now. "I misspoke." She shrugged. "Don Tomás read to me and I parroted his words."

"I heard no one speaking in his study except you."

"You eavesdropped?" Indignant, she jabbed her finger at him. "With your ear to the door?"

He backed away. Beatriz advanced with them going in circles, him looking frightened again, her railing. "What do you think Don Tomás would do if he knew you were at his door listening? Would you like me to tell him?"

"I insist you to stay away from the man."

"How do you propose I do so when he owns this castle and has a right to be wherever he wants within these walls?"

Nuncio glared. "With you always nearby. I see what goes on. You keep trying to tempt him."

Keep? Beatriz had succeeded beyond her wildest dreams without trying in the least. "Nothing untoward happened between us."

He glanced at her cap.

The thing kept slipping forward, nearly covering her right eye. She set it straight over her braid. "Don Tomás read to me and I repeated his words. That. Is. All. Knowing how much you worry, I left before he could even think to make a move, since a man's passion is my burden, not his. How lucky to be born male." She crossed her arms beneath her breasts and lifted her chin. "The room is still quite dusty. I had no chance to finish my work."

"Little wonder considering what I heard from there." Nuncio mimicked a moan and whimper.

Coming from him the noises sounded comical and vaguely repulsive. "El Cid's woes nearly drove me to tears. I fled before Don Tomás could see. I had no wish to upset him."

"Did you now? How thoughtful of you to spare him a few womanly tears. A warrior who has seen men torn apart in battle and witnessed countless deaths of Spain's finest soldiers, many of them his dearest friends. You are kind."

She wanted to thrash him. "May I return to my work?"

"I expect you to leave this castle immediately."

Her fury dissolved beneath stark fear. "I did nothing wrong. Don Tomás will tell you as much. Ask him."

"I have no intention of troubling the master with this."

"Fine. I will." Tomás would never send her away at anyone's request. He ruled here, not Nuncio.

The moment she reached the door, Nuncio grabbed her upper arm and pulled her back.

She clenched her jaw. "Release me."

"I forbid you to speak to Don Tomás."

"You expect me to leave with only the clothes on my back, possibly starve without work, but say nothing to my patrón? I think not." She yanked her arm from him.

Nuncio edged past her and blocked the door. "I can inquire about positions for you at other estates."

She flushed hot, then went cold. Not for a second had she called his bluff by promising to speak to Tomás. Nuncio seemed determined to see her go, no matter what she threatened.

For her to leave the estate would mean never seeing Tomás again. The only thing making her days bearable was to be nearby when he strolled across the grounds, strode down a hall, read a missive, and spoke to the other servants. She didn't want to leave and wouldn't. Nuncio would have to throw her out bodily. Given how old and bony he was, she didn't think he could overpower her for long. "No."

He straightened even more, looking down his nose.

She did the same. "Your search for another position for me could take weeks and may come to nothing."

"I have other connections. With your reading skill, you could work as a tutor in the city."

Bile rose to her throat. She swallowed hard, forcing the hideous taste down. "No. Never. I told you, I merely repeated the words Don Tomás read. The only work I can do is what Señora Cisneros has tasked me with here. I must stay. If you throw me out, you may be responsible for my demise."

He arched one eyebrow. "What of your mamá? What keeps you from returning to her?"

"The living I make here. I send her money so she can survive. Her death will also be on your head if you force me to leave. Do you want to risk your place in heaven by being so cruel to two helpless women?"

"Helpless? I gave you a warning, yet you refused to heed my words."

"Were you there?"

"I heard."

Ah yes, she'd forgotten he'd eavesdropped. "Allow me to stay and I promise to keep away from Don Tomás even if he follows me like ducklings with their mamá."

"This time, I can make certain you do so."

She leaned away. "What do you mean?"

"You can remain at the castle until I locate another position for you elsewhere, so my conscience is clear and my soul is ready for paradise. However, your days of dusting our master's study and the bedchambers have come to an end."

* * * *

Tomás's mood couldn't have been deadlier. Already, he'd suffered through two days with the señoritas buzzing around him like bees on a flower, refusing him a moment's peace or privacy. From dawn to well past midnight, they bombarded him with their chatter and wheedled him relentlessly until he agreed to play checkers, chess, whisk, all fours, and other card games until he was ready to run off, shrieking like one who was demon possessed.

If such behavior had dissuaded them from staying here, he would have played the part well. Unfortunately, nothing seemed to deter them from seeking a betrothal. He kept fending them off while also trying to find Beatriz.

The few times he checked the bedchambers and his study she wasn't around. Nuncio was, advising Tomás to return to the señoritas immediately lest they think him rude for ignoring them.

He hardly cared, though safety did become a concern when they tried their skill at archery. Their wayward arrows came perilously close to his servants who delivered refreshments to the mamás. With that trouble over, the señoritas now played hoodman's blind.

Ines wore the blindfold and tried to catch the others who laughed and scurried away. With her hands sweeping air, Ines ran heedlessly into a servant. The poor girl toppled over a bush, bumped her head, and scraped her elbows.

Ines yanked off the blindfold and gave her a mean scowl. "Stay out of my way, do you hear?"

Nuncio edged closer to Tomás. "Best you keep an eye on your guests or risk losing one of the help."

He already had. "Have you seen Beatriz?"

"Not out here."

He tightened his fists. "I can see as much. Where is she?"

"Tending to her duties as servants do."

"She has yet to dust my study. Send her there at once." Tomás proceeded to the room determined to wait for her. Given how they'd parted, they had to speak, touch, kiss again, and share so much more.

He waited for what seemed hours. Footfalls finally approached. Another servant, barely past childhood, offered a nervous smile from the doorway. He frowned. "Why are you here?"

He looked past her for Beatriz. Perhaps she was training the girl on the intricacies of dusting.

"To tidy your study, Patrón."

"Wait." He held up his hand to keep her from entering. "Who sent you here?"

"Señor Nuncio."

Unspeakable irritation raced through Tomás. "Where is Beatriz?"

The girl stared at his fists and lifted her shoulders.

"Return to your other duties." He strode past.

Outside, he remained in shadows, making certain his guests didn't notice him. He hardly wanted them to pull him into their silly play. Nuncio wasn't with the others.

Tomás checked the man's bedchamber next. Empty. He wasn't in the public rooms or dining hall.

At last, Tomás strode toward his study. Nuncio was at the open door, peering inside, his back to Tomás.

Of all the outrageous behavior. "Checking up on me?"

Nuncio flinched and looked over, his mood inscrutable. However, his complexion was ashier than normal.

"I came to check on your study." He offered a stiff smile. "The room appears quite clean now. Does the appearance meet with your approval?"

"No. I have yet to see Beatriz inside. What have you done with her?"

His smile disappeared. "Nothing. What about you?"

Tomás approached, forcing Nuncio to enter the room or risk a physical confrontation if they touched. The time for fair play was at an end. He slammed the door. "Where is she? Precisely."

"Seeing to her duties as you should see to yours."

"What I do is none of your concern. Do you understand?"

Sweat beaded on Nuncio's forehead. In his haste to put distance between himself and Tomás, he bumped into a chair. "Are you actually going to strike me?"

"I promise to strangle you if you keep avoiding my question."

"I thought you valued my advice."

"I do. When I seek you out, not when you try to force your will on me."

"Someone has to see to your welfare as you refuse to do so."

Tomás threw up his hands. "There you go again, meddling. Did you send Beatriz away?"

"And risk having you murder me?" He stepped behind a box chair. "I had Señora Cisneros assign her new duties."

"In one of the villages I own?"

"If only such a thing were possible."

Tomás growled.

Nuncio sighed. "The other night, Beatriz ran from your study with you chasing after her. Explain that."

As though they were father and son with Tomás not yet of age. He kept himself from yelling. "Gladly. We were playing a new game. We call it annoy Nuncio until he minds his own business or dies at my hands."

"Make light of this if you will, but the girl is naught but trouble for you."

"How? By being my friend? Is such a thing so tragic?"

Nuncio pressed his hand to his throat. "You intend to be her friend? A servant? Why?"

"For the same reason you and I are friends. We are, no?"

The man's face went bright red. "I served long and well with your family. I earned my spot. Beatriz is a relative stranger."

Not to Tomás. He seemed to have known her forever, liking how she made him smile and laugh, enjoying how comfortable she was to be around. Thrilling too. Everything a man could desire in a woman. What he wanted in a manservant was another matter entirely, though he couldn't get into that now with Nuncio looking close to a swoon. Tomás tempered his aggravation. "No one can ever replace you. Unless I have to murder you for an answer. For your own survival tell me where you sent her."

Nuncio exhaled loudly and seemed to shrink with the lost air. For the first time, he seemed more than ancient. He looked frail.

Tomás backed off. "Is she still in the castle, or did you send her to the stable?"

"I asked Señora Cisneros to put her to work in the kitchen."

"Baking?" Of course, the same as her late papá.

"No."

He frowned. "What then?"

"As a scullery maid."

* * * *

Gritting her teeth, Beatriz prayed for more strength than she possessed. The bucket she carried was impossibly heavy. Water sloshed over the sides with each step she took. She was several feet from the area she needed to scrub when her knees wobbled uncontrollably and her arms shook.

"Watch what you do," another servant said. She frowned at the puddles Beatriz had trailed into the kitchen. "If one of us slips and hurts ourselves, Cook will look to you to take our place."

They'd have to pull her off the floor first. Never had she been as tired. Every part of her ached. She'd scoured, scrubbed, washed, and polished until she figured everlasting damnation couldn't be worse. Give her Hell's fire any day over this misery. "What happened to the scullery maid whose place I took?"

"Over there." The woman inclined her head to a sturdy girl Beatriz guessed to be no more than fifteen. She gutted a hog with apparent glee. Blood and entrails had splashed on the floor.

"Leonor has much to learn." The woman salted her meat. "Until she does, you need to clean up the mess she makes. Watch her carefully. One day you can pluck chickens, scale fish, and gut animals as she does."

Only if she lived that long. Well short of her goal, Beatriz sank to her knees.

Rufio lifted his eyebrows, his smirk widening. He sat on the other end of the wide table where Leonor worked, swinging his legs back and forth. "Having trouble?" he asked Beatriz. "Need my help?"

At any other time, she would have rather died than obligate herself to him. Unfortunately, pride had no place here. "Please."

"After you work here awhile, buckets of water and animal carcasses will give you no trouble at all. You should see Leonor. She can carry nearly as much as I can."

Besotted, the girl smiled at him.

Ignoring Leonor, Rufio jumped off the table and lifted the bucket as easily as he would a feather, even swinging the thing back and forth, sloshing water everywhere. "Where do you want this?"

On his head would have been nice. No, wait. Nuncio's. He'd caused this. "By the blood on the floor." Obviously.

Rufio gave her a lewd grin, followed by a wink, and settled the bucket where she'd asked.

"*Gracias.*"

"Let me know what else you need." He came as close as possible and took her in possessively, lingering on her breasts and mouth despite the others here. "I can make things easy for you."

Or impossible if she dared cross him. Not knowing what to say, she simply nodded.

He left the room whistling.

She scrubbed Leonor's messes for what seemed like days, sensing the girl was deliberately careless in her work, dropping guts on the floor because Rufio hadn't given her his undivided attention.

If Beatriz hadn't been so tired, she would have begged Leonor to wed Rufio quickly and keep him busy for always.

Once she'd finished cleaning the floor, her other duties waited. Countless pots, pans, and dishes needed washing. She had barely started on the pile when Señora Cisneros hurried into the room. "Beatriz."

What now? There were fields to plow, another castle to build? She leaned against the counter. "Sí?"

The woman motioned her over. Beatriz was too sore to move swiftly.

During the wait, Señora Cisneros twisted her mouth, which made her mustache more prominent. "Did you hurt your feet?"

"No. I can stand and work all night if you need me."

"Go to your bed and rest. Tomorrow, you get new tasks."

What? No. Tomorrow was her day off. She only had one a week, the same as everyone else, and needed the time to wash her things and prepare for more dreadful labor in this horrible kitchen. Unless the new tasks were somewhere else...somewhere worse, like the stable. "What will I be doing now?"

"Tomorrow will be soon enough for you to find out."

"Have I done such a poor job here?" Fearing the unknown more, Beatriz didn't want to leave the hellish place.

Señora Cisneros patted her arm. "You did nearly as good as Yolanda." Beatriz hung her head. Yolanda was only twelve years old. "Give me time. I can do better."

"Not here. Go. Now."

She backed away as quickly as she could and climbed the steps to the servant quarters with the vitality of the near dead. Upon reaching her narrow mattress, she wanted to curl into a ball and cry over what she'd lost because of her papá, a cruel, selfish man who'd never given her a moment's consideration. To him, she'd always been nothing but property to do with as he desired.

She hadn't been able to live that way and had run instead.

Now, she was on her own with no friends, family, money, or time for sorrow and regret. She'd have to endure and survive whatever new torment Nuncio had devised to keep her away from Tomás. How foolish her attraction must have seemed to Nuncio who knew, as she did, there would be no happy ending for her.

The brief moments she'd shared with Tomás, teasing, smiling, laughing, and kissing were all she had left now.

She recalled those wonderful times as she washed her clothes and hung them to dry. Given her aching muscles, the task took twice as long as usual, depleting her remaining energy. At last, she dropped onto her bed and fell into an exhausted sleep.

* * * *

Beatriz frowned at a hand on her arm, shaking her quite rudely. She rolled away and hugged the edge of her mattress.

"Wake up, please." Yolanda shook Beatriz again.

She rubbed her eyes and looked over. Despite Yolanda's rough touch, she was lovelier than an angel with big brown eyes, black hair, and a complexion rivaling the finest cream. In a few years, she'd transform from a skinny child into a beautiful woman. Right now, though, she was dressed in livery for work rather than a nightgown for bed. Alarm shot through Beatriz. "Did I oversleep?"

Heaven help her if she was late for the torture Nuncio had planned for today.

"No. You must get dressed and go to the stable."

She'd guessed correctly that her new task was shoveling manure. With all the will she possessed, Beatriz pushed to a sitting position. Light haloed around the wooden screen over the window. "Is it well past dawn?"

"Nearly midday. You must hurry." Yolanda backed away. "Make certain to wear your own clothes, not your livery."

Of course. Nuncio wanted her to soil her garments. Beatriz would never have guessed he could be so cruel, but was determined to do exactly what he wished.

"Wait." She held out her hand to Yolanda.

When she returned, Beatriz hugged her. "Make certain to ask Rufio to lift anything heavy for you."

"For me? He would surely laugh in my face. Calls me brat rather than my name and never once looks my way or answers any question I may have. Just as well. I can carry most pigs already and I have yet to reach thirteen. Someday, I hope to lift a fully grown hog."

She patted Yolanda's back. "Until the day comes, please ask for help, even if it has to be from him."

"Not likely it will make a difference. He only wants to do things for you." Giggling, she ran from the room.

With no other choice, Beatriz prepared for her day, wearing her chemise, a simple blue gown, and yellow tunic she'd stolen before coming here. The only clothing she had left in the world. Along with her freedom. Nothing was more important than ruling her life, living the destiny she sought.

Matters could be worse than now, and had been in the city.

She left the castle from the side entrance, not wanting to run into Rufio in the kitchen. Once outside, she braced herself for the señoritas' gay laughter, them surrounding and touching Tomás with privilege she'd never have.

The lawn was eerily quiet save for crying birds, the breeze rustling leaves, cattle bellowing in the distance.

The guests must have been amusing themselves in the parlor.

She took another route to the stable so she wouldn't have to pass the windows and witness Tomás playing checkers or chess with a young woman. Or worse, them reading to him from El Cid's tale.

They'd better not. The story belonged to her and to him, no one else. No matter how irrational, she needed to keep the fantasy alive.

Legs sore and heart heavy, she lumbered across the grounds, wishing her life were different on such a glorious day. The air was a soft caress, heated and sweet smelling from the surrounding gardens. The sun made everything seem clean and bright. Flowers she couldn't identify raised their blossoms to the brilliant rays, the orange and red petals wiggling in the breeze. She picked a bloom, smiling at its pleasant fragrance. After rubbing the scent on her neck, to help her withstand the manure stench, she tucked the crushed blossom inside her sleeve. She needed to keep something pleasant from this day.

The stable, imposing and Moorish in design, had an enormous arched entrance. The doors were open. Columns supported the domed roof. Individual stalls sported carved doors, the dark wood gleaming. She counted thirty stalls on one side, sixty in all. Cleaning fifteen would most likely take the entire day.

She forged ahead and stopped at the entrance. Horses nickered or neighed, announcing her presence to no one in particular. There wasn't one stable hand around to tell her what to do, leaving her to figure it out on her own.

She wanted to run but entered the cool, shady stable. A door creaked to the left. She whirled.

Tomás left the stall.

Her breath spilled out.

He wore a long linen shirt, dark hose, and a leather belt, along with ankle boots. No doublet or robe. His muscular calves and thighs called to everything female within her. His wind-tousled hair begged her to ease those silky, blond waves off his forehead. He smiled and offered his hand.

Beatriz rushed to him, her pulse pounding crazily. She didn't understand what was happening. This was too wonderful. Surely, she'd died and gone to heaven.

His palm was warm and dry against hers, skin calloused from warfare and physical activity, his touch gentle. He kissed her knuckles, his lips unbearably soft, breath hot. "Buenas tardes."

She opened her mouth but couldn't speak.

"You wonder what this is about."

She nodded, hoping he'd explain.

"Today, neither of us works." He played with her fingers. "We get to know each other."

In what way? She didn't think he meant in the usual carnal sense. Tenderness, not lust, filled his eyes. "Why?"

"I want us to be friends."

"What?"

"Friends. After we ride to our destination—wait, you do ride, no?"

She did, or rather had at one time, and nodded.

He beamed. "Once we reach this spot I know of, we can enjoy our meal and read about El Cid's triumphs." He gestured to a basket, the book on top.

Theirs alone, no one else's.

He leaned in. "I have to warn you of something."

Nothing he could say would worry her at this point, unless he told her the señoritas would join them. "What?"

"El Cid has nothing on me. My adventures will dazzle you with the force of a star shooting across the sky, the crash of thunder above your head, the wail of the wind trying to blow in a door." He wagged his finger. "Mind you, what I say is no mere boast."

Beatriz didn't believe she could ever like another man more. She was in far too much danger of laughing, weeping, and throwing her arms around him. Controlling herself, she ran her thumb over his. "Someone should write several epic poems about you. Volumes and volumes." She paused and stopped stroking him, wary of a matter that still concerned. "Perhaps the señoritas can manage such a feat."

"I sent them on their way this morning as you slept, leaving the task of an epic poem for you. I have writing materials packed with the other items. Wait. You can write, no?"

She nodded readily, loving him for getting rid of the other women. One might someday be his wife, though not now. These moments were theirs.

Tomás squeezed her hand lightly. "Come." He led her to another stall, the mare inside already saddled. "We need to begin our day."

Chapter 4

Everything was perfect, the mild breeze fluttering Tomás's hair and Beatriz's skirt, just as he'd envisioned. Sun bathed them in its golden glow, clouds nowhere in sight. Past the wide clearing, cork, mulberry, olive trees, bushes, and flowers, cultivated or wild, perfumed the air with scents only nature could create.

He'd never been happier to be alive or with any other woman. Beatriz's eyes sparkled. The same pleasure coursed through him, though he wasn't completely content. Although she hadn't worn her livery, she'd pushed her hair beneath her servant's cap, hiding the lovely tresses from him. "What happens if you unbraid your hair?"

She stopped studying his thigh and looked up, her cheeks rosy with embarrassment or excitement, perhaps both. "What?"

"If you were to take off your cap and loosen your hair, what would happen?"

She considered his question, then matched his playful smile. "Shall we see?"

"We should. Would you like me to hold your reins as you tend to things?"

"I can manage both."

She held her reins in one hand and pulled off her cap with the other.

He reached for the hat.

"I have this." After pushing the cap into her sleeve, she removed the pins holding her braid and offered them to him.

The small wooden pieces were simple in design, nothing like the ivory and jeweled pins noblewomen wore. He found these more precious than ones studded with pearls or diamonds, wanting to lift them to his nose to see if they bore her scent. He controlled himself, lest she think him odd.

She uncoiled her dark hair and worked her fingers nimbly through the braid until she'd loosened the tresses. They framed her face, making her complexion even paler, the ends cascading to her waist. Thick, shiny waves he longed to touch and smell.

She held out her hand. "My pins, please."

"I have them." He slipped the items into his pouch. "I promise to protect the pins with my life."

She regarded the sheathed dagger and arming sword hanging from his belt.

"Ignore the weapons. They mean nothing. Who taught you to ride so well?" She seemed born to a horse, the same as him, easily riding astride rather than sidesaddle. Good thing. He hadn't had one to offer.

She looked past him, brow furrowed in thought or dismay. "He did."

"Who?"

She tensed, fists clenched. "My papá."

Her dislike for the man surprised him. Their relationship must have been awful for her to harbor such resentment after his death.

Tomás wanted to know more but could hardly pry. He needed her happy and at peace. "Have you had recent news of your mamá? Is she still feeling well?"

Beatriz lifted her face to a bird flying past. "She is."

He nodded, wanting her to look at him rather than the bird or anything else. "Does your mother grow ill with the same malady each time or something new? I only ask because I may be able to find a remedy for her. I was near death when a potion saved me."

"What? Oh no, you nearly died?"

Her concern surprised and pleased him, proving how much she cared. Not that she should. He shouldn't either but couldn't help himself. He hungered for the smallest information about her, wanted only to please, and couldn't have been more thrilled to be at her side. "I recovered fully." He threw out his arms to prove how robust he was, his weight the same as before he'd fallen ill.

Her lovely features tensed. "Did you have the fever?"

"And a cough so ghastly I could scarcely breathe. I was at the fortaleza then. My men sent for the *sacerdote* to anoint me as no one expected I would live."

Beatriz clutched her throat. "Has the cough returned?"

"Not at all. No need to fret." Grateful for her worry, he smiled softly. "Once my…ah…that is, the physician arrived and ministered to me, I slowly grew better."

"What was in the cure he gave you?"

Tomás had no idea, recalling nothing more than how awful the potions had tasted. Sancha had risked her life to save him, and he'd nearly said her name to Beatriz, revealing how Sancha healed in secret. If the Inquisition ever found out...

He didn't want to consider such a thing. "I recall little of my illness. However, I will ask about the ingredients if your mamá should ever need the remedy. Had you planned to visit her today? Do you usually do so during the times you have free?"

He'd hoped to surprise Beatriz with this ride and their meal, not keep her from her daughterly duties.

She stroked her horse's mane even though the mare needed no comfort. The ride was uneventful and quite leisurely, his gelding and her mount ambling along, enjoying themselves as much as he was.

"I visit when I can." She lifted her shoulders. "Not often."

"Because you lack a horse?" If Beatriz had come from a village, as stated, and he sorely wanted to believe her on the matter, then surely the community was one he owned and under his protection. "Is your mamá's home far?"

"Too far for me to walk to easily or readily."

"If you need to visit or when you care to do so, let me know. I can provide a horse or my carriage if you prefer."

Her smile looked more pained than appreciative.

"What have I said?"

"Nothing. I was picturing Señor Nuncio's face if I were to ride from the castle on your fine Arabian or in your carriage, the guards chasing after me, swords drawn, arrows flying at his request."

Tomás laughed. "No need to worry about them or him. Nuncio and I had a talk. Beginning tomorrow, you return to dusting my study and your original duties. His meddling and the kitchen are in the past."

She gave him a sidelong glance. "Señora Cisneros said I performed nearly as well there as Yolanda, who has yet to turn thirteen."

He'd already heard the same. Señora Cisneros had seemed eager to get Beatriz out of the kitchen. "Did you hurt yourself while you were there? Show me your hands." He pushed up in his saddle and craned his neck to get a better look at them.

"I am quite well." She hid her fingers within her sleeves. "May I ask you something?"

"No need. I have no doubt you were as extraordinary in the kitchen as you are riding a horse even with your hands buried in your clothes as they are now."

She laughed quietly. "I could barely lift a bucket of water."

"Did you break your fingers trying?"

Beatriz pressed her face to her shoulder, her newest laughter muted.

Tomás smiled. "Come, show me your injuries."

"I have none." She displayed one hand, then the other. Outside of a small cut on a knuckle and her skin being slightly pink, she was well on the road to recovery.

"What was your question?"

"Yolanda is still a child. Might you find less difficult work for her? If not, I would rather stay in the kitchen to help her out."

And neglect the dust in his study, along with their time together to read and talk? Never. "The moment we return, Señora Cisneros and I will have a word about Yolanda."

"Gracias. May I ask something else?"

"I want no one except you to dust my study. I trust your abilities."

Beatriz rolled her eyes. "Were your other servants so horrible that you find my service good in comparison?"

"Not at all. I find you perfect in every way. Lovelier than the dawn, brighter than the sun, more enchanting than a moonlit night. Was that your question?"

She blushed prettily. "No. Are you expecting trouble?" She gestured to his weapons.

"I always carry my dagger and sword with me whenever I leave the castle. A habit I learned when I left my father's estate at seven and became a page."

"So young?"

"I had no choice."

She made a face. "Why? Did your father force you out? Is he a brute?"

"Practical. Do you know anything about Spain's current laws of primogeniture?"

Beatriz opened her mouth only to close it. She smoothed her hair and pushed strands behind her ear before she shook her head.

Tomás wasn't certain what to make of her delayed response. If she didn't know, why not admit it readily? No need for shame, especially when the law affected nobles and affluent merchants, rather than villagers who lived simply. He considered her background, the details still not fitting. Nothing about her was unrefined or lacking. She was exceptional in every way. Too bad he couldn't tell her so, and everything else in his heart, without running her off. "According to the law, the first born inherits everything, leaving the others to scramble for a living. Women can join an order or marry well. Men can become priests or fight for the Crown to earn their wealth. As the youngest of six brothers with little chance to ever inherit, I became a warrior to build my future."

She frowned at the lush surroundings, vineyards, fields, and orchards extending to the horizon. "You risked your life repeatedly and without thought for this estate?"

He considered his land quite beautiful. "I had no wish to become a priest."

"You could have died. Were you ever hurt?"

Numerous times. He'd often boasted to señoritas about his battles, loving the fire in their eyes at his bloody tales.

Beatriz searched his face, her complexion paler than usual, expression pained.

He shrugged. "I have a few scars."

She regarded his chest, thighs, and groin, lingering there the most. His shaft stiffened, sac tightening from the intense heat pouring through him.

She glanced up. "Were you afraid?"

He patted his horse's mane. His gelding exhaled at the unexpected attention. "At times." He lifted his shoulders, feeling foolish for admitting any weakness. "Not even the bravest warrior looks forward to death."

Her eyes rounded. "How close did you come? How many times?"

During every battle with swords clashing, arrows sailing, arquebuses firing. "If a man stopped and considered such things before a conflict, fear would kill him. A soldier blinds himself to everything except doing what he must."

"For this?" She gestured at his estate.

"Not entirely. Mainly for the Crown. Every warrior has a duty to protect Spain, just as El Cid had. You find his tale quite rousing."

"In a book written after he survived, not when he was young enough to risk death." She shook her head. "Your eldest brother should have shared his inheritance with you and your other siblings."

Tomás tried to imagine such a thing and couldn't. "He has yet to receive all the properties. Papá is very much alive."

"Do you resent him?"

"My father?"

"No. Your brother. For having everything given to him when you had to risk your life for years."

"I hardly faced death every day. My men and I had some free moments to enjoy ourselves." Tomás stopped short of telling her about the women and drinking between battles. He did smile, though, liking her spirited defense on his behalf. "I never envied Enrique, my eldest brother. He was as caught up in the situation as the rest of us were. As a boy, he wanted to be a warrior. Instead, our father forced him to learn numerous languages and nearly every subject on earth. While the rest of us rode or swam, he was stuck in a room with his books. Papá hounded him relentlessly, never giving him a moment's peace or the simple joy of being idle. He learned to accept his fate. We all did. You do what you must."

"Or change things. Men only care about property and wealth, gaining favor with the Crown, ruling others. People never matter to them, only things."

"Are you including me in your judgment?"

Her features slackened. "No. Never. I was talking about... You must find me awful for saying what I had."

Not at all. She reminded him of Sancha and Isabella, intelligent and spirited women who hardly cared about convention. He recalled Fernando's initial complaints about Isabella's independence, her determination to do what she wanted whether he approved or not. Fernando wouldn't have fallen in love with a lesser woman. Certainly not foolish señoritas like Ines, Zita, and the others. The same with Enrique. Sancha loved him but he didn't rule her. She would never have allowed such a thing. They stood shoulder to shoulder, respecting each other's wishes and beliefs. "No."

"No, what?"

"You asked if I found you awful. I could never think of you in anyway except dazzling."

She got a faraway look in her eyes, somewhat dreamy but also marred with unease.

He guessed what she thought. "As a friend." Hardly all he wanted, but he was determined to be as positive about their arrangement as possible. "As such, I must point out how noisy your belly is."

She pressed her growling stomach.

"No good. You need to eat." He inclined his head to the right. "We can share our first meal together over there."

* * * *

Beatriz adored the secluded location, the hillside view spectacular. The valley stretched beneath them, endless wheat fields undulating in the wind. A large section was green, a small portion golden and ready for harvest, the lighter color seeming to advance before her eyes.

After Tomás tethered the horses to cork trees, he carried the basket to a clearing for their first meal together. He'd spoken with confidence that they'd do this again.

Perhaps they would, but their shared days would never last. He'd either ask her more questions about her parents and she'd reveal the truth, or he'd tire of their friendship, want more, and seek other women.

Sadness tightened her throat. She pushed the feeling aside, not wanting anything to ruin this day. During these few moments, he belonged to her.

He spread a soft brown blanket over the grass and secured the corners with rocks. Once he'd placed the basket in the center, he put his weapons to the side. The breeze pushed his shirt against his broad, muscular chest. He was more stirring than El Cid and certainly more handsome.

He offered his hand.

She accepted his help readily, her earlier aches disappearing beneath delight.

They sat side by side, arms touching, wildflowers in purple, blue, and white surrounding them, the basket in front like a longed for gift they both wanted to open.

Beatriz could barely keep still. "What did you bring?"

"I have no idea. Cook packed this. I did tell her not to include the carcass Leonor gutted yesterday while you scrubbed the floor. Cook said you kept frowning at the thing."

Beatriz laughed and bumped his arm. "You two discussed me. Wait. You made light of me."

"I did. She frowned quite a bit. Ah, look here." He tore through the basket. "We have cold pork, chicken, cheese, boiled eggs, olives, oranges, bread, and wine."

With each word, he'd removed the food and placed containers in her arms.

Struggling not to drop any, she pressed the dishes against her breasts. "Such a feast. What do you intend to eat?"

He winked.

Immeasurable pleasure coursed through her with his gesture, far different from Rufio's. She'd sensed an undercurrent of cruelty in his playfulness. Not Tomás's. Though large and powerful, he was unmistakably gentle too.

After relieving her of the food and spreading the containers before them, he slipped his hand beneath her chin.

Her scalp tingled.

He leaned in and brushed a small slice of pork over her lips. "Eat."

She tongued the meat into her mouth, licking his fingers as she did so. Whether the fare was flavorful or not, she had no idea. Tasting him was what mattered.

He stroked her throat.

Her lids slid down.

"Good?"

She'd never had a more enchanting meal. "Sí. You now." She eased a sliver of chicken between his lips.

He chewed and swallowed, and then he wrapped his hand around hers and licked her fingers quite slowly, lingering on each. "Wonderful. Cook knows how to roast a bird." He sucked her forefinger.

She tried to catch her breath but couldn't, resigned to overwhelming dizziness as long as he was near. "Should we see how well she prepared the other items?"

"We must, or risk hurting her feelings."

"I could never be so cruel."

"Nor I."

They feasted, washing down the fare with sweet wine before returning for more, their attention on each other, nothing else. His locks were almost white in the sun, a delightful contrast to his bronze skin and dark eyebrows.

She kept fighting an urge to stroke his lips and smooth back his windblown hair, repeatedly lifting her hand, then pausing at what she was about to do. Rather than touch him, she brushed her skirt even though she'd swept crumbs away earlier. He was the same, reaching for her tresses only to stop and push back his hair instead.

Once their food had run out, she couldn't have eaten another bite, her appetite sated, but not her desire. She was taut with need.

Tomás cleared his throat. "Had enough?"

Never. She would always desire him. "My belly should be quiet for the rest of the day. You?"

"Filled to bursting." He sagged to the blanket, arm pillowing his head, and took her in.

A pulse beat hard in Beatriz's throat. Surely, he could see her desire, as great as his, his features flooded with yearning, eyes hooded.

She'd never faced a moment such as this with another friend. Lightheaded, she tried to control herself. "Would you like me to read to you now?"

"If you want."

What she wanted had nothing to do with El Cid's tale. She opened the book to the page where they left off. Her hands trembled, her hunger for him spiking again, growing unruly. She cleared her throat and began to read, not hearing anything she said. Blood kept rushing in her ears, her pulse pounding loudly.

Somehow, she reached the end of the page and turned to the next.

Tomás captured a tress.

His touch registered in her core. Stoically, she resumed reading. He wound her lock around his fingers. Pretending not to notice, she pressed on.

So did he, winding her hair around his hand, easing her closer.

She dropped the book and fit her mouth to his.

Growling, he drove his fingers through her hair.

Only death would pull her away.

With his face cradled in her hands, she drew her thumbs over his bristly cheeks and parted her lips to his, demanding he fill her.

Tomás speared his tongue inside. She suckled him greedily, her mouth pressed so firmly to his, her teeth dug into her bottom lip. She suffered the pain without complaint, angling her head to the right and left, trying to get closer, unable to do so.

He made an uncivilized noise, slightly feral, decidedly base.

Excitement made her hot. Yearning made her weak.

He rolled them over. She squealed.

Once on top, he muffled whatever sounds she made with his impassioned kiss. She rested her leg on his and held him tightly so he couldn't get away. He cupped her breast as he had in his study, though bolder now, squeezing, dragging his thumb over her nipple.

A pleasant ache registered between her thighs.

He ground his hips against hers, his shaft thick, hard, insistent, everything she required and couldn't have.

Unsettled, she released him and pulled her mouth free before they lay together and she brought him scandal or shame. Tears stung her eyes.

Concern tightened his features. "You have nothing to fear."

"We have everything to fear."

"No. Listen to me. I would never compromise your virginity. I promise you."

She didn't understand. "What then? We kiss as we have been until we drive ourselves mad?"

"Hardly." His shoulders shook with suppressed laughter.

She frowned. "Are you making fun of me?"

"Never." He grew serious. "We can enjoy each other without regret."

Only if they were married.

Her hope soared and crashed as quickly. He could never wed her. Even if he were reckless enough to suggest such a thing, she wasn't free to wed him. Surely, he meant something else. "What are you talking about?"

"If I touch you with naught but my lips, tongue, and hands, nothing untoward will happen." He rested his palm on her mound.

Heat shot to her face, though not from shame. Exquisite feelings barreled through her, overwhelming need she hadn't known until now. Longing so rich she couldn't imagine how she'd survived without it. "What a genius you are. I want to do the same with you." She touched his rigid shaft.

Tomás trembled. "Of course—wait. You do know what this involves, no?"

"You pleasure me with your hands, mouth, and tongue and I do the same to you. I had no idea such a thing was possible."

"Most women refuse to allow such things."

"I consider them fools."

"Remove your clothes." He tugged her to a sitting position and pulled up his shirt.

"Wait."

"Why?"

She glanced over both shoulders. "What if someone comes upon us?"

"No one will. All the servants' tasks keep them far from this spot. Nuncio knows better than to approach, unless he wants me to toss him off the hill." Tomás wiggled his eyebrows. "This is what friends do for each other."

Beatriz giggled, not caring how foolish she sounded. No one could hear or see how she behaved. The Church and society would certainly condemn her for the coming pleasure, calling her vulgar. She had too little time to spend with Tomás to worry about decency. Her future held naught but loneliness. For these few moments, she wanted him to desire, pleasure, and love her beyond belief.

After pulling off her shoes, stockings, and tunic, she set to work on the endless laces on her gown.

Tomás piled boots and clothes nearby.

She stilled at his male beauty. Smooth bronze skin taut with youth, his muscles superbly defined. His biceps spoke of a man who'd known hard physical labor for years on end. His tiny nipples were dark brown, resembling newly tilled earth, a faint scar near the right one, another on his firm belly below his navel.

Wanting to touch every part of him and not knowing where to begin, she simply gaped.

He rested his hand on her thigh. "Are you pleased?"

His rigid member jutted from a thatch of brown curls, the crown plump and reddened with passion, the shaft thick with lust. Veins traveled up the magnificent column, each so prominent she wanted to touch and lick them.

She nodded. "Exceedingly pleased."

"Good. Do the rest of your clothes come off, or do I only guess at your beauty?"

Laughing, she plucked her laces. "Can you help me with the rest of these?"

Together, they pulled the gown and chemise off, baring her to him.

Pleasure radiated from Tomás, widening his smile, quickening his breath. Her nipples constricted at his arousal. More moisture bathed the folds between her legs, proving how much she wanted this.

No other man had seen her naked. She'd always imagined feeling timid, shamed, repulsed at the prospect.

Not with Tomás. Her desire for him made her bold. She melted into his arms and kissed him first, slipping her tongue into his mouth. He groaned and suckled her greedily.

They sagged to the blanket, Tomás on top, his hand sweeping over her nudity, Beatriz touching his, their musk mingling and scenting the air. She traced the small scar near his nipple, circled his navel, and stroked the thick thatch on his groin.

On a wild growl, he tore his mouth from hers. Before she could ask why, he slipped down and latched on to her nipple, suckling and tonguing the tip. Heat and desire sped through her, astonishing in its power. She'd never experienced such passion and excitement, or being so sensitive to touch.

He fastened his mouth on her other nipple, running his tongue over the rosy halo, lapping the tip lazily before he returned to the first one. Breathless, she pushed her fingers through his hair, soft as she'd hoped, and kept him to her.

He suckled hard, which she liked, and slipped his hand down her torso. She quivered. When he reached the dark curls between her legs, she parted her thighs, inviting him to explore.

A low groan poured from him, signaling what sounded like pleasure. He cupped her mound possessively and stroked her small nub, outrageously susceptible to his touch.

A lifetime of carnal sin wouldn't have prepared Beatriz for the feeling he'd generated within her… sweet tension that nagged and teased, unlike anything she'd believed possible. Unable to resist, she alternately pushed into him, then tried to pull away when the delight grew too intense.

He settled the matter by ending their kiss and crawling between her legs. "Bend your knees and push your hips up."

Her cheeks stung, again from elation not embarrassment.

The moment she lifted her buttocks he slipped his hands beneath them and settled his mouth on her folds, tonguing them, her opening, and erect nub.

Reckless with need, she pushed closer.

Her wantonness seemed to excite him further. He suckled her kernel, ran his fingers down the furrow between her cheeks, and stroked her tightest opening.

She craved more, helpless against her desire.

He worked her well, alternately licking, suckling, and tonguing her nub, giving her no rest. An inner frenzy gathered strength, wanting to break free.

In order to prolong these moments, she fought the delicious tension building inside.

Tomás suckled harder, faster, stroking her other opening, remaining there, tempting and teasing her vulnerable flesh.

Beatriz lost control, the world spinning too fast for her to keep up. She gripped his shoulders needing an anchor against what was happening. Breathing proved hard, speech impossible, her limbs tensed, then trembled. A pulse ticked within her sheath.

She shuddered.

Surprising warmth filled her. Heat so comforting and needed she never wanted to feel anything else.

Tomás licked her nub one last time. She thrashed wildly.

He leaned up and smiled. "Will you live?"

She laughed, surprised she could, considering how spent she was. "I fear not."

His brow furrowed. "Why?"

"I need this again and again."

"Good. Wait. Have you forgotten me?" He gave her a withering look. "You have. And here I thought you were my friend."

Poor man. "I shall tend to you before you dissolve into tears."

"Before I what?"

She muffled her yawn with her hand. "Very well." Fighting fatigue, she pushed up and let excitement rule. "Weep all you want." She put her hands on his chest.

"What? Hold on. What are you doing?"

"This." She shoved.

Taken off guard, Tomás toppled over, arms shooting out to catch himself. The hair in his pits was dark and silky, surely scented with his musk. Crazed with need, she crawled to his side. "Spread your legs." She ran her fingertips up his hairy thigh.

He groaned.

She smiled. "Bend your knees."

"Tell me why first."

"Do you have so little faith in me?"

"An untried virgin?" He placed his hand over his shaft and sac. "I might pay dearly for any mistake you make."

"Very well, I shall nap." She yawned loudly and crawled away.

He grabbed her ankle. "Get back here."

"Sí, my lord." She returned to his side. "One day I may tell you a fantasy I have regarding you, with me as the conquered maiden."

"Sounds as though you made me a warrior."

"What else?"

He smiled. "Is this the way you treat a battle-weary soldier and friend, making him wait endlessly for pleasure?"

In answer, she cupped his sac, fascinated with the male power it represented, the ruddy skin lightly furred.

He groaned softly.

Lover's music that thrilled, increasing her boundless joy, encouraging her to press her face to the pelt above his shaft. He smelled exactly as she'd hoped, clean, musky, and completely masculine, intensifying her desire.

After her first lick on his rigid column, she traced the veins with her tongue. He pushed toward her, murmuring Arabic words that sounded like praise.

She never wanted to do anything except give him pleasure. Until they'd met, she hadn't believed a man like him existed. He was generous, kind, playful. She envied the woman who would capture his heart, and wished she could stop time so he could be hers for eternity.

A foolish and sad notion.

She had nothing more than these few moments and needed to make them count for the dark days ahead.

She lapped his crown, pausing frequently to gauge his reaction. He whispered something she couldn't hear. She grew bolder, flicking her tongue over the entire head, at last reaching the back. He stiffened and made a passionate sound.

She'd found the spot that pleased him most, paying great attention to it, then brushed his sac lightly.

He shouted and a bird took wing.

Tomás would have no escape from her. She licked his shaft fully, liking its faint saltiness, the same as the moisture that escaped the small opening in the crown. He made pleasant rather than uncivilized noises.

That wouldn't do. She wanted him as wild and helpless as she'd been when he was between her legs.

With one hand fondling his sac, she lifted his member and took him in her mouth.

He bellowed heartily, pushing himself toward her.

Although Beatriz was untried with men, she sensed he wanted her to take his entire shaft inside her mouth, mirroring what her sheath would do. How could she not? He hadn't forced her as most nobles would have done. He offered to protect her virginity, treating her with kindness and respect.

As a friend would.

Tomás was already far more to her. She had to give him her best.

She eased his shaft as deeply into her mouth as she could, then took still more, not content until she had nearly all his length inside.

New sounds poured from him, similar to when they'd kissed, only these were more spirited. Encouraged, she allowed his shaft to slip from her mouth except for the crown. Holding it between her lips, she licked his most sensitive area.

He cried out repeatedly, each louder than the last.

She took his sex within her mouth and ran her thumbnail over his sac. Explosive noises burst from him.

She tempted and teased as he'd done with her, pacing herself so he wouldn't reach the end for minutes, perhaps hours. Given her innocence in these matters, she had no idea how long a man could last.

Perspiration bathed his face, throat, and chest. His features had twisted into what looked like anguish...or pleasure so intense he found the feelings impossible to bear.

His shaft grew harder and thicker. Tirelessly, she glided her tongue over his member, increasing her pace, then pausing, not allowing him to know what her next move would be.

He tugged his hair, his growls sounding frantic, his roar pleased. His creamy seed spurted into her mouth. She didn't recoil. Her feelings for him were too deep to reject anything he had to give.

With tender regard, she accepted his offering, swallowing every drop, licking him clean. Despite his ragged breaths, he looked drunk with joy.

"You can breathe easy." She stroked his thigh. "I left you unharmed."

Tomás laughed with little strength. "You honored me."

As a friend. She had to be happy for that. "Did I give you great pleasure?"

"You were perfect."

"Just perfect? No comparing me to the sun, wind, moon, and stars?"

"When I regain my strength." He opened his arms. "Come to me."

She nestled close, hand on his chest, face against his neck.

His heart drummed hard in time with hers.

Finished with his yawn, he nuzzled close. "We must do this again."

For all time.

Chapter 5

Although Tomás objected, Beatriz dismounted far short of the stable. He did the same, even though she insisted on walking alone to the castle.

"No one should see us together." She folded her hands primly. "The same as earlier. Wherever you sent the stable hands, they must have returned to their work by now. Discretion is best."

She was right but he had a hard time letting her go. "They may wonder why I have two horses, both of them saddled, no?"

"Let them think what everyone else will. One of the señoritas returned, stormed the castle, and you had no choice except to coax her out here for a ride so you could toss her over the hill."

Laughing, he led Beatriz to a copse of cork trees.

She pointed in the other direction. "The castle is that way."

"And will still be there when we finish."

Once hidden within the trees, he tethered the horses and trailed kisses over her silky cheek and throat.

She sagged into him, wearing his scent as he did hers.

He inhaled deeply. "Tonight you come to my study to dust."

She parted her lips to his, accepting his tongue. From the beginning, they'd fit so well. Now they molded to each other with even greater ease. He cupped her buttocks. She held him close and played with his hair.

When they finished their kiss, she rested her forehead on his shoulder, her hand over his hammering heart. "No."

He stopped nibbling her ear. "You want me to kiss your neck instead? Very well, anything to please you."

She eased back before he could enjoy any part of her. "I meant no to dusting tonight. If I leave the servant quarters to go to your study, the others may wonder why and talk. I should be enjoying my time away from work, not doing more."

"You had a bad time today? What we did was mere work to you?"

She kissed him brazenly in answer. Breathless, he held on to her and she clung to him, both needing each other for support. On the hillside, she'd satisfied him to exhaustion, arousing him repeatedly until he could barely walk to their horses.

"What am I to do tonight with you so far away?" He eased a stray tress behind her ear and adjusted her cap to where the thing should be. "Do you want to see me buried in dust before you return to work?"

Her laughter filled the fragrant air. "No. However, you could use the time to speak to Señora Cisneros concerning Yolanda. You did promise."

Indeed, he had. "Tomorrow evening you return to my study. No argument, hear?"

She returned his fiery kiss for only a moment before pulling free and racing up the path to the castle.

Tomás leaned against a rough trunk, giving her an opportunity to reach her destination before he followed.

The stable hands weren't foolish enough to ask why he had a mare and a gelding without a second rider in sight. If they wondered, he didn't care.

Once in the castle, he lifted his face to the ceiling, wishing he could see through wood and stone to her in the servant quarters. Too bad he couldn't move her into his bedchamber. Even if she agreed to such a scheme, which she wouldn't, the arrangement would have tongues wagging.

Pity everyone couldn't mind their own business.

After a brief search, he found Señora Cisneros in the parlor, her back to him. She ran her fingers over the windowsill, inspected them, and nodded. At the next window, she did the same and made a displeased sound.

The smallest speck of dust had always disturbed her.

He cleared his throat. "I need a word."

"Sí, Patrón."

He gestured her to the far end of the room, so no one would overhear them, and warned himself to approach the subject delicately. "What would you say is the easiest household task? One even a grandmother could handle without causing any strain?"

She drew her bushy eyebrows together. "Is Beatriz now having difficulty with dusting and changing or washing linens?"

Heat crept up Tomás's neck. He feigned indifference to her question. "This is about Yolanda, the young girl who works in the kitchen."

"The best scullery maid I ever hired." Señora Cisneros grinned broadly. "In no time, Yolanda will be gutting animals next to Leonor."

Tomás tried not to stare at the hairs on the woman's chin. "Given how young Yolanda is, it might be best if she has less tiring work until she grows older."

"Has she complained to you?"

He had no idea what the girl looked like or that she'd even existed until Beatriz had mentioned her. "No. I, ah, saw her struggling with a bucket of water and thought she seemed too frail for kitchen work. There must be an easier task for her to do."

"Would you like her to take Beatriz's place?"

"Never. That is, no."

Señora Cisneros tapped her hairy chin, her features pensive. At last, she lifted her forefinger. "I suppose she could help the chandler, unless you prefer Yolanda serves you at meals, washing your hands after you dine."

He wasn't certain if she was making light of him or not. Unlike many nobles who were helpless to the extreme, Tomás could wash himself, unless Beatriz wanted to do the job. "Candles it is for Yolanda, with the chandler. Make certain she begins the new work immediately."

"At the same wage she earns now?"

He had no idea. "Certainly not less. Pay her whatever you would an apprentice."

Her eyebrows shot up. "So much?"

"You decide what she should earn." He patted her fleshy shoulder. "I have full faith in whatever you do."

He left the parlor hoping Beatriz wouldn't want to spare other servants their loathsome labor. He'd have to rearrange the entire household staff to keep her from toiling at their side. What a mess that would be...though in the end a minor matter if he made her happy.

He couldn't imagine doing anything less. These last hours with her had given him a glimpse into what life should be like, not what protocol or the Church ordained. He wasn't a devout man and had never cared for rigid custom, either. Not like those nobles who'd had everything handed to them, as Beatriz had said. They seemed the most devoted to keeping change at bay.

Perhaps because they had always been sheltered from horror, had no idea how the real world worked.

After Tomás had felled his first Moor, he hadn't whooped with delight as the older nobles said he would, many having no experience in battle. The gore had appalled him, the blood never seeming to end. The young man's family had surely waited for his return only to learn they'd lost him forever.

Killing did become easier, only because he wanted to survive, but he never looked at warfare the same. As a boy, he'd found the battles exciting. Upon becoming a man, he understood the enormity of loss.

His love for Spain, not the wealth he might earn, had kept him at the task. In many ways, Tomás agreed with what Beatriz had said about men coveting things more than they did people. A sorry way to live and a tradition he wanted no part of.

He retired to his study, finding the room too large and empty without her. In no time at all, he'd become completely besotted. Foolish that. When she had to move on to another friend, lover, husband, he wouldn't be able to stop her.

She was young and unbelievably lovely. Other men wouldn't wait to make their moves until Tomás had his fill, if he ever would. The male servants had already noticed her, especially Rufio. He, especially, seemed eager to make her his.

She'd shown no interest in the young man, but others would eventually come into service here. One might catch her eye and capture her heart.

Tomás muttered an oath, not wanting to consider his hopeless situation. Even though he ruled here and could do whatever he willed, even to take Beatriz as his bride, his actions would cost her dearly. He'd hold her up to ridicule to the servants she once worked with and the nobles who made up his world.

They'd never accept her no matter her beauty, intelligence, and wit. Although he hardly cared what they thought, she certainly would. He'd be a beast to subject her to their scorn at gatherings. Nor could she stay here while he attended those functions alone. He'd merely fuel gossip that his wife wasn't good enough to associate with her betters. She might grow to hate him for the anguish he'd put her through when he should have known better and considered her feelings rather than his desire.

He should stop the impending sorrow now and refuse to see her again, depriving himself of her laughter, smile, touch, scent. All he had to do was live without those things.

Tomás sank to his chair, head in his hands, knowing he couldn't. He needed a few more days with her, at least. A week perhaps. No, a month. Possibly more.

He wasn't a pious man, but soon found himself praying for time.

* * * *

The following morning, Beatriz was the only one who congratulated Yolanda on her new position. The other servants seemed confused, stunned, or were outwardly jealous, muttering that the girl wasn't special, never had been, and hardly deserved such a lofty job that should have gone to them.

By late afternoon, the cruel barbs had taken their toll, Yolanda no longer her buoyant self.

Beatriz searched the child's lovely face. "What happened?"

"I fear everyone hates me now."

She slipped her arm around Yolanda's narrow shoulders, chiding herself for having mucked things up. She'd only wanted to help, not bring her pain. "Surely the others will adjust."

"I hope they do. Too many times today, I got shoved, tripped, pinched, and burned."

"Burned? Who did that? Where?"

"My wrist is fine now." She held her arm to her chest. "The hot grease stung for no more than a few minutes."

Beatriz rubbed her forehead. "Would you like to work as a scullery maid again? Were you happier?"

"No. I earn more now than I had before and my tasks are easier than yours."

Thanks to Tomás. She cupped Yolanda's chin. "Then smile."

Yolanda did, making her even lovelier, but quickly backed away. "I must be off. I have so much to learn. Tonight I keep watch on the tallow and wax." She bolted away, skirt flying.

Beatriz returned to cleaning those bedchambers the señoritas and their mamás had used. The lot had manners worse than a common villager. They'd left food on the floor to rot, spilled wine on the fine linens, tracked in mud, and ruined two pillows, sending the feathers everywhere.

By the time she'd finished, the hour was late, her chance to dust Tomás's study finally at hand. Excitement dashed through her, making her giddy with expectation. All day she'd waited for this moment.

She darted from the last chamber and nearly collided with Nuncio in the hall.

He reared back. So did she.

"Forgive me." Beatriz pressed her hand to her chest. "I had no idea you were lurking about in the dark without a candle to guide you."

Nuncio curled his upper lip. "I was walking, as is my right."

She gave him a sweet smile. "Of course. The fault, as always, is mine. Can you possibly forgive me?"

He lifted his chin. "What spirit you seemed to have gained since we last spoke. Remember these moments well. They will not last. They never do, no matter what Don Tomás may have said." He strode past.

"Wait." He practically ran. Beatriz grabbed a candle from the cabinet and caught up. "What do you mean they never do?"

Nuncio had led her to believe that Tomás hadn't behaved with anyone here as he had with her. Before that, he'd been away fighting the Moors, his actions at the fortaleza not Nuncio's concern, including any girls Tomás had taken there in between his battles.

Her stomach sank. Tomás had said he'd enjoyed life, which surely meant women, during those times he hadn't fought for the Crown. Perhaps Nuncio had referred to that. Perhaps not.

He gave her a cold smile and disappeared into the darkness.

As eager as she'd been to see Tomás, she was now as reluctant. Picturing him with another woman gave her pause, when it shouldn't have.

Men had lovers and mistresses even after they wed. Still, she'd hoped to be the first servant Tomás had desired here or anywhere else. Not much to ask for when her future with him was stillborn.

Heartsick, she finally slogged down the stairs, her candle providing scant illumination. The castle was dark, cool, and quiet, the other servants in their quarters or at their tasks in a far part of the structure.

She reached the hall prior to Tomás's study. A figure skulked in the shadows. She stopped short, her breath catching. Nuncio? She lifted her candle.

Rufio. He stalked toward her, smiling suggestively.

Her skin crawled. She wanted to flee but sensed he might consider her escape a game and run her down. If she bolted to the study, he would surely follow and might start rumors about her and Tomás.

Acting on impulse, she hurried to him before he could reach her. "How fortunate to see you here." She grabbed his sleeve and pulled him farther away from the study. "We must speak."

Surprise crossed his face. "We can go to the kitchen. No one is there."

She released him. "Here is fine. As you know, I fear Nuncio."

Rufio rocked on his heels, his chest puffed out. "I can handle him."

"And lose your position if he catches you with me at this hour? I beg you, protect yourself and Yolanda."

"That annoying brat? Why her?"

Beatriz told him what Yolanda had said. "Please check on her for me. Yolanda has to keep an eye on the tallow and wax. Make certain no one lurks around bothering or hurting her. Guard the entrance to where she works all night if you must."

Rufio made a face. "What do I get if I do?"

"You can have my wages as soon as I receive them."

"What if I want something else?"

She forced herself not to step back, showing fear or disgust. "The wages will have to do. Take them or leave them."

He shrugged. "After I waste my night protecting her, you best pay up."

Again, he'd proven he was like most men, thinking only of himself and money. "You have my word. Go, please."

"In good time." He stepped closer.

She backed away and stopped at movement past his shoulder. "Leave now." She spoke softly. "Señor Nuncio is behind you."

Rather than handling the old man as he'd promised, Rufio looked over, pivoted, and hurried away. Beatriz didn't bother to speak to Nuncio or try to explain herself. He already thought the worst of her.

Before anyone else crossed her path, she rushed to the study and stopped outside the door, cold with dread, her throat tight. She had to end this now before she lost her heart and couldn't recover. To repeat what she and Tomás had shared on the hillside would be madness given what Nuncio had implied.

Braced for pain, she slipped inside the study and closed the door.

Tomás looked up. He was in in his chair, elbows on his knees, hands clasped either in prayer or as he troubled over something. Beatriz lowered her candle to a cabinet, their silence lengthening. The air grew thick, charged with emotion she needed to fight but couldn't.

He stood and crossed the room to her, she to him. Their embrace was as heated as their kiss, her fingers buried in his hair, his hand on her breast. She melted into him, knowing she was damned, her good intentions forgotten already. Until he or circumstances forced her to leave, she had to have moments like this.

He pulled his mouth free and gulped air, his forehead against hers. "Take off your cap. Take off everything, please. I have to taste you again."

As she did him, though not now. She sidled away.

He made a face. "What are you doing? Get back here."

"Shhh." She inclined her head to the door.

He pressed his mouth to her ear. "Is someone out there listening?"

"Perhaps. On the way to your study, Rufio then Señor Nuncio came upon me."

"What was Rufio doing in this part of the castle? Is he now following you?"

"He hasn't just started. He's done so since I began working here."

Tomás eased back and frowned. "You should have told me."

"I am now. Both of them hound my moves. I need to dust and go."

"No. Never. We need to kiss, enjoy each other, and read. Stay here as I tend to things."

"Wait." She grabbed his sleeve. "What are you going to do?"

"Make certain neither comes near my study."

"Are you going to let Rufio go? He has a mean streak and could exact revenge against you."

Tomás laughed quietly. "That will be the day." He rested his hand on her neck, his thumb stroking her jaw.

She leaned into his touch, defenseless against him. "Heed my words, please."

"I have no intention of dismissing Rufio. There are countless tasks to keep him away from you, this room, or anywhere near these halls."

"Leaving you to deal with Señor Nuncio. Do you plan to throw him off the hill?"

"Him I'd prefer to strangle."

She fought a smile. "As much as I dislike him, he does mean well. He has your best interests at heart."

"I am not his to worry about. Dust if you want, but prepare yourself for pleasure when I return." He left the room, closing the door quietly.

Beatriz tried not to worry, but his absence dragged on. The candles grew short. She paced until her legs hurt and checked the hall several times to see if anyone was there. The area remained deserted and dark.

Her stomach rolled. She worried that Rufio had waylaid Tomás, until she considered how ridiculous that would be. Rufio was a menace to her, not a man. He'd fled readily upon seeing Nuncio, exactly as a coward would. He wouldn't dare do anything to hurt Tomás.

Exhausted, she curled up in his chair, El Cid's tale on her lap to keep her company.

* * * *

His talk with Señora Cisneros had taken far longer than Tomás had wanted. First, he had to wake her and apologize for doing so. Next, he had to make small talk about her work and everyone's duties so he could finally circle around to Rufio. Getting him away from Beatriz without the señora guessing that Tomás was trying to protect her.

The woman was no fool. "I told the boy many times to quit chasing the women."

"Perhaps he should have listened. Make certain he does from now on."

After much deliberation, she suggested Rufio work with the outside laborers, rather than anywhere in the castle.

Tomás agreed.

"For the same wage?" she asked.

"Of course."

With Rufio's future settled, Tomás had searched for Nuncio and found the man in his bed, where he should have been hours ago.

"I know you were following Beatriz tonight." Tomás planted his hands on his hips. "Never do so again. Stay away from her. This is my last warning."

"Are you going to dismiss me?"

"I plan to throw you out the window if you refuse to heed my word."

"What of Rufio?" Nuncio held his bedsheet to his scrawny throat. "He was following her earlier."

"He no longer works in the castle. His duties will be outside with the other laborers. Would you care to join them, rather than remain in this luxury?"

Nuncio's room was nearly as fine as Tomás's. The bed large, mattress and pillow soft, beautiful tapestries on the walls, Persian rugs on the floor.

"I shall do as you wish." Nuncio offered a pained smile. "Even if you come to harm."

"How gracious of you to allow me to meet my ruin. Have a pleasant evening." Tomás was determined to do so.

He returned to his study. Curled up in his chair, Beatriz was fast asleep, looking small and defenseless, like a little girl. Tenderness poured through him. He closed the door carefully to avoid waking her.

She did anyway, blinking at his approach. She pushed up. "What happened?"

"Nothing untoward." He offered his hand. Once he'd helped her to her feet, he sat and pulled her onto his lap. "Go on, sleep."

"Like this?"

He couldn't think of a better way unless they were naked and sharing a bed. Not likely this night or any other. Earlier, he'd prayed for more time with her and was now content to have her back in his arms. "Sí."

He eased her head to his shoulder.

She rested her palm on his chest. "Did all go well?"

"From now on, Rufio will work outside with the other laborers. Nuncio too, if he bothers you again. Both are out of your life forever, never to come near this room or you."

She finished her yawn. "We can look forward to pleasure?"

"Tomorrow." He stroked her arm. "For now, I want you to rest."

"Only for a moment. You must wake me."

"I promise."

She snuggled into him, fitting perfectly, and fell asleep. Tomás drifted off.

* * * *

They awoke near dawn, sore from having slept in the chair. Tomás welcomed the hurt, loving how she'd kept him warm, delighted to smell her scent before anything else.

After groaning and stretching, Beatriz gave him a chaste kiss, then straightened her cap. "I must go and get ready for the day."

"The evening too. Remember, you owe me pleasure."

She smiled. "As you do with me."

Nothing would keep him from her. He spent an endless day going over the castle's receipts with the accountant, listening to problems regarding the cattle, fields, vineyards, and horses, and answering missives from the mamás who'd visited, with them pushing for a return invitation.

Tomás wrote that he was leaving the area to see his papá in the north and had no idea when he might return. Finished at last, he awaited Beatriz's arrival.

Her footfalls finally sounded in the hall.

Like the other times, she carried a lone candle. Her lips parted at the dozens he'd lit in preparation for their time together.

He couldn't wait to begin. "Close the door."

The moment she had, he came around his desk and stood before her. "You said you have a fantasy about being a conquered maiden."

Her blush was obvious in the light. "I do."

"With me as the warrior who captured you."

She ran her fingertips down his shirt. "Sí."

"Sí? Is that how you answer the man who owns you?"

Beatriz smiled slowly and quite sensually. She inclined her head in submission. "No, master."

He liked this game, but suppressed his smile to play his lordly role. "Take off your cap and unpin your hair. Now."

She placed the linen and pins in his palm. He put them on his desk and returned to her. Beatriz's tresses fell in soft waves to her waist, the dark locks glossy in the light, beckoning him to press his face to them.

He controlled himself for now. With his hands behind his back, legs parted, he affected a conqueror's stance. "Remove your clothes."

Bold lust burned in her eyes. She worked her laces faster than she had on the hill, dropped the items to the side, and stood naked before him. Her skin shone golden and flawless in the candlelight, nipples tight, the folds between her legs surely damp with passion.

"On your knees. Legs parted."

She sank to the floor and looked up at him. Her irises reflected the flames, giving her an unearthly appearance.

He wanted to devour her, but held himself in check and circled at a slow pace, drinking in her nudity, wanting Beatriz to feel how naked she was.

Her face was bright red, but a wanton smile curled her lips.

He paused behind her, yearning to kiss the dimples above her buttocks. Restraining himself, he stepped closer. She stilled, not even breathing.

No matter how much air Tomás pulled in, the room still swayed. He had to have relief soon from his burgeoning passion or lose his mind. He stopped in front and lifted his shirt above his hose. His shaft was so erect it hurt, his sac pulled tight to his body, his need insatiable. "Tend to me."

She kissed his belly, enticing him with her silky lips and comforting heat. He had to tense his legs to keep upright. Making a pleased sound, she untied the laces on his hose and braies, then eased both garments down.

His member sprang free, his flesh thick and hard.

A low moan flowed from her. She cupped his buttocks and pressed her face to his dark curls.

Warmth rushed through Tomás in an endless flood, prickling his skin. He lifted his face to the ceiling, teeth clenched.

On a wanton sound, she squeezed his cheeks and rubbed her nose in his thatch. He lost what little air he'd taken, unable to make another noise. Her shameless caress stole his breath and all thought.

She brushed her lips over his length, her touch gentle as a sigh, her tongue hot and wet. At last, she reached the head and took him inside her mouth.

Tomás fought for control. She'd imprisoned him in the best way, short of her sheath. He pushed his fingers through her hair, crushing the silky strands in his fists.

Encouraging his carnal hunger, she ran her tongue over the most sensitive part on his crown, then eased his sex deeper into her mouth. He shuddered at her incredible heat. She kept at her task, not stopping until she'd taken in his entire member.

Every part of him rejoiced.

She worked her mouth up and down the hard column, licking his full length, doing what her channel never could.

The room spun. Sweat rolled down his face and chest.

Beatriz stroked his buttocks and tight opening. An incredible move he liked. She suckled and licked his shaft, then let it slip past her lips.

No, no, no. She shouldn't have stopped. He was her master, she the conquered maiden, required to do whatever he commanded. "Continue. Now. I mean it."

"As you wish." She lapped his sac.

Unimaginable pleasure dashed through him. Delight he'd never known, rapture one should only experience past death. Rarely, had he been as alive, nearing the peak, the precipice at hand.

She took his member back between her lips, her movement quick, licking endless, while she also caressed his sac. Her gentle fondling and persistent suckling undid him. He shattered, his seed pouring into her mouth.

She accepted him without hesitation, swallowing every trace. Finished, she looked up.

He sank to his knees, chest heaving with his ragged breaths. With his arms around her waist, he rested his chin on her shoulder. "Tend to me."

They sagged to the floor. Beatriz held him as he drifted toward sleep, her loving embrace, wondrous scent, and unparalleled heat conquering him.

* * * *

She spent her days dreaming about the evenings, her nights stripped bare in his study, playing their wicked games.

On their sixth evening together, he gave her a challenge. "I want a new fantasy. Devise one for the morrow. No work for either of us, remember? We have the whole day to ourselves."

"On the hillside?"

He winked. "I intend to surprise you and expect the same in return."

"Surprise me how?"

"Wait until morning and see."

The night passed too slowly, Beatriz eager to be in his arms again. As she dressed the next morning, Yolanda ran to her, cheeks flushed. "Hurry. You must go to the stable."

Of course, she must. Tomás waited there to take her to a new spot as a surprise. Perhaps to a pond on his property where they'd enjoy a meal, then each other. She stroked Yolanda's arm. "Do you like making candles?"

She bounced in place. "I do. Hurry."

Beatriz took a shorter path than she had the previous time, no longer worried about running into anyone. For the past week, no one had followed her to the study.

She smiled at the morning sky, only a few clouds hugging the horizon. Flowers scented the air, birds called to each other, the wind tugged her locks in every direction. She hadn't worn her cap or braided her hair today. No need. As Tomás had said, they wouldn't toil this day.

The stable was only a short distance but she couldn't wait any longer. She broke into a run, smiling so hard her cheeks hurt. No workers milled about, the same as the last time she and Tomás had played this game. Breathless, she dashed into the structure and considered trying each stall, coming upon him before he could do so with her.

Liking such sport, she raced to the other end, thinking to catch him there.

The horses neighed and whinnied.

A door squeaked behind her. Laughing, she swung around, arms open.

Rufio strode from the stall, shirt damp with sweat, mud and straw on his boots, his features icy.

She cringed. "What are you doing here?"

"Guess you thought the master would be here, instead, as he was the last time when you two rode off. Not likely."

What had Rufio done? "Where is he?"

"My, how familiar you sound when you speak of the master." Rage swept his features. "You always did think you was better than the rest of us. You had him send me here and ruined everything for me. No more. Now, you pay."

He pounced. Hand over her mouth, he dragged her into the stall.

Chapter 6

Tomás could barely keep still in his study, eager to begin his day with Beatriz. Minutes before, he'd sent for Yolanda and awaited her now. Better to have the child, rather than him, go to the servant quarters to tell Beatriz where she had to be in order to learn his newest surprise. One he'd worked on for days.

Once she saw what he'd prepared, she'd surely come up with a delightful fantasy for them to engage in.

Light footfalls sounded in the hall. A young girl, no doubt Yolanda, stopped in the doorway to his study, cheeks flushed, mood expectant.

He gestured her into the room. "I have a task for you. Can I trust you to carry out what I ask?"

"Sí, Patrón. I would never fail you."

He liked her eagerness and lack of guile. Nuncio could take lessons from her on how a servant should behave. "I need you to deliver a message to Beatriz. I understand the two of you are friends."

"We are. The only one I have left."

He wasn't certain what she meant and didn't have time to ask. "As her friend, I want you to keep this message a secret from everyone else. Can you do so?"

"I already have twice."

"What do you mean?"

"Last week I told her to go to the stable as Señora Cisneros said I should. A few minutes ago, I did the same."

"Did the same what?"

"Told Beatriz to go to the stable. I told none of the servants, just as you wanted."

"Just as I…" He frowned. "What are you talking about?"

She pulled in her shoulders. "You wanted me to give your message to Beatriz a few minutes ago. Rufio said you—"

"Rufio?" Tomás's chest tightened. "What has he to do with this?"

"He said to tell Beatriz to go to the stable. You wanted her there and no one should know."

Tomás ran from the room and down the hall to the entryway. Nuncio gaped at him. Tomás skidded to a stop. "Alert the guards. Tell them to go to the stable."

Nuncio rushed in the other direction.

Tomás bolted outside and tore across the grounds, rage mingling with fear. Beatriz had warned that Rufio would exact revenge. Tomás should have heeded her words. If anything happened to her…if that beast laid one hand on…

He sprinted to the stable, racing inside. Horses snorted loudly. Several squealed.

The brute was on top, holding Beatriz down. She punched and kicked futilely, her sleeve torn.

He yanked Rufio off her. The young man staggered back, arms flailing. Tomás stomped toward him. "*Puto.*"

The foulest word in the Spanish language.

Rufio breathed hard, his ruddy face going white. "You misunderstand, Patrón. We were playing a game. She wanted me to do this."

Tomás slammed his fist into Rufio's jaw.

His head snapped back. He staggered but didn't fall, and twisted around to run.

Tomás landed a solid punch in his side, then his belly.

Gagging, Rufio dropped to his knees, his lip split, blood dirtying his chin.

Three guards raced inside, swords drawn.

"Remove this thing from my estate." Tomás flung his hand at Rufio. "Take him to the *hermandad*. Have them deal with him." He strode to Beatriz.

"No." Rufio staggered to his feet. "I did nothing wrong."

Tomás bunched his shoulders, fury pulsing through him. "Take the animal now."

Rufio sidestepped the men. "Will you have the whore go to the hermandad too to explain how she seduced—"

"Puto." Tomás lunged.

Rufio backed into a stall door, arms over his head, bent at the waist to protect himself. "If I go, she does too, to prove what you think I did. All lies. She wanted the game."

Tomás stilled, not throwing his next blow. Beatriz huddled against the back wall, knees to her chest, face lowered.

A dull pain pulsed in his belly. Asking her to prove her purity to men she didn't know was more than he feared she could bear. However, he had to give her the chance to decide on her own.

He sank to one knee at her side. "Do you want to go?"

She shook her head.

He turned to his guards. "Throw the puto off my estate with no more than his belongings."

"Wait." Rufio stayed clear of the men. "What of my wages?"

"You forfeited them when you attacked the señorita."

"She is a whore."

Tomás left the stall. "Take this rubbish away before I kill him. No one speaks of what happened here to anyone, understand?"

His men nodded.

"Even you know she lies," Rufio said. "Why else would you keep this a secret?"

Tomás spat. "You are filth. If you tell anyone of your service here, hoping to gain another position, I promise to warn your new master to get rid of you immediately."

"Please Patrón. Without your good word, I can never work again."

"If you starve, the outcome would be too good for you."

The guards hauled Rufio from the building. His pleas shifted to crude oaths.

Tomás returned to Beatriz and gathered her in his arms. She stiffened, then squirmed, trying to break free. The pain in his belly worsened. "Forgive me. I mean no harm." He loosened his hold. "Should I send for the physician?" He spoke quietly. "How badly did Rufio hurt you?"

She kept her face lowered, tears dripping from her chin. "You came before he could do his worst." Her shoulders trembled. "I thought you sent for me like the last time. He was on me so quickly, I…"

"Rufio will never bother you again."

Tomás stroked her hair. Straw stuck to her tresses, tunic, and gown. Although the horses had quieted somewhat, they were still agitated, the stable hands nowhere in sight. He guessed Rufio had lied to keep them well away from this place so he could attack her. "Let me bring you back to the castle."

"No. The others will see how I look."

"Only if you return to the servant quarters. I have another place in mind. Where I intended to bring you for your surprise today."

She eased back, her eyes reddened. "Intended? You no longer want me?"

Oh Beatriz. "Of course, I do." He hugged her even harder. "Never question my feelings. I just thought…" He didn't know how to continue.

"What? Tell me."

"Rufio showed you the worst way a man can behave. Do you still want me?"

She kissed him deeply, her lips salty with tears, her caress desperate, not letting him go. When she finally finished, she pressed her cheek to his. "I want you as I never will another man. I need you to take me in every possible way."

Tomás wasn't certain what she meant, or if she realized what she'd said. "Do you mean our coupling?"

She cupped his face. "From the start, I wanted nothing more. If Rufio had succeeded, he would have been my first. I would have lost that moment with you." Her expression grew more pained. "One I can hold dear for all time."

After they parted. She was already saying goodbye.

He clasped her to him, unwilling to allow such an outcome. "We have many moments, starting now. Are you able to walk or do you need me to carry you?"

"To your study?"

"No. A hidden place within the castle. Only Señora Cisneros knows its location. I had her clean the spot we'll use."

"Hidden why?"

"Let me show you." He helped Beatriz to her feet. In addition to her torn sleeve, she'd lost a shoe.

He helped her to make things right, even picking straw from her hair. When he slipped his arm around her waist, she pulled away. He brought her back. "The others will never see us together. The entrance is on the other side of the castle, far away from the usual areas, planned that way deliberately."

"By you?"

He smiled. "The Moor who once owned this land."

"Are we going to his study?"

Tomás laughed softly. "No. Let me show you."

He led her from the stable.

With no one about, she pressed against him, her arm firmly around his waist. Her complexion had almost returned to normal, tears at an end. They reached the entrance he'd mentioned. Tall bushes shielded the area and wooden door from notice.

She pressed her mouth to his ear. "Is this where the Moor kept his prisoners?"

"In a manner of speaking."

She searched his face. "Can you explain further for a simple servant like me?"

He could, but wanted to surprise her. "Never refer to yourself as simple or as a servant. The highest-ranking ladies in the kingdom are not nearly as noble as you."

Her brow wrinkled.

He had no idea why and wasn't about to question her. No matter how much she might have argued, she was the finest woman he'd ever known. Today, she'd be his.

A reckless decision if he didn't intend on them sharing their lives. Somehow, he'd have to see they did, find a way to make them fit together, not only here but in his world too.

With her hand in his, he led Beatriz inside. The walls and polished stone floor were cool to the touch, the ceiling arched. He'd lit an oil lamp earlier in preparation for this, just as the Moor who'd once lived here would have done. Today, everything needed to be magical. If Rufio had ravished her, Tomás would have never forgiven himself. Her first time with a man should be a breathtaking act with such intense joy she'd always want more.

They strolled deeper into the space. The hall widened into a large chamber that led to an interior courtyard. There was no access to this spot from the castle. No one except Señora Cisneros knew the place existed.

Beatriz eased from him and explored. Instead of heavy Spanish chairs, benches, and tables, low platforms with thin mattresses, large vases, and exquisitely designed rugs in red, blue, and gold dominated the area. Silk sheets covered each mattress. Colorful pillows lay strewn about. Intricate latticework screens stood next to arched windows and doors, opened now to allow an unrestricted view of the small courtyard. Flowers in every color, lush green plants, and towering trees created a veritable Eden.

Her eyes glittered. "Is this, or was this, what I think it is?"

"A prison?"

"In a manner of speaking. A harem, no?"

Yes. This room, and the ones beyond it, spoke of a woman's willing surrender to the man who owned her. Sensuality permeated the space. Tomás wanted Beatriz nude and reclined over the purple silk nearest her. Arms above her head, baring her breasts, legs parted to expose her folds, dewy and plump with arousal, begging for a man's sex. He had to lock his knees to keep standing. "Are you offended, appalled, incensed—"

"Delighted. Did Señora Cisneros feel the same when she saw this, or was she dismayed at having to clean this room on her own?"

"The castle parlor is far larger and I did pay her well."

Beatriz regarded the silk-covered mattresses. "Did you tell her why you wanted her to take care of this?"

"You mean as a den of desire for you and me?"

She laughed.

Every horrible thing in the past faded with the sound. "I told her I wanted to use this space to get away from the constraints and demands of my estate. And to avoid Nuncio whenever I could."

"How clever. What did you tell the men who tended the courtyard?" She gestured to the vegetation.

"I took care of the plants on my own."

"And the pools?"

Two depressed areas of moderate size lay in the stone floor, clean water sparkling in each. Harem women had probably used them, rather than tubs, to bathe. "Sí."

"You did so much work by yourself?"

She made him sound incapable of hauling water from the courtyard well or tending soil. Next, he feared she'd suggest Yolanda wash his hands after meals. "I had to amuse myself with something during the endless days. You waited far into each night to dust my study and tend to me."

"Forgive me for being so thoughtless of your feelings. Is that for me?" She inclined her head to the large basket he'd left on a red silk sheet.

"I thought we might share. Are you hungry?"

"For every part of you, always."

His cheeks heated at her words. Despite being a virgin, she thought like a man. He liked that.

She stroked his nipples and suckled his neck.

His legs wavered from fierce desire whipping through him. "Does your hunger for me involve a new fantasy?"

She purred and eased back. "Several. Beginning with you as my master in the harem, teaching me what to expect as your slave."

He pulled her into him, her mound against his thickened shaft. "You mean, conquering you."

"Using me for your pleasure, delivering ecstasy neither of us can resist."

A delightful idea. However, she was still untried. He ran his thumb over her cheek, tracing the tracks from her dried tears. "I want you to be honest with me. Are you afraid to lie with a man?"

"Not you. I offer my virginity without regret."

"You can never go back once the deed is done."

"Why would I want to? I was unhappy and lonely before we met. You gave me a reason to smile."

He hurt for her. "Was your life so terrible? Tell me. I want to know."

"I want to forget. Help me to do so, please."

Tomás wanted to ask more, but kept his peace, giving her what she needed now. He kissed her with all the longing he possessed. She responded eagerly. They made noises only lovers could, filling the room with passionate sounds as old as time.

He cupped her neck and pulled his mouth free. Her lips were wet from their kiss, bruised with their desire.

"You willingly become my slave in here?"

"From this moment forward."

"I can do with you as I will?"

"Use me well and never deny yourself. In these rooms, everything is possible, nothing forbidden. This is our world."

He never wanted to go anywhere else. Her desire stirred him deeply, her passion coming from deep within, not a game like other señoritas who expected a betrothal or marriage in return. Beatriz wanted him for the man he was, flawed and lacking in so many ways.

She didn't see his imperfections.

He embraced her as fiercely as he dared, not wanting to hurt her.

"Are you all right?" She hugged him. "Have I spoken out of turn?"

"Never. You continue to amaze me."

"I have yet to do anything."

"You will." He released her. "Undress me."

She regarded his clothing. "Such an easy task."

"In time my demands will grow far more difficult." He leaned down until their noses nearly touched. "Some might say hard."

Color crept up her throat to her cheeks. Studiously, she avoided his gaze. After unbuckling his belt, she hung it over her shoulder. "So heavy." She stroked the fine leather. "How do you manage to wear this every day?"

"A man learns to carry many weighty things around."

She glanced at his groin. "Surely, you must grow tired of such a burden and need relief at times."

He did right now. His member strained against his braies and hose, wanting inside her sheath so badly he feared harming them both with his desire. "Are you tempting me?"

"Undressing you." She put his belt on the floor, pulled his shirt off, and dropped the garment on silk striped blue and gold.

On her knees, she tugged off his shoes and hose, placing each item on the other, undressing him far more slowly than he would have liked. Fevered and wanting, he could barely stand still. His muscles kept bunching, demanding action like the warrior he was, the master who owned her body and soul.

He wanted her heart. Unwilling to settle for anything less, he held himself in check.

At length, she relieved him of his braies, and lowered it to his other things. With him finally nude, she kissed a particularly long battle scar and looked up, her mouth close to his rigid sex, her breaths skipping over the thickened rod.

He snatched a meager amount of air. Taking more was beyond his capabilities. "On your feet." He was determined to give her a fantasy she'd never forget even if he died waiting for his own pleasure. "Take off your clothes."

Her knowing smile fueled his need for everything she was. Bright, kind, seductive, his. Tomás wouldn't consider any other outcome for them. They belonged together.

She placed her shoes, stockings, and tunic next to his garments. When she touched her torn sleeve from Rufio's violence, her mouth turned down.

"Would you like me to help?" He didn't want anything dampening her spirits. "Or do you want to kill me with the wait?"

Beatriz laughed, his teasing having the desired effect. She worked the laces. As always, there seemed to be no end to them. In the future, he'd insist she never wear clothes on their days together. Perhaps he'd give his entire staff the same time off, leaving him and Beatriz free to roam the castle nude.

He grinned at his outrageous fantasy.

She gave him an odd look and tossed her gown and chemise on the other clothing. Gloriously naked at last. No harem girl could match her beauty, dark hair against milky skin, her nipples rosy, breasts ripe, hips lavish. She was beyond temptation, more womanly than a man's most indecent dreams.

Her scent captivated. The hint of musk enthralled.

She cocked her head. "What are you thinking?"

Better to show than to tell. He pulled silk from the wall, the fabric light as air, tinted yellow and green. "Give me your hands, wrists together."

She kept her arms at her sides. "What?"

"Already you tire of being my slave?"

"No...I..." She put out her hands.

Tomás wrapped the fabric around her wrists and secured it with a knot. Using the silk as he might a rope, he led her to a screen next to an open window. Sun spilled inside, slanting across her hip and the dark curls between her legs, already damp with her arousal.

His shoulders and chest grew increasingly taut, his escalating need difficult to ignore. "Raise your arms above your head."

She looked at the screen. "Is this what a Moor does in his harem?"

"If not, he should."

She laughed and lifted her arms. He secured her wrists to the screen and stepped back, regarding her nudity, how vulnerable she was to his will and touch.

* * * *

She softened beneath his gaze, eager to have him fill her. They'd careened toward these moments since their first kiss. Rufio had simply hurried matters along. When he'd pressed himself against her, she'd feared surviving his attack more than she had death. A lifetime would never erase the memory of a man mounting her against her will.

She'd escaped the city to avoid such a future.

She couldn't deny herself or Tomás any longer. Her virginity meant nothing if she had to lie with someone she didn't love or respect. To live out her life without having known Tomás's touch, strength, and passion was too awful to imagine. Whatever happened in the future, she'd always have these moments.

Lust flooded his features, along with awe and tenderness. She wasn't simply a means to an end. She mattered to him. He'd proven himself when he'd fought Rufio, helped Yolanda, tended the garden here, and carried in fresh water.

He'd worked hard to make her happy, giving Beatriz the greatest gift a man could.

She loved him. Foolish, of course. Tradition said she should feel shame for losing her virginity, especially without marriage first. Wonder filled her. Never would she regret this day or any others they might have.

He touched the silk around her wrists and slid his fingers down the insides of her arms. She laughed. "That tickles."

"Then I must do something else."

He licked her nipple and eased the tip inside his mouth.

Heaven. She raised her face to the ceiling. Each swirl of his tongue sent warmth surging to her mound, dampening her folds even more.

He suckled her other nipple, his mouth hot, hand between her legs, gliding over her slippery cleft. His growl sounded pleased and aroused.

The most exciting thing she'd ever heard.

He sank to his knees, exposing her sex to his view and touch.

She couldn't have been more naked or owned more completely. He tongued her opening and licked her nub. Delight erupted within her. Eager to give herself to him, she pushed closer.

He gripped her hips, giving her no peace or release, slowing his licks and pausing, then beginning anew before she'd caught her breath. Whenever she was ready to fall over the edge and soar, he stopped, allowing the feelings to fade.

She burned with frustration, then went soft with submission each time he briefly gave her what she needed. All too soon, she was certain she'd lose her mind. "Please, give me relief."

"In time."

She might not survive that long. Abruptly, he pulled his mouth from her sex and stroked her instead. Touch firm, movements quick.

Release whisked through her, her sheath pulsing rhythmically. Her head fell forward, knees bent, every part of her so weak that standing proved a trial.

Tomás shot to his feet, untied her wrists, and swept her into his arms.

She curled into him, her cheek to his shoulder, breath heating his neck.

He lowered her to a mattress draped in gold silk. The fabric shimmered in light streaming across the room. With her wrists cuffed in one hand, he imprisoned her arms over her head and settled between her legs, trapping her further.

She'd never known such freedom, a curious weightlessness, the dark days she'd lived finally in the past. "Fill me, please, before we both burst. Especially you."

His features were tight with passion, muscles tense, blond tresses falling over his forehead. The image he created was more beautiful than an angel. And as tortured as the damned, his color rising. "Why do you wait?"

"Our coupling may hurt at first."

"Followed by pleasure, no?"

"More than you can imagine."

"Show me. Teach me."

She needed him to love her and pulled back her legs, inviting him to take what she offered.

He regarded her for a long moment, their intimacy reaching her soul. He lifted his shaft to her opening, bathed the crown in her moisture, and entered fully.

She started but didn't cry out, welcoming the sting, Tomás making her his. He was a large man, his member stretching her sheath to the limit, filling her completely.

He huffed out several breaths, pulled in more, and kissed her shoulder.

"Will you live?"

"Will you?"

"I have no intention of dying at this point." He pulled out of her until only his crown remained inside, then plunged again. Their curls touched for a moment before he pumped once more.

The sting faded beneath new tension building within her sheath. Her opening seemed smaller, congested somehow. On an impulse, she squeezed her channel around his shaft.

He groaned loudly, pumped faster, and stroked her nub.

She shuddered from the intense pleasure. Her sheath tightened around his sex, adding to the friction between them. They rocked in time with his thrusts, breathing ragged, sounds reduced to moans, whimpers, grunts, and growls.

Beatriz yielded first, trembling from the delight he'd delivered. Soaring as she'd never done before.

* * * *

Tomás couldn't get close enough to her no matter how hard he tried. Coupling with Beatriz wasn't enough. He needed to be a part of her blood and marrow, so deep within that nothing would ever separate them.

He drove his sex into hers, its tightness and heat precisely what he needed, the same as her response. Her sheath pulsed around his rod, proving her satisfaction. Reaching release a second time, she moaned roughly, caught up in pleasure that overshadowed convention.

Beatriz enjoyed coupling as much as a man did. She was more than perfect. She was a miracle.

He lost himself completely between her legs, lust consuming him. Her breasts shook with his powerful thrusts, the faint slap of their bodies the most beautiful sounds he'd ever heard. He fought release as relentlessly as he'd battled the Moors, wanting this to last forever.

His passion betrayed him at each step. Pressure built within his shaft and sac to an unmanageable level, pleasure wanting its due. He tightened his shoulders, squeezed his lids, and surrendered, roaring like an uncivilized beast.

Seconds later, he trembled like a newborn, his strength drained fully.

He sank down and supported his weight on his elbows to avoid crushing her.

She smoothed back his hair and tightened her sheath around his shaft once more.

He shuddered. "Squeeze again and I may die."

"Forgive me. I had no idea how fragile you are."

He laughed tiredly and lifted his head with great effort. "Have I shown and taught you well?"

Her smile was luminous. "I may need more lessons."

Chapter 7

Beatriz hadn't believed Tomás could surprise her more than he already had. She was wrong. "You and I will go to Hell for this."

He grinned at her from across the narrow pool, his elbows resting on the edge, legs stretched out. Beneath the water, his shaft looked even thicker and longer, his sac luscious.

"I see no sin in bathing." He gave her an innocent look. "Do you?"

She arched one eyebrow. "Is that what you call this?"

He'd posed her quite indecently, her legs parted and bent at the knees, sex displayed, breasts skimming the water.

He sighed noisily. "I call this heaven."

Even paradise couldn't match the splendor of this moment or place. A soft breeze flowed through the airy room, ruffling the silk hangings, delivering sweetness from flowers, freshness from vegetation. Birds sang. Water slapped gently against stone.

Tomás's peaceful mood matched her contentment.

She breathed deeply. "How can we return to work after this?"

"We always have your nights dusting."

"Reading too and writing an epic poem about your grand adventures."

"Are you glad we became friends?"

Her spirit would have died without him. Even with her newfound freedom, she'd found her future difficult to face. Having nothing to look forward to except toiling endlessly without hope for true happiness, constant worry about losing her position and not finding another, someone discovering who she really was and returning her to a man she loathed.

Tomás had changed everything for her, at least during this brief slice of time. When they finally parted, she'd have to move on alone, though she would be richer for having known him.

She pushed melancholy aside. "Indeed, I am. After being in service to you, I will never look at dusting the same way again."

He laughed heartily and slapped the water, sending a wave in her direction. She squealed and did the same to him. They played like children, each trying to make the other wet, finally wrestling in the pool, their behavior boisterous and silly. She was no match for his strength. However, she did know how to pinch and twisted the skin on his ribs.

He yelped and pulled back, hands lifted. "I surrender before you draw blood."

"A wise choice." She clawed wet hair from her face. "Though I must say, you were an almost worthy opponent."

Tomás hugged her fiercely. "You have to stop making me laugh so much."

"Would you like another pinch?"

"A kiss." He fitted his mouth to hers, his desire surprisingly tender and exploring, seeming to stop time.

Beatriz embraced him with love, her tongue stroking his, the noises they made pleasant and happy.

When he broke free, he rested his face against her neck, lips skimming her skin, his breath heating her more than the sun ever could.

She burned these moments in her mind and eased her fingers through his damp hair.

"That feels good." He sighed. "You must always tend to me like this."

She couldn't imagine doing anything else during the time they had left. "Of course. What are friends for?"

"Some might say to get to know each other better." He stroked her nipple.

The tip hardened, halo constricting, pleasure coursing through her. "I may be wrong, but bathing as we are should mean we crossed the line from reserve to familiarity."

"Not in every way. I want to know about you."

Her stomach clenched.

He kissed her jaw. "Tell me why you were unhappy until we met."

A chill ran through her, the tepid water suddenly seeming cold, the breeze icy.

"Was your mamá difficult to care for during her illness?"

She recalled her mother, the real woman, not the fiction she'd created to convince Señora Cisneros to hire her. Those rare times her mamá had laughed were unbelievably precious to Beatriz, even though her mother had always put on a brave front, smiling despite the sorrow in her eyes. No matter how bad their home life had become, she'd tried to make Beatriz's days pleasant.

She was only fourteen when her mother had fallen gravely ill. The physician claimed a bad case of the fever had taken hold. Beatriz knew better. Her mamá had finally given up on living and welcomed peace.

On her deathbed, she'd embraced Beatriz as much as she could, given how frail she'd become.

"Always remember how much I love you and wanted you to be happy." She'd spoken haltingly, no louder than a whisper. "Never let him destroy you. He is not what you think. Be stronger than I was and win against him."

Beatriz had witnessed her father's cruelty firsthand, had finally learned the full extent of what he'd done to her mother, and realized exactly what he was. She shook her head in answer to Tomás's question. "She had never been any trouble. I tended to her gladly."

"Would you like to have her here with you?"

"What?" Blood drained from her face, leaving her dizzy. "In the castle?"

"Where else?" He eased damp hair off her cheek. "You can keep an eye on her here, rather than making infrequent visits to the village. She may even like a position, something easy to avoid burdening her."

"No. Impossible."

"Why?"

The woman he spoke of didn't exist. "She would never leave the village."

"Not even to be with you?"

"She likes her home. Women her age grow set in their ways. Besides, what would the other servants think if she were here?"

"I hardly know and care even less."

"Because you never have to deal with them on their level rather than as their patrón."

He grew thoughtful and nodded. "Was your sadness because of your papá? Was he a brute to you?"

Not when others could see. He was unfailingly decent in public, his reputation stellar. He'd saved his rages and true nature for when he was behind closed doors. Beatriz couldn't count the times her friends had said how much they'd envied her for having such a sweet papá.

Her mother had lived the awful truth and had died to get away from him.

"We were never as close as I would have liked." She held Tomás more tightly. "Perhaps if I had been a son…"

With his hand beneath her chin, he lifted her face to his. "Is that why he taught you to read and ride? He wanted you to be like a boy?"

"I suppose. I never asked."

"Why not teach you to bake too? I suspect if he had, everyone in my castle would be eating your bread."

Caught in another lie, she searched for an answer. "Only a son would do in the shop. Business is a man's right, not a woman's. Most likely he thought me too stupid to follow even the simplest recipe."

"Forgive me for saying this, but he was a fool not to have worshipped you."

She laughed sadly at such an impossible notion. "What of you?" She ran her finger around his flat nipple and the scar nearby. "Are you and your mamá close?"

"She died when I was a boy."

"Oh no. Forgive me for bringing up such a terrible moment."

"No need. I remember her fondly, cherishing the times we did have. Tell me more about you."

She tensed again. "I have nothing else to share. My life was simple and tedious until I met you."

"What of the dreams you had for the future?"

There hadn't been any except for her desire to escape. "Dreams are for those who can afford such luxuries. As long as I had a bed to sleep in and enough to eat, I was content."

"You want nothing more now?"

She wasn't certain what he meant and wouldn't ask, risking more lies. After what he'd done for her, he deserved better than her continuing deception.

"You mean other than this?" She gestured to the lovely room. "A meal would be nice."

He glanced at their untouched basket. "I forgot to feed you."

She trailed her fingers down his neck, liking how the ridge in his throat bobbed with his swallow. "You were busy making me a woman."

"Are you sore?" He cupped her face. "I should have asked but forgot. Are you?"

"If I die from hunger, what will a little stinging matter?"

He threw up his hands. "Again, I forgot our food." He pointed. "Stay where you are as I serve you."

He left the pool. Water coursed down him, leaving puddles as he padded to the basket. He glanced over twice.

Checking to see if she'd obeyed and stayed put?

Feeling playful, she waited until he'd dug through the basket before she slipped beneath the surface.

Water filled her ears. She waited. He didn't shout with worry no matter how long she stayed down. When her lungs burned for air, she finally surfaced and gasped.

Tomás was on one knee at the edge, his expression sour.

She affected an innocent look. "I swooned from hunger."

He made a disbelieving noise and pushed a piece of bread at her. "Eat."

She licked his thumb.

His shoulders trembled with laughter. "Will you never learn to obey?"

"You have much to teach me."

* * * *

Tomás fed her on a mattress covered with dark blue silk, numerous pillows behind her shoulders. He'd posed her as a sultan might have done with an odalisque, her nudity exhibited for a man's pleasure. Water dripped from her hair, beaded on her nipples, and sparkled on the curls between her legs.

His shaft was hard and aching for her.

Ignoring his discomfort, he slipped orange slices, boiled eggs, crispy white bread, and roasted beef between her lips. She ate the fare quickly, then lingered on his fingers to lick away sweet juice and stray crumbs.

After he'd given her half the food and offered still more, she grabbed his wrist. "You need to eat too." She pushed his hand to his mouth. "You need to maintain your strength if you intend to keep up with me."

He threw the bread to the side. "Is that so? You think me frail?"

She regarded his shaft, so rigid his crown pointed at her cleft. "How can I say until you prove your strength?"

Ah, she sought to challenge him. He pushed the basket off the mattress and flipped Beatriz on her belly, her buttocks exposed.

She looked over, eyes rounded. "What are you doing?"

"Proving my vigor. On your hands and knees, legs spread, back arched. Present your sex to your master for him to take, use, and enjoy."

She grinned. "I think I like this."

He stifled a laugh. "Did I say you could speak?"

"No, my lord, forgive me. I shall be quiet from here on out." She achieved the position he wanted and looked over. "Is this about right?"

She'd spread her lovely cheeks quite nicely, revealing her tight, pink ring and cleft, her sex wet with arousal. He hardened himself against impossible need. "Are you talking again?"

"Forgive me. No sound will pass my lips from this point forward."

Silly girl. His satisfaction wouldn't come until she shrieked in delight and screamed for more.

He mounted her, swift and deep, until they touched. Her flesh hugged his. He grunted to show his approval. She moaned throatily.

Not enough. He demanded everything she had to give. "Tighten your opening around my shaft."

She squeezed his sex repeatedly, her rapid pace keeping time with his heart's frenzied beat, driving him wild. "No, no, no, slow down."

"Like this?" She squeezed for a long moment, rested briefly, and resumed.

She was going to kill him with nothing more than her channel. Sweat stung his eyes. If he clenched his teeth any harder, they might break. His chest and shoulders hurt from trying to restrain himself. "Slower."

She tightened her muscles around him again. He waited for her to relax. She didn't.

"Slow enough?" she asked.

He pounded into her, crazed with lust. She was equally lost to pleasure, pushing into him on each thrust, forcing him to tunnel deeper. Once he had, she shouted in delight. Never had he known a more unrestrained woman.

Tomás pumped, staving off release far longer than what should have been possible, and stroked her nub again. Jubilant cries rushed from her.

He finally threw back his head and howled with naked indulgence.

The sounds echoed through the chamber.

Wobbly, he sank to the side, bringing Beatriz with him, his arm around her waist, his sex still filling her.

They struggled for breath. He cuddled closer, loving how she nestled into him. With his carnal needs sated, he wanted only good thoughts lulling him to sleep.

What she'd revealed about her parents intruded instead.

He didn't understand her reluctance to share any information about a mother she adored. Unmistakable love had sounded in her voice. Tenderness softened her features.

Distaste for her father had been equally evident.

If the man thought so poorly of her, why teach Beatriz anything, especially how to read and write. Those were far harder skills for her to learn than following a recipe. Yet, he'd gone to the trouble to educate her, almost as a lady. Seeing to her future like a father would do with a boy, then dismissing her from having anything to do with his business.

Either her father had been a most unusual man or she was lying. Tomás couldn't imagine why but wanted to find out. He had to.

She was in his blood now. He required her as much as he needed food and drink, and had to make his plans.

* * * *

Shortly after he and Beatriz had returned to the castle, Yolanda came to his study unbidden. The child seemed far less confident than she'd been this morning, now shifting from foot to foot.

Little wonder. Servants never came to his study to speak to him. They went through Señora Cisneros.

When the girl didn't say anything, he had to. "What is it?"

"Am I in trouble? Will I no longer work with the chandler? Are you going to dismiss me?"

"Did you start a fire with the wax or tallow?"

She gaped. "I would never do such a thing. Are you angry with me for believing Rufio? I saw Beatriz's sleeve. She said one of the horses nipped her and when she tried to get away, the fabric tore. My wages should pay for the damage. If not, I can work extra until I can afford to buy her a new gown."

Tomás warned himself not to smile. He certainly didn't want Yolanda thinking he'd made light of her. She had a good heart. In many ways, she reminded him of how Beatriz must have been as a child. Loving yet spirited with an admirable sense of fair play. No wonder they'd befriended each other…and had probably shared their pasts.

He leaned back in his chair. "No need to worry about the gown. Since my horse ruined her garment, I should handle the repair. Your position is also safe. However, I do want to speak with you. Close the door and sit." He gestured to a bench next to his desk.

She perched on the edge, hands clasped, her face grim as an undertaker's.

He rubbed his mouth so he wouldn't chuckle at how solemn she looked. "Before I begin, I need your word not to repeat to anyone anything said in here, especially Beatriz."

"I would never."

He believed her. "Has Beatriz told you much about her past? What village she came from? Her family? She seems alone to me and I worry for her."

"She only spoke to me about an ailing mother who was better for a time, then grew ill once more. Or was she hardy and grew ill only to become hardy again?" Yolanda became thoughtful, then frowned.

He hoped the rest of what she knew would be more fruitful. "Did she say which village she came from?"

"The one to the east, I think. Or maybe the south."

"Too far to walk from here?"

"Not for me or any other servant." She grew pensive again and shrugged. "Maybe Señor Nuncio."

Because he was old when Beatriz was young and quite fit. She'd tested Tomás's stamina repeatedly today. If walking to those villages proved no problem for Yolanda, Beatriz should have found the journey equally easy, not difficult as she'd told him. Of course, Yolanda could have been mistaken in what Beatriz had told her.

"What about the communities beyond the nearest ones?" he asked. "How far are they?"

"Only been to them once. Took me several hours at most even with stopping to rest."

Time enough for Beatriz to arrive by late morning, visit her mamá, and walk back here well before the end of the day. "And those even farther?"

"Never been there."

Beatriz might have grown up in one. "Please find Señor Nuncio and ask him to come in here."

"At once." She raced from the study.

Nuncio must have been prowling nearby as he came in quickly. "Do you need the guards again?"

"No. Close the door and take a seat."

He remained far away. "I have not been anywhere near Beatriz."

Tomás looked past him to the open door. "And you want to make certain the rest of the servants know as much?"

Nuncio closed the door. "Whatever Beatriz told you, she has the wrong idea. I have no idea where she is or what she might be doing."

"Good. Keep it up. How familiar are you with the villages on my estate?"

"Not at all."

Of course not. If he were, that would make this quest too easy. The same as Tomás asking Beatriz straight out where she'd come from, why she was reluctant to speak of it, and what she might be hiding. Deep down, he sensed his questions would push her away. Better to find out on his own. "Learn as much as you can about them, near and far. I want to know where every servant hails from and if there are bakers selling their wares in any of those places."

He suspected Beatriz's mother had sold her husband's shop upon his death. If she had, though, Beatriz wouldn't have needed to work here to support her. Could be the new owner had cheated them. Maybe that's why she'd worried about a place to sleep and enough to eat, making her unhappy until she met him.

Nuncio looked pained. "You want me to question each servant?"

"Start with Señora Cisneros. Surely, she knows the most about the people she hired. With those she fails to account for, strike up a conversation with them to get the information."

"A conversation?"

Tomás smiled. "You know, speaking with another person as though you actually care what they say in return."

Nuncio lifted his chin. "May I ask why you need me to do this?"

"Do I have your word not to repeat what I say?"

"Of course." He looked appalled Tomás had even brought up the subject. "I never repeat anything you tell me."

"Good. Beatriz's background concerns me."

"I knew it." He finally joined Tomás at his desk and sat on the same bench Yolanda had. "At last, you realize what I have all along. The woman is trouble. Why go through this instead of simply getting rid of her?"

Tomás frowned. "Impossible."

"Why? Has she threatened you?"

"Worse. She bewitched me. I love her."

* * * *

During the following days, everyone looked at Beatriz hostilely or suspiciously, especially Nuncio. She might as well have worn a sign proclaiming what had happened between her and Rufio in the stable, followed by what she and Tomás had shared in the harem. The few times she and Nuncio crossed paths, he stared, and glared a little too, but said nothing, always hurrying away.

Leonor didn't try to mask her hatred. Beatriz figured the girl blamed her for Rufio's sudden departure from the estate. Every time she and Leonor were in the servant quarters, Leonor made certain to pass too close and rammed her shoulder into hers.

After the last time, Yolanda had bounced on her heels. "You best take care with her. A knife in her hand can be deadly to animal and man."

Beatriz kept even more to herself than usual, not telling Tomás what had occurred. When he questioned the bruises Leonor had left on her shoulder, Beatriz had to lie, as usual.

"I was carrying linens, turned a corner too quickly, and ran into the wall."

He kissed the purplish spots. "You need to be more careful."

She struggled not to laugh. As he'd given his warning, he was undressing her in his study when she should have been dusting, not engaging in carnal acts with him. "Careful is keeping my clothes on in here and staying far away from you."

He cupped her naked breasts. "Is that what you want?" He suckled her nipples.

She trembled, wanting more.

They spent a good part of each evening with him mounting her from the front, the back, and any other way he could devise. When he finished, they were as sore as untried virgins.

He didn't complain, nor did she.

Given their lust, Beatriz feared she had surely conceived and waited for the signs other women had discussed. Illness in the morning, dizziness, weeping uncontrollably for no reason, or for the very best…carrying a child while unwed.

She experienced no symptoms.

To her surprise and relief, her flow came as usual, giving her and Tomás another chance to guard against doom. A matter she was determined to discuss with him as soon as he returned from business involving his land.

They'd been lovers for too short a time, but she had no choice. They had to return to being no more than friends.

* * * *

Unlike his brother, Enrique, Tomás didn't care to run a large estate. He found the complexities of crops and cattle exceedingly tedious. Give him the opportunity to plan a battle any day. Now there was an activity to engage a man's mind.

Not only did this work bore him, the endless discussions kept him from Beatriz.

He'd been away for a week before he finally finished his business and returned to the castle.

Nuncio greeted him in the grand entrance hall, cheeks pink, hair disheveled. Certainly not by a dalliance with a maid.

"How eager you were for my return." Tomás removed his robe. "Going so far as to watch for my arrival from the parapet. Never deny it. The wind mussed your hair. Wait." He leaned in. "Perhaps a servant girl played with your locks."

Nuncio smoothed the strands. "The wind did, and yes, I was on the parapet searching for you. I live for your presence. Would you care to know what I learned in your absence?"

"Not here." They were too many servants around who pretended indifference but listened to everything. "My study."

Once inside, Tomás tossed his robe and doublet on a chair, then braced himself. Good or bad, he had to know what Nuncio had discovered. "Tell me."

"Only one village has a baker who sells his wares. He and Beatriz have different surnames."

Tomás shrugged. "Her family might have sold their concern to someone else."

"The baker is older than I am and has never done anything else."

"Was this village close to here?"

"The farthest away."

And not easy for her to walk to. Tomás didn't allow the news to rattle him. "Her family must have closed the business they had."

"The current baker is the only one who ever served that area."

So what. Perhaps Beatriz had grown up in the nearest village and found walking between there and here far too taxing. "What of the other communities? Surely, they had someone selling baked goods."

"No one has a business in any of them. Everyone tends to their own families or barters."

"Aha." He pointed at Nuncio. "What we consider barter they might consider a business."

"If you wish to believe so."

He didn't much like the man's attitude. "What of the other information I asked you to get?"

"I made a list of the servants and where they came from." He gestured to the desk. "I left the paper in your top drawer, not wanting Beatriz to come across it in my bedchamber when she cleaned there."

Good thinking. Tomás read the list. Everyone who worked here had come from similar locations, meaning some of them had to know Beatriz if she hailed from the same village they had. "Did Señora Cisneros say which of these places Beatriz came from?"

"The one in the north or the west."

Yolanda had said the east or south.

"I did have a conversation with some of the servants." Nuncio rocked on his heels. "I mentioned several names to them, including Beatriz's, asking if they had grown up together. All said they shared childhoods with one or another on the list. None of them had ever known Beatriz before she came here."

"So?" Tomás tore up the list and threw the pieces into the hearth. "The information means nothing."

"If you wish to believe so."

"I believe she came from a village, her papá was a baker who liked to read, taught her the skill, and she deserves more than your suspicion. You had better watch your step around her."

"Why? Are you intending to make her your manservant because you love her?"

"No. I intend to wed her."

Nuncio gaped. "No. Impossible."

"I informed you of my plans. I hardly asked for your permission."

"Beatriz is a servant. A lying one at that." He put up his hand before Tomás could get any closer. "Strike me if you must, throw me out the window, and then dismiss me, but she came here on a pretense."

"You think I care?"

"I can see your feelings have clouded your judgment. Even if you could make this marriage happen, how would she fare with the people you know?"

"Beatriz is brighter than all of them. In no time she can learn the conduct she needs to fit into my world. You can teach her how to be suspicious and stab people in the back. Quite useful at court."

Nuncio narrowed his eyes. "This is not a game."

"How right you are. This is my life and I refuse to spend my days without her."

"Who said you must? Especially if you continue with your reckless desire for her. When she conceives, you can hide the fact by marrying her off to one of the other servants. When you wed a noblewoman, you can keep Beatriz as your mistress. Done all the time."

Tomás clenched his teeth. "Not with me. Not to her. Suggest such a thing again and—"

"I know. You dismiss me or I die at your hands. I give up."

"Good. Keep everyone away from my study. I intend to speak to Beatriz without interruption."

Shaking his head, Nuncio left the room.

Tomás paced, wanting to see her so badly he didn't care about her past in the least. There had to be a reasonable explanation as to what she'd told the others. No matter what it might be, her history wasn't their business, anyway. She might be ashamed of where she'd come from, how she'd lived, and told a more acceptable tale in order to hold her head high. Who could blame her?

His wait seemed endless, but at last the hour for her dusting had arrived. Her footfalls sounded in the hall.

The moment she was inside and had closed the door, he crossed the room, pulling her into his arms. "I missed you so much I thought of little else."

He kissed her deeply, tenderly, then passionately, unable to decide what he needed most. He swung her around, set her on her feet, and trailed kisses over her temple, cheeks, forehead, and the tip of her nose. "Did you miss me?"

Tears shone in her eyes.

"You did." He hugged her as hard as he could without harming her. "We need to talk. I have something to say."

"I do too."

He stilled at her forlorn tone and eased back. "Are you with child?"

She shook her head quickly, her cap slipping to the side.

He righted the thing for her. "Are you ill?"

"No."

"Your mamá is ailing again?"

"No. If you let me speak, I can tell you."

"I have to go first. Please." He held her hands. "I love you. I have from the moment we met. These last days have been unbearable without you. I want you near to me always, as my wife."

She stared harder than Nuncio had. "What?"

Tomás grinned at how he'd surprised her this time, even better than their day in the harem. "Wed me."

The color drained from her face. She pulled away. "No. Never."

Chapter 8

Tomás's smile faded slowly replaced by surprise, then confusion.

The way any sane man would have reacted. She'd behaved wantonly with him, repeatedly proving her desire. Yet when he'd offered her a privileged life at his side, she'd refused.

He loved her.

Joy bubbled up in Beatriz, followed by anguish. She'd never hoped for his heart and had to stop this now without telling him why or offering comfort. Tenderness would only confuse him more.

Tears clouded her vision. She backed away.

"No?" He stared. "Never?"

She couldn't answer, not wanting to hurt him any more than she had or lose control and reveal her secret.

He frowned. "Did you hear what I said?" He looked past her. "You must not have." A slight smile replaced his scowl. "I want us to marry."

She shook her head.

His arched eyebrows registered more surprise. "How can you refuse me after what we shared? You enjoyed our moments together as much as I had. You nearly killed me with your passion."

"What we had could never last."

"Had?" He stepped back, shock on his face. "Are you saying even our desire is in the past? Where did your feelings for me go while I was gone? Wait." He held up his hand. "I know what this is about." His complexion darkened. "Nuncio."

"What?"

"He stopped you before you came in here and threatened to do something if you accepted me." Tomás slammed his fist into his palm. "This is the last time he interferes with you, me, or us."

"You told Nuncio you planned to ask for my hand?"

"How else would he have known? He did stop you before you came in here, no?"

"No. Yesterday was the last time I saw him." She frowned. "You discussed me with him? Why?"

He averted his gaze.

She grew clammy. "Everyone has been looking at me oddly since you left. On more than one occasion, Nuncio spoke to the other servants when he never has before. Was he telling them about your plans or was he asking them about me?"

Tomás still didn't look at her.

Queasiness washed over Beatriz. He'd guessed her secret from the lies she'd told the others. No wait. If he'd learned her past, why would he have offered marriage? "Are you going to answer me or not?"

His shoulders slumped. "Nuncio knew I planned to ask for your hand and gave his word not to tell anyone."

"He lied to you."

"No. His conversations with the servants had nothing to do with our marriage."

He hadn't heard a word she'd said. There wouldn't be a wedding. Her nausea returned. "What was he speaking to them about if not us? Why would he approach the other servants but fail to include me in his conversations?"

"I warned him not to bother you."

She bounced on her heels, fear overwhelming her. "You keep refusing to answer my question. What was he speaking to them about?"

"Beatriz, please." He reached for her.

She pushed his hands away. "I want an answer. Was he asking them about me?"

"Why would he? Is there a reason for him to have done so?"

Surely, he didn't expect her to confess. "You said his conversations had nothing to do with your decision to ask for my hand. How could you know what he said to the servants unless you told him to talk to them? About what?"

"Must we discuss this?"

"Answer me, or do I need to go to him?"

Tomás swore softly.

"Very well." She crossed the room to the door.

He stopped her before she could leave. "I told him to ask them about Rufio."

"What? Why him?"

"You said Rufio was the kind to exact revenge, which he did in the stable. I wanted Nuncio to check with the others to see whether Rufio had tried to gain access to the castle."

"With guards at the walls and gate?"

Tomás lifted his face to the ceiling and took a deep breath. "He fooled Yolanda and you. I feared he might do the same with someone else. I merely wanted to take care and asked Nuncio not to alarm you. Silly me." He looked at her. "You seem more upset now than I would have ever believed possible, clearly because I asked for your hand. Why are you refusing my offer?"

She couldn't reveal the truth and hadn't a ready lie to satisfy him without causing more hurt.

He crossed his arms over his chest. "If we have to stay here all night until you answer me, we will."

"Nuncio should have talked you out of this."

"He tried. I told him to keep his tongue or risk losing the vile thing. You keep avoiding my question. Why? Do you find me so loathsome you could never deign to wed me?"

"How can you say or even think that? You are a man among men, a warrior with no equal, a god on earth."

He regarded her and smiled. "I see my manner of speaking rubbed off on you."

Beatriz wanted to laugh, cry, and shriek at the same time. She wilted. "You have nothing to do with my refusal."

"Which leaves you. I confessed my love and heard naught in return. You have no love to give or find me too lacking to ever claim your heart?"

She had to leave.

"Oh no." He brought her right back to face him. "I demand an answer. What are your feelings for me?"

Right now, she wanted to scream at him for putting her into such an impossible position and kiss him breathless for returning her love. Neither action was possible. She struggled for an answer, at last remembering the most obvious.

"Have you forgotten my station?" She pulled away from him and gestured to her livery.

He ignored what she wore. "I keep listening but have yet to hear the word love, hate, indifference, or any other feeling you may have in regard to me."

"My feelings matter not. Your nobility does."

"Is that the only thing troubling you? Easily remedied."

"You intend to give this up?" She swung out her arms, taking in the grand room.

"No need. Once you change, everything will fall into place for us."

Not with that attitude. "Change? How?"

"Your clothes, of course, and your hair, conduct, what you say, how you—"

"How awful of me to be so lacking, and here I thought I was perfect in every way. Lovelier than the sun, brighter than the night, more enchanting than a storm."

"You have my comparisons mixed up. Outside of that, you are perfect. For me. If the choice were mine, you could stay hidden here forever, never seeing anyone."

"Hidden? Like a creature too monstrous for a noble to view lest the sight of me upsets the precious one's delicate stomach?"

Tomás huffed. "You keep taking my words and twisting them."

"Because I lack the sense to understand a noble's brilliant mind?"

"No. Because you keep trying to start a fight and I refuse to battle you. By change I mean no more than you wearing fine silks and velvets, having a servant do your hair in the same style as the other ladies, knowing what manner of address is required for a duke, marquis, count, or any other noble, and to watch what you say so no one can stab you in the back later with your own words. Ones spoken at gatherings you and I will attend with me showing you off proudly as my *esposa*. I know, I know, what a beast I am to ask such things of you."

He was too wonderful, proving how awful she was for duping him. "What you want would never work."

"Why not?" He eased close. "I see how you look at and touch me. No woman has ever wanted me as badly as you seem to, yet you refuse to speak of love or even mild affection. Is the problem your mamá? Does she hate nobles? Did one do something unspeakable to her?"

Several had with her father's full consent and willingness. "She could never hate you."

He hugged her. "We could bring her here and give her a life of leisure. A physician I know could care for her if she falls ill again. Let me make everything better for you and her, giving both of you whatever you want. Say yes."

If only the answer were possible. The moment he posted banns, what she was hiding would come out and their world would crash down. If she confessed now, she'd put the burden on him as to whether he should act on her confession, as honor demanded, or help keep her secret. In either event, they could never have a life together, certainly not one in the open.

She never should have let things get this far, hungering for their first kiss, caress, coupling. Now, even friendship would have to be in the past.

Beatriz pulled away. He eased her back into his arms.

"No." She twisted away again and put distance between them. "I want nothing of your wealth or position. Neither means anything to me."

"What about me? Do I matter at all?"

She'd gladly die for him and would do all she could not to ruin his life. "I can never wed you or any man."

Tomás stared, then laughed.

She frowned.

"Why are you unable to wed any man? Were you planning on the nunnery after your service here?" He sobered. "After our adventure in the harem, joining the order may be a mistake for you."

"What we did was wrong."

"How?" He advanced, crowding her.

She stepped back and ran into his desk, which cut off further escape.

He looked pleased. "You have yet to answer me. Are you saying we were wrong to enjoy each other as God and nature intended a man and woman to do?"

"Only after they wed."

"Ah, but I asked and you refused. Not only me but every other man on earth with your decision certainly including another servant. Tell me, what could keep you from wedding a man of your station?"

"I want no one to rule me."

"As though I have. Have you forgotten my offer to help you carry linens and dust this room so we could read and play our games instead? What a swine I am."

Her mouth trembled with laughter and sorrow.

At her first tear, his shoulders slumped. "Now, I made you weep? Are you deliberately trying to kill me?"

She covered her face.

He touched her wrist, his sigh sounding as sad as hers. "I thought we were the best sort of lovers and friends."

"We can be neither any longer."

"What?" He stopped touching her. "Are you saying we have no more nights in here or days on the hillside and harem?"

"To what end?"

"Marriage and a family. What else?"

She growled in frustration. "What you want can never be. How many times must I tell you?"

His mood changed, growing hurt, then cold. "This last one will be sufficient. I will never ask again."

Tears streamed down her face, his sadness and anger killing her. "Are you going to throw me out of your castle now?"

"Do you want that too?"

"Not without a new position in hand. I have nowhere to go."

"What do you mean? What of your village and mamá? Has she already forced you from her home? Is that why you never visit her?"

"Do I stay here or not? Does my position depend upon me lying with you?"

Tomás stepped back, offense on his face. "I have never forced myself on any woman. Stay if you want. Ending your service is up to you."

She nodded. "Gracias."

"You thank me now? I never should have returned from my business. Leave this room."

Suddenly, she couldn't move.

He pointed at the door. "Go!"

She bolted from his study and passed Nuncio in the entrance hall. He skittered back. She stopped and rushed to him. "Please tell Señora Cisneros to find another servant to see to Patrón's study, beginning immediately. I appreciate what you did about Rufio. Gracias."

Unable to speak further, she took off for a place where she could cry alone and pull herself together before having to go to the servant quarters.

* * * *

The door opened.

Tomás whirled around, hoping to see Beatriz, even though he'd just thrown her out. Already he missed her, wanted her to run into his arms, tell him she'd changed her mind. She did want him in every way.

Nuncio came in.

Tomás sank to a bench, forearms resting on his thighs. "What do you want? Wait. Did I hear you knock?"

"Forgive me for being unacceptably rude. Is everything all right?"

"Do I look happy?"

He stood at Tomás's side. "She refused your offer?"

Tomás clenched his jaw.

"How could she?" Nuncio made a face. "I thought...she seemed... most women in her position would..."

"Beatriz is hardly most women. I already told you as much."

Tina Donahue

"Did she give you a reason for turning you down?"

None Tomás could accept. He'd been certain she loved him as much as he did her. Why else would she behave as she had during their times together. If her intent had been to charm him into marriage, she'd accomplished her goal readily. Then turned around and spurned him.

Her behavior didn't make sense. None of this did.

"She simply said no when you offered your hand?" Nuncio's eyes widened "And then she left?"

"No. We argued. She wants nothing of my wealth or position. They mean nothing to her."

Nuncio sucked in a breath. "She is extraordinary."

Tomás glared at him. "Now you find her acceptable because she refused me?"

"I thought she was after what you have, the same as all servants and the señoritas who came here. I readily admit how wrong I was. Rather than allowing avarice to guide her, she understands the folly of becoming a part of your world and came to the right decision."

Tomás made a face. "Right decision? Because she can never be as magnificent as the nobles I know who fail to pay their debts, eat and drink too much, ruin each other's reputations because of perceived slights, gossip about which husbands are cheating on which wives, and fail to provide for their bastard children? Are those the nobles you have in mind?"

"They were born to privilege. She was not. Nothing can change the matter. However, she did earn my esteem tonight." He squeezed Tomás's shoulder. "Beatriz spared you endless humiliation with the people you know over who knows how many years. Be grateful."

He knocked Nuncio's hand away. "Only when I get what I want."

"You mean her?" He made a pained sound. "How do you intend to court Beatriz in light of her refusal? She wants nothing to do with you."

Tomás stood and advanced on the man. Nuncio danced back.

"How would you know how she feels about me? Were you listening at the door?"

"No. Before I came in here, she asked me to speak to Señora Cisneros immediately about getting another servant to clean your study."

Tomás gripped his desk to keep from swaying. A blow couldn't have hit him harder than this news. At the very least, he'd expected to see Beatriz in here each night. He'd hoped to coax her into reading El Cid's tale again and ask her to begin the epic poem they both forgot about, charming and wooing her to his side once more.

That dream was over now, leaving him with nothing. Unless he wanted to haunt her every move in the hope she'd throw a glance his way or deign to kiss him.

"She also thanked me for what I did about Rufio." Nuncio shook his head. "I have no idea what she meant. Will you tell me?"

He ran his hand down his face. "She noticed you speaking with the other servants and asked if I was checking into her. I told her I wanted you to find out if Rufio had tried to sneak back onto the grounds for revenge. If she questions you about what I said, tell her the same lie, understand?"

"Of course."

"Leave me."

"Will you be all right?"

He had to make things so. Tomás had survived horrifying battles and a near-fatal illness. He wasn't about to let tonight destroy or defeat him.

* * * *

Señora Cisneros tasked Garbine with dusting Tomás's study. As one of the oldest servants, Garbine was rather frail but quite sweet, making her easy to approach. Beatriz took her meals next to the woman, hoping she might share some news of Tomás.

Garbine never mentioned him. Not even a brief anecdote of seeing Tomás in the study or him entering the room while she worked. He might as well have been a fantasy Beatriz had concocted to make her time here less dreary.

Days turned into weeks without her seeing or hearing anything about where he was, what he did, who he shared his time with. After their fight, she'd feared he'd see reason and invite the señoritas back, choosing one for his bride.

No visitors came.

She worked herself to exhaustion, hoping for some peace at night, but lay awake, missing him so badly she began to want their time together more than freedom. What did liberty matter when she was as miserable now as when she'd escaped everything she hated?

On those few days she had time to herself, she walked to the hillside to see if the area had changed. If anything, the view was more exquisite than she recalled, enticing couples to fall in love all over again.

She slipped away to the harem once and returned to the chamber where Tomás had taken her virginity. Pillows and silk panels lay where they'd left them. The pool water had evaporated somewhat. A few leaves floated on the surface.

She found an orange peel they'd failed to put into the basket. Beatriz pressed the rind to her nose, wanting the fragrance to return her to their day here, giving her a chance to hear his laughter and teasing again, water splashing from their play.

The day remained quiet, even the birds and breeze forsaking the spot.

Beatriz slipped the peel into her sleeve, a memento more precious to her than jewels or silks. She didn't return to the harem again. Recalling times past merely made each day harder for her.

She tried to forget him but couldn't. Every time footfalls sounded, she held her breath, hoping they might be his. His scent seemed to be in every chamber. More than once, she stopped near the hallway leading to his study and listened for his rumbling voice.

Silence answered.

Her time here had to end. She couldn't abide the unending heartache. Prior to her next day off, she stopped Yolanda outside the kitchen before they went in for their meal. "Can we have a word?"

"Always. Has Leonor started knocking into you again?"

Not for weeks. A new boy in the kitchen had the girl's eye. Beatriz was again invisible to her. "No. I wanted to ask you about the village closest to the castle."

"East or west?"

She had no idea. "Which is the largest?"

"The west one."

"Can work be found there?" She'd come to the point where she was ready to labor in the fields, hoping to prove herself more capable than a child.

"Who needs work?"

Beatriz didn't want to reveal her plans, fearing Señora Cisneros might find out and let her go before she found a new position. "A woman I grew up with. On my last day off, I was on the road between the fields and chanced to see her again. Her skills would never be fine enough for the castle, but I thought she might find something in the village, on one of the peasants' farms. Do you know of anyone who might need help?"

"She could work the patrón's land. To hear others talk, he always needs someone for the crops or cattle."

"The village would be better for her. Would work there be possible?"

"I suppose. The only way to be certain is for her to go there and ask around."

* * * *

Two days later, Beatriz left at dawn with Yolanda's map in hand. Yolanda couldn't read or write, but she had an excellent memory and drew lines to show the road. Large X's represented landmarks, including a copse of olive trees, an untended orange grove, and a small pond.

When Beatriz had asked Yolanda to create the map, she'd explained the drawing was for her friend. Yolanda hadn't questioned the lie or looked the least suspicious.

Once past the castle gate and wall, Beatriz regretted not having eaten or taken food from the kitchen. She hadn't wanted anyone to stop and question her as to where she'd spend her day off.

The sun was behind her, the morning pleasantly cool. She shuffled down the descending road. Her trip back would be far more arduous as the castle stood on the highest hill overseeing the valley, the day's heat would be at its greatest, and she might be hungrier and thirstier than she'd been since coming here.

She checked the map to see how far the groves were, hoping to find a few oranges to eat. From what Yolanda had drawn, Beatriz wouldn't reach the spot for an hour, perhaps more.

The road leveled off, leading past fields and vineyards. She hoped no one would see her passing and gossip with those at the castle. As far as she could tell, no workers toiled nearby.

The land stretched far beyond the point where she could see its end. Birds flew in and out of the wheat, this golden crop near harvest. She considered how much a sickle or scythe might weigh and if she'd be able to manage cutting grain for hours.

Her belly rumbled from hunger.

In order to eat, she'd have to withstand anything. Perhaps after weeks in a field, she'd no longer think about Tomás or her increasingly bleak future and would finally sleep.

A short distance into the journey, her lids grew heavy, the slumber she'd missed catching up with her. She craned her neck hoping to see the groves closer than what the map showed. To rest as she ate sweet fruit sounded like paradise.

Wheat fields, cork trees, and bushes stretched before her, offering no relief.

She tucked the map in one sleeve and fingered the rind in her other.

A noise ahead stopped her. She listened hard, unable to identify the rattling sound. Ahead, the road rose sharply, not showing what was on the other side. On instinct, she hid within tall bushes and waited.

A simply designed cart appeared with one wheel in front and two in back, pulled by a goat and directed by a young boy. His hat, tunic, hose, and bare feet marked him as a peasant.

Her stomach growled again until he neared, his cart heaped with dung, not food. The revolting odor slammed into her. She forced down swallow after swallow, hoping she wouldn't be ill.

As he passed, the boy stared, then twisted around to keep looking at her. His frown said she was the oddest creature he'd ever witnessed.

When he disappeared over another hill, she returned to the road, her feet and calves aching from the climb and pitted terrain. She had to take care not to step the wrong way and twist her ankle.

The sun was high enough now to bear down on her back and neck. She'd braided her hair, wearing the coil on top without her servant cap. Unable to afford such a luxury, she owned no hat.

At the top of an incline, she wanted to drop to the ground. More fields, but no groves as far as she could see. Her throat was parched, limbs heavy. Ignoring her discomfort, she kept on until she came to a turn. She checked her map and slumped. The groves were still quite a distance.

Hot and tired, she spied trees some length past the road. Farther than she wanted to walk, but the relative seclusion and shade called to her for a short rest. Upon reaching the area, she sank to the ground, her back against a trunk, face damp with perspiration. Her lids slid down.

* * * *

A cramp in her shoulder stirred Beatriz from sleep. Her belly rumbled and ached, adding to her distress. To have to walk again without knowing if she'd find food overwhelmed her.

Fighting tears, she opened her eyes and flinched.

Tomás was on one knee at her side, his gelding tethered to the next tree. Without comment, he offered her a *bota*. She expected to taste wine, not cold milk. Pleased, she drank greedily. Once she'd finished, he handed her bread and beef from his *alforjas*.

Tears ran down her face. "Gracias."

He peeled an orange.

Trying not to cry, she gobbled the fare he'd given her.

He offered her three orange slices and looked at the road. "Where are you heading?"

She didn't want to tell him.

He separated another slice. "I can give you a ride."

"I was just out walking."

"This far, without food, drink, or even a hat?"

Her mouth trembled.

"You could have been hurt out here by Rufio or someone like him. You never thought of that?"

Feeling like a fool, she lowered her face.

He handed her boiled eggs and cheese, waiting patiently until she finished. On his feet, he looked down at her, the breeze tugging his hair, his noble station evident in his fine green doublet and robe. "Do you want to continue on your own or ride back with me?"

She didn't want to walk another step. "With you."

He offered his hand. Her belly fluttered at his warm, dry skin, her joy sinking when he released her quickly. With the bota and alforjas secured to the saddle, he helped her onto the gelding, untied the reins, and mounted behind her, his arm around her waist.

Unable to resist, she leaned into him, savoring his solid body, his powerful thighs hugging hers.

He wheeled the horse around and rode back. They traveled in silence, his arm keeping her close, her hand on his, their breaths and scents mingling.

She wanted to drown in his love, lose herself in his embrace, knowing neither was possible.

More swiftly than she would have liked, they neared the castle wall and gate.

Tomás stopped short of where his men stood guard. "Would you like to continue to the castle or dismount here?"

She never wanted to leave his side but hadn't the right to a future with him. "It would be best if you leave me here."

He held out his arm to help her dismount.

Once on the ground, she looked up. "Gracias, Tomás."

He wheeled around and took the way they'd come, the horse's hooves stirring up dust.

Chapter 9

Tomás rode hard to the village. What he guessed had been Beatriz's destination.

Having her near him had nearly undone his restraint. He'd almost mentioned love once more, marriage, a family, their future together. He'd wanted to capture her mouth, losing himself in her softness and heat. Their last conversation kept him from making any move. Not because he feared she'd hurt his pride again. He didn't want to push her farther away.

He pressed his palm to his face, hoping to smell her scent. Her fragrance eluded him the same as she kept doing.

He'd been afraid to run her off today, so he'd followed at a distance to assure her safety. Men and animals could become unpredictable quickly. She'd seemed oblivious to danger, not even carrying a stick to protect herself, much less having a dagger or knife at the ready as the other servants would have. Bringing food and drink had also escaped her notice.

Given how she'd gobbled what he'd provided, she hadn't bothered to eat prior to leaving the castle.

Every other servant would have gladly enjoyed the ample food he offered, especially before walking to the village. Since his talk with Yolanda, he'd learned the nearest community was more than a league away. Hardly an idle stroll, especially on an empty belly.

Giving Beatriz the food he'd packed was the easiest thing he'd ever done. Finding the right words to say escaped him.

They'd been lovers in every conceivable way, their intimacy exceeding what most couples probably experienced in a lifetime. Yet, meeting each other's gaze, speaking from the heart, seemed to defeat them.

During these last weeks, he'd discussed the matter with Enrique and Fernando, joining them to celebrate Enrique and Sancha's first child. A boy they'd named Bartolomé to honor Sancha's late father.

When Tomás had confessed his love for Beatriz, a troubled glance had passed between his brothers. His outrage followed. "She isn't an uneducated peasant. She can read and write as well as I can. Perhaps better. She has a lady's manners."

Fernando lifted his hands. "As long as you love her…"

Enrique elbowed Tomás. "How does she feel about you?"

He regretted having brought her up. He finally told them she'd refused his offer, along with her reasons.

"She sounds like Sancha," Enrique said. "Especially the part about riches meaning nothing and no man ruling her."

Fernando nodded. "I finally gave up trying to tame Isabella. She continues to reward me for backing off."

"Sancha too. Our nights and days are filled with endless pleasure."

"How wonderful for both of you," Tomás said. "How did you get your women to the altar?"

Fernando spoke first. "With great difficulty. Isabella fought me every step of the way."

"Same with Sancha." Enrique clamped Tomás's shoulder. "Your only choice is to wear her down as we did with our wives."

If Beatriz didn't flee before then.

The village was ahead, offering nothing more than mud huts, penned goats and pigs, along with chickens scurrying about. Peasants tended small patches of vegetables and grain. Children played in the road, their bare feet stirring up dust, tiny voices raised in laughter.

Goats and mules, along with crudely hewn carts, seemed to be the only means of transport. There weren't any horses, a blacksmith, or a structure to indicate a baker or any other business in the area. There were so few people no commerce was necessary. Everyone could have bartered to get needed items.

Tomás couldn't imagine these people knowing how to read and write or having a love for books. Unless they had a Bible, none had probably ever seen the printed word.

Surely she hadn't wanted to come here to visit her mamá. Even if she had, she'd proven this had been too far for her to walk, as she'd once told him.

He dismounted and led his horse through the village. A sturdy man approached, sickle in hand, his face weather-beaten, clothes homespun. He inclined his head in greeting. "Patrón."

"Buenas tardes. I heard a woman named Beatriz lives here or used to live here with her mamá. Can you point out the hut to me?"

"No one by that name lives here."

"Now. What of the past?"

The peasant shook his head. "I grew up in the village and never knew a woman by that name."

"Is there labor to be had here?"

"Only for family." He gestured to the surrounding area. "Our community is simple as you can see. Many leave here to work at the castle."

He gave the man a few coins for his trouble. "If your community needs better tools, let Nofre know." Nofre was Tomás's overseer and far more familiar with the land than him. "He can help."

"Gracias, Patrón."

A girl, surely no more three, ran up. She bumped into Tomás's leg and squealed happily.

"No, no, no." The peasant waved the child back. "Watch where you go."

"No harm done." Tomás patted the little girl's head, picturing Beatriz at this age. Innocent of the world and the restrictions faced by status or being born female.

When Fernando and Enrique had first mentioned their wives' desire for freedom even within marriage, Tomás hadn't understood what they meant or how restrictive women found their lives. Meeting Beatriz had changed his view.

She had no transport, home, status, or means to earn a living and support her mamá without his or another man's good will. Although, he was a fair master, she'd mentioned having to lie with him to keep her position.

He sensed she'd chosen this village to find work. Not because she was afraid he wouldn't keep his word about staying away, but because she couldn't endure their forced separation any more than he could. Their times together had been too sweet.

Today, she'd failed to reach her goal. Next week might be a different story if she walked to the village in the opposite direction.

The ache in his belly and chest returned, along with hopelessness. He couldn't forbid her to leave. Nor could he lose her, which put him in an intolerable position.

His brothers had suggested he wear her down. Easy for them to say. Tomás had no idea how to do so. Or what magic he might need in order to convince her to become his.

* * * *

After Tomás had given her a ride, Beatriz suddenly ran into him everywhere. When she hauled linen down the halls, he'd approach from the opposite direction, Nuncio or Señora Cisneros always at his side, their voices low, keeping her from knowing what they discussed. Even when

Beatriz was only inches away, Tomás kept his full focus on the servant he was with, not glancing at her.

Each time he disappeared from view, her heart cramped.

Wherever she dusted, he was soon there with other servants, ordering them to fix something, directing them to lug cabinets from one end of the room to the other, showing them where a new wall hanging should go. Not once did he look at her.

Whenever she was outside beating rugs, he showed up, telling his men where he wanted new flowers or bushes, what trees they had to prune.

She didn't understand the change in him.

During their intimate moments, he'd confessed how he hated being a landowner, preferring to fight every Moor in Granada instead. Apparently, he'd gotten over his distaste for these tasks as he now spoke endlessly with the workers about what he required. Not once did he seem to notice she was also outside, even though she beat every rug with all her might. The whapping sounds were loud enough to scare several birds and caused the men to glance her way.

Tomás seemed immune to the noise or determined to pretend she didn't exist.

More than once, she'd wanted to throw the carpet beater at him and confess her love, but kept her tongue and maintained an outward calm. The distance he kept between them was for the best even if she longed for a brief glance.

He never gave her one.

She began to yearn for time away to avoid seeing him.

On the afternoon before her day off, he was unexpectedly gone again, not showing up in the rooms she cleaned. Perhaps he'd tired of having the servants move cabinets and hang tapestries, or they'd run out of things to fix. She was dusting a windowsill when footfalls sounded in the hall. Beatriz didn't pay much attention until the steps neared and stopped.

She looked over.

Tomás stood in the hall, alone, and actually looked at her. Gone was the longing and passion she'd seen in times past. He regarded her with indifference, the way a noble lord would with any servant.

Her pulse stopped racing, melancholy setting in. "Patrón."

He strode to her like the noble he was, his red doublet and robe complementing his beautiful hair. His cheeks, chin, and upper lip were bristly, his beard returning as it always did during the afternoon. Gray hose hugged his muscular calves and thighs to the point Beatriz had to keep from staring, longing for his nudity pressed against hers, bodies and mouths joined, their scents mingling.

"I have a task that needs doing. I thought of you."

She hid her surprise, unable to imagine what task could have made him consider her or fail to go through Señora Cisneros. Unless… Maybe he needed a missive penned or wanted her to scour his agriculture books, pulling out needed portions to tell him the best time to prune trees and plant flowers.

She looked at him expectantly.

He glanced at the hall.

Her pulse quickened. Whatever he intended to say must be a secret he wanted kept between them. Perhaps he would ask her to write the epic poem at last. An innocent project, allowing them to share time as chaste friends…the only situation she could hope for at this point.

With no one in the hall listening to what went on in here, he faced her. "The harem needs tending. Rather than have Señora Cisneros clean again, I thought you might like to earn what I paid her, so you can use the funds for your mamá. You should be able to do a fine job, knowing the place as well as you do. Although I prefer the task done today, the hour is late. You can start tomorrow, early morning. Wait." He frowned. "Your day off, I forgot. Surely, you have plans."

Her cheeks stung at how casually he'd said she knew the harem. Of course, she did. She'd offered him her virginity there and he'd gladly accepted, treating her with passion and tenderness. A far cry from now.

When she didn't comment, he looked past her. "If you plan to visit a village, I can let you use a mare or my carriage so you actually get to your destination."

She gritted her teeth.

"I can also have Cook pack food for you. Along with a knife or dagger for protection. I may be too busy to assist you as I did the last time."

Beatriz pulled back her shoulders. "I have no plans. I can clean your harem."

His expression darkened.

She wasn't about to take back what she'd said. The harem was his, not theirs. Not any longer.

"Excellent. Make certain the pools are dry and the silk is kept away from the sun."

She knew how to protect fine fabrics. Her service here had also taught her how to clean and tend to other things. "Would you care to make a list for me, specifying your concerns?"

"A list? Wait. You can read."

She wanted to slap him for pretending he'd forgotten. Holding back, she dug her nails into her palms.

"I can start on the list immediately." He crossed the chamber and stopped at the doorway. "Are you sure you want to give up your day?"

"The villages will still be there next week and the next."

He returned to her. For a moment, heat flared in his eyes, along with yearning she'd recalled.

He hid both quickly. "The items you need, a bucket, carpet beater, dust cloths, and more, will be in the chamber when you arrive tomorrow. The list will be in my top desk drawer within the hour. Garbine cleans my study at the same time you used to. If you want to avoid any questions or gossip, make certain not to run into her."

He left.

* * * *

Tomás tensed with such need he could scarcely draw a breath. He couldn't recall his shoulders ever hurting more. His fists ached from clenching them.

In his determination to wear Beatriz down, he was killing himself.

He sank into the chair in his study, head in his hands.

The only thing he'd accomplished thus far was to stop her from seeking work at a village and leaving here. Of course, the communities would still be there in the following weeks, months, and years. He wasn't certain he could think of enough tasks for her to do to keep her away from them and close to him.

Pity he wasn't a sultan. If she'd been his concubine, he would have stripped her bare, shackled her to a bed, and mounted her without pause. She'd never get away from him. He'd own her mouth, breasts, and sheath, but not her willingness or her heart.

He ground his fists into his eyes.

Without her ready consent and love, physical intimacy meant nothing. In the past, he'd used other women for relief the same as they'd done with him. A pleasant affair, but those acts had never come close to the moments he and Beatriz had known.

"Why do you fight me?" He pushed his fingers through his hair. "What are you so afraid of?"

She claimed to want freedom and an end to everything they'd been, yet when he complied, treating her as he would any other servant, Beatriz seemed heartsore. She kept sneaking glances at him when he failed to acknowledge her presence. Her expression was always forlorn when she wasn't aware he was nearby, watching. She'd beat the poor rugs ruthlessly, in what he guessed was an effort to get his attention. If she kept that up, she'd hurt herself or put a hole in the fabrics.

He wanted to talk to her again, man to woman, lover to loved, but sensed she'd only pull away. The only option he could see was to be around her frequently, tempting her until she couldn't refuse what they both wanted, and she became a part of his life once more.

* * * *

The following morning, Beatriz slipped Tomás's list in her sleeve and joined the other servants in the kitchen for breakfast. Her last excursion away from the castle had taught her not to leave without a full belly. Apparently, she should have also taken a knife for protection.

He must have considered her a hopeless fool, not even knowing how to do her work. His list was endless, detailing everything as one would for an imbecile too stupid to figure out how to fold silk, beat mattresses, empty water.

The tasks wouldn't be easy on her clothes. Her mended sleeve might rip again today. However, she hadn't wanted to wear livery and have the other servants asking why she was working on her day off or where the task might be.

Yolanda finished her milk, leaving a white mustache on her upper lip. "Have any plans for today?"

Beatriz smiled. "The workers planted new flowers. I may walk among them or explore the grounds."

Although her comment seemed casual, she'd chosen her words carefully. If anyone spied her crossing the lawn to the harem, that person wouldn't question her movements.

Yolanda grabbed three figs and an orange. "I must be off. Enjoy your day."

"You too."

The other servants chatted amongst themselves, not deliberately excluding Beatriz, but they'd never grown close to her, either. They seemed to know she was different than they were. Not as open, lying constantly about her past, steering converse back to them rather than having to share anything regarding herself.

Her actions made for a lonely existence, except for dear Yolanda. However, Beatriz saw no other choice.

Once she'd filled her belly, she asked Cook's permission to take enough food for her next meal. Gaining the woman's approval, Beatriz wrapped three oranges, several slices of bread and pork, a mound of olives, and a large cheese wedge.

Cook eyed the feast. "You get so hungry simply walking around?"

Hauling water from the pools would probably make her ravenous in no time. "This should be all I need until tomorrow morning."

"Off with you then."

The sun hadn't yet dried the grass. Dew dampened Beatriz's skirt. On a whim, she slipped off her shoes and stockings and held them to her chest with the fare she'd packed. The lawn was deliciously cool beneath her toes.

She wanted to linger but couldn't, glancing over her shoulder repeatedly. To her relief, no one was behind her or in front. For the most part, the sky was clear, though there were a few smeared clouds in the distance. Birds flew past the sun, the light turning their bodies to dark outlines.

In times past, the Moor's women might have seen sights like this, if they ever ventured farther than the harem and courtyard. How sad if they hadn't. They would have known luxury but had never actually lived, imprisoned for carnal use, having to share a man they might have come to love.

Beatriz couldn't have stomached being here if Tomás wooed and claimed another woman. She should have gone to the village today, rather than dragging out her departure. If she delayed too long, she'd eventually be standing in line with the other servants, waiting to greet his new wife, trying not to wince at the smile he gave the woman, the love he showed.

She reached the hidden door, heart aching at what she could have had with him but lost because of her papá. Even without her father being at the castle, he'd killed her future so easily.

She retraced her steps from the other visits she'd made and stood in the chamber, picturing Tomás taking her here on their wedding night, them using this place not for its grandeur, but as a sanctuary against the outside world. Here, they could be themselves, him hating anything to do with running an estate, her unafraid to proclaim her love.

Even though she was no more than his servant now, she'd want him until her dying breath.

The bucket, carpet beater, and other tools lay to the side. She read his list, another memento she meant to keep, and saw to the silk first. She beat the mattresses as well as those she'd tended in the castle, getting through only half before she stopped, tired and sweaty. Heated air and sun poured into the room. Hours gone already.

She slumped. At this rate, she wouldn't finish until tomorrow morning.

Her stomach growled repeatedly. Ignoring her fare, she kept to her task, finishing the other mattresses by the time the sun had passed the highest point in the sky and had started its descent.

Unable to continue without food and rest, she sat with her legs in the stone pool, eating her meal, pushing the floating leaves aside with her feet. If Tomás had been here, they might have made this a game, seeing who could push the leaves fastest to the far end. They'd battle in earnest, laugh themselves silly no matter who had won, then embrace, kiss, and make love.

She covered her eyes, fighting tears. Her throat was so tight she could barely swallow the cheese. A sob caught in her throat. She waved her hands in front of her face, pushing sadness away. There was too much work for her to sit here and weep about losing him.

Sniffing, she put her remaining food to the side. She pushed up her sleeves, filled a bucket to drain the pools, and dumped the water in the courtyard as Tomás's instructions had ordered. After her tenth trip, her arms and back ached. She eyed the mattresses longingly, wanting a brief nap, but continued.

By the time she'd finished with the pools, the sun cast long shadows. Slumped against a column, she pushed her sleeves down and froze, not feeling her orange peel.

She checked inside her sleeve past her elbow but couldn't find the rind she'd carried for weeks as a keepsake.

She slipped her hand between the silk sheets, lugged the mattresses away from each other, and stood in the stone pools to check the damp corners.

The rind was inexplicably gone.

She'd lost everything and now she didn't even have the memento to comfort her when Tomás would be nothing more than a wonderful memory, wed to another.

She checked the mattresses and silk a second time, then ran into chambers she'd never been in.

Hands fisted, she cried, "Where are you?"

Squatting, she searched crevices in the latticework screens, knowing how foolish she was behaving but couldn't stop. She'd asked for so little, wanting only to keep a memory of the most wondrous day she'd ever known.

No matter where she looked, the orange peel remained elusive.

At last, she tore out to the courtyard where she'd dumped the water. Puddles covered the ground, the sun so low rays no longer shone within the space. On her knees, she searched bushes, flowers, grass, and mud.

* * * *

Tomás strode across the grounds, unable to wait any longer for Beatriz's return. She should have come back well before now. The sun had nearly set.

He'd left the oil lamp in the harem, but no means for her to light the thing. He'd only used the lamp on the day they'd first coupled to strike a sensual mood, giving her a taste of a Moor's territory. When the sun was up, the hall to the chambers was easy to navigate. In the darkness though... She couldn't be working by moonlight.

Using another oil lamp, he reached the wooden door and slipped inside. "Beatriz."

Nothing.

Uneasy, he ran down the hall, praying she hadn't fallen into the water. "Beatriz!"

He stopped at the stone depressions, both empty, mattresses stacked to the side, the silk piled next to them. Ready to call her name once more, Tomás lifted the lamp.

She knelt in the courtyard, head down.

He put the lamp on the floor and raced to her. "What happened? Did you hurt yourself?"

She lifted her face, her cheeks damp with tears that glistened in the waning light. "I lost it."

"What?"

She trembled. "It was all I had of our day here."

He touched her shoulder. "What do you mean? Tell me and I can help you look for whatever you lost."

"The orange peel! You forgot to put it in the basket before we left. I came back and found it." Her mouth trembled. "So little to ask for when I lost you. I only wanted..."

He gathered her close. "You never lost me."

"I have." She gripped his shoulders, tears rolling down her cheeks.

He helped her to her feet and swept her into his arms. She clung to him as though drowning. They both were without each other. Their separation had to end.

Back in the chamber, he lowered Beatriz to her feet and put a mattress on a platform. "Lie down."

"No. I have to look for the peel."

"We will later, I promise." He pulled her down to the mattress.

She threw her arms around him, her kisses hungry. They fell back, tearing at each other's clothes, trying to keep their mouths together. Soon, they lay on the mattress naked, Tomás between her legs. He mounted her quickly, thrusting deep.

She captured his mouth.

Given their savage passion, one would have thought decades, rather than weeks, had separated them. He couldn't get deep enough inside her to quell his desire. She couldn't seem to sate her hunger for his mouth. They rocked in time, breaths mingled, joyous cries combined to make one glorious sound.

Panting, he rolled over until she was on top, her weight and heat comforting him.

He fought sleep, fearing she'd disappear if he closed his eyes. He didn't think he could survive another estrangement from her. "We have to settle this. I refuse to go back to these past days. What of you?"

She tightened her hold. "I feel the same."

He lifted her chin so she'd have to look at him. In the faint light, she was a mixture of golden skin and dark hair, a creature of passion, the loveliest woman he'd ever known. "Tell me precisely what you mean. I want to hear the words."

He needed Beatriz to declare her love and promise to be his wife.

She looked so solemn he grew uneasy.

"Do you intend to leave the castle because we had each other again?" His skin prickled. "Do you intend never to see me again?"

"I want to be with you. God help me, I have to…though not as your wife."

"You want us to remain friends? What happens when you conceive?"

"I would do the very best for our child."

"On your own?" Everything was slipping away again, and so quickly, he couldn't keep up. "Without me?"

"Our son or daughter would bear your name. I would keep your memory alive. I would never want anything else."

He couldn't believe she'd actually said what she had. "You expect me to allow you to take our child away?"

"We could stay here until the time came for us to leave."

"When would that be?"

"When you wed."

"You expect me to wed someone else when I love you and to let you take our son or daughter from me?"

"You would always be a part of our child's life, if you wanted to do so. You and I could still see each other."

"Have you gone mad? How?"

"I would be your mistress."

Chapter 10

Tomás rolled them over until she was beneath him. He left the mattress and backed away. "No. Never. How dare you suggest such a thing."

"This is the only way." Leaving him forever wasn't possible any longer. She'd have to share him with another woman in order to have him in her life at all.

"You have gone mad." He threw up his hands. "You expect us to live in the shadows, hiding. From what? Why? Because of your station? Position means nothing to me. I want you as my wife, not my mistress."

Beatriz wanted the same, but their desire didn't matter, a future together wasn't possible. She reached for him. "I love you. I will never want another."

His outrage changed to yearning. He sank to one knee by the mattress and pressed his lips to her knuckles.

A tear ran down her cheek. "Please say you agree."

"No. How can you even ask?" An anguished sound rushed from him. "Why are you doing this to us? Tell me. We can solve anything provided I know the truth."

If he did, their time together would end. "I want no man to rule me. This way, I can be free and you can too."

He released her hand. "Except for my ties to my future wife. Have you forgotten her?"

She'd have to push her feelings aside, never wanting to know if the other woman was pretty or plain, whether her voice was sweet, how she and Tomás behaved together. Whether they touched freely, smiled, and became lost in each other's gazes.

Beatriz wanted to die, but pulled herself together. She had no other choice. "Many in the kingdom have loveless marriages with the husbands and wives seeking pleasure elsewhere."

"How true. But what if I fall in love with my wife? What then?"

She'd never recover. She lowered her face, hiding her torment. "I would have your child or children to remember you."

"You would also have your precious freedom." He stood. "Put on your clothes. We need to quit this place."

She couldn't move.

He yanked on his shirt and reached for his braies. "Did you hear what I said?"

"Please reconsider."

"No. Never mention such a vile thing to me again, understand? From this day forward, you and I are nothing to each other. Without marriage, you will never have my love or my child. Get dressed. Now."

She forced back tears. Her hands shook so badly she could barely manage to pull on her clothes or work her laces. Tomás didn't offer to help. He fetched the oil lamp and remained away, waiting for her.

Once she'd finished, he led the way from the harem and across the grounds.

She held back. "Wait. My clothes are muddy. My hair…" During their passion, he'd loosened her braid. The breeze blew tendrils across her cheeks and forehead.

He stopped finally, his hair ashy in the moonlight, the locks and his shirt quivering in the light wind. He returned to her. "If anyone notices how you look, tell them you became lost in the darkness and fell. I heard your cries for help. Let them think what they will." He proceeded to the castle.

Beatriz had to run to keep up.

* * * *

Tomás was finished with her. He had to stop this madness now. Beatriz thought so little of him she was willing to share him with another woman in order to retain her precious freedom.

So be it. Never again would he offer her his heart, nor did he want to see her every day to remind him how foolish he'd been. He hated this estate and the endless, boring tasks. He wanted to fight again for Spain. Die for his country if need be.

When he'd been at Enrique's castle, they'd heard from their other brother, Pedro, about the Crown's advance on the Moors. Spain had already taken Cuxar, only two leagues from Baza, the next goal. Tomás's destination after tonight.

He reached the back entrance. Light glowed in the kitchen, with a possible audience to his fury. He rounded the castle to enter from the front. Nuncio stood at the door, waiting for him.

Tomás frowned. "Go away."

Nuncio took in Beatriz's tear-streaked face, muddy clothing, and messy hair. "Don Tomás, you must listen to me."

"Not now."

Nuncio stood in his way. "You have a visitor." He inclined his head to a carriage and men to the side, then glanced at Beatriz. "You need to speak with him."

"I said, not now."

For the first time in his service to Tomás, Nuncio wouldn't retreat. He leaned close and whispered, "This is about her."

Tomás grew cold. He looked over at Beatriz. "Go to your bed."

"No." Nuncio kept his voice low. "She needs to stay down here."

Tomás went unsteady with foreboding. He waved her away. "Go to my study. Remain there until I say otherwise."

She stared at him and Nuncio.

Tomás frowned. "Now."

The moment she entered the castle, he crowded Nuncio. "Speak. Explain."

"While you were gone, Señor Don Larnaz Telles arrived at the gate, demanding entrance."

"And you let his carriage in? Tell him and his servants to go."

"He awaits you in the parlor."

"You let him in the castle?"

"I had no choice. The man is a marquis."

"He could be king for all I care. I never heard of him. This has to be a mistake. Tell him to leave. Call the guards and have them throw him out if you must."

"He demanded we bring Beatriz to him."

Tomás's belly clenched. "He spoke her name?"

"Quite clearly."

"Beatriz, my servant? Surely, the man wants another woman called the same."

"He expressly demanded her, Beatriz González y Serrano."

"Have you lost all good sense? That is not her surname."

"I told him as much. He gave me this to prove what he said and to show you."

Nuncio handed him a portrait miniature, no larger than Tomás's palm. He couldn't look at the thing. Didn't want to.

"The face is hers." Nuncio pulled a torch from its holder and held the light closer to Tomás.

The artist must have painted Beatriz a few years earlier. She looked slightly younger. However, her features and hair were the same. He tried to understand this but couldn't. "Was she in service to the marquis? Did she steal from him?"

"What servant has the means to have a portrait created?"

"How should I know? She might have tutored his children. Maybe she was an important part of the family. Nothing else makes sense."

"You need to speak with him to find out."

Squeezing the portrait, Tomás forced himself to go inside, and entered the parlor.

A corpulent man of perhaps sixty lumbered to his feet. Chin lifted, he glared at Tomás's disheveled hair and soiled shirt, then wrinkled his nose. "I insisted on speaking to the master. Not a fool servant."

Nuncio rushed up. "Allow me to introduce Don Tomás to you. He rules here."

Don Larnaz's florid cheeks went as dark as his wine-colored doublet and robe. He puffed out his chest, straining his already snug garments. "Don Tomás. We meet at last."

"Why should we meet at all?"

Larnaz's mouth fell open, making his sagging jowls more prominent. He frowned at Tomás's fist. "You have my portrait. Return it at once." He thrust out his hand.

Tomás ignored him, hating the man already for how he looked, behaved, and the way he'd said Beatriz's portrait belonged to him. "How did you come to be here?" He stepped closer. "Who told you to barge in on my estate?"

The man's shaggy eyebrows shot up. He recovered quickly, frowning. "I had no intention of requesting an audience with you. To answer your question, I believe the man's name is Rufio."

Tomás had to keep from reacting. Beatriz had warned him that Rufio would exact revenge. "How does he fit into this?"

"If you must know, I offered a reward for information leading to Beatriz's whereabouts. I had her likeness posted at various areas in the city, even the ones where peasants gather, hoping for work. Rufio recognized her, had someone read what I had written, and appreciated the sum I offered for what he knew."

"Beatriz worked for you? She stole money or property?"

His expression darkened. "She and I are betrothed."

Nuncio gasped.

Tomás couldn't breathe. This wasn't possible. Yet her refusal finally made sense. If she'd accepted his marriage offer, the moment the banns were posted, Larnaz would have found out where she was and would have dragged her back.

Tomás curbed his outrage. "She ran from you."

Larnaz sneered. "Beatriz and I had a quarrel, easily remedied. She adores her papá and wants what he does. He chose me for her. She agreed. I have the contract."

Her father was alive? "He chose you? Are you saying Beatriz is noble born?"

He stroked his gray-streaked beard. "If only such a miracle were possible. Her beauty, however, does make up for her poor lineage to some degree. Her papá is one of the most prosperous merchants in the city. I agreed to take her off his hands."

Tomás wanted to run the puto through. "Nuncio, ask Beatriz to come in here. Say I want to see her, not that the marquis has arrived."

Nuncio backed away slowly.

Larnaz scowled. "Be quick about it."

Nuncio wasn't, but finally left the room.

Larnaz faced Tomás. "I have my men waiting outside should she try to slip away again. Beatriz can be quite headstrong at times. A lesson I learned too late. She needs a firm hand, which I intend to give until she learns to obey. Never again will she escape my reach." He cleared his throat. "All this needless explanation is making me quite thirsty. I require a drop of wine."

Tomás would die before giving him a sniff. "You can taste your own store once you leave."

The man huffed.

Beatriz entered the parlor and stopped short. Her face deathly white, she stared at Larnaz as one would a demon.

Larnaz scowled. "What have you done to yourself? How dare you put me to such trouble only to have you look this way? Come here at once."

She recoiled.

"Very well. I will go to you." He stormed across the room.

Tomás stood between him and Beatriz. "Leave now. Never come here again."

"As though we would. Once Beatriz and I take our leave from—"

"She stays."

Deep red patches spread across Larnaz's cheeks. "You have no say in this. She and I are betrothed. I have the contract."

"If you had an order from the king, my answer would be the same. I asked for Beatriz's hand. She accepted."

* * * *

Beatriz's vision dimmed. The room swayed.

Nuncio rushed to her side and took her hand. She gripped his fingers, surprised yet grateful for his comfort.

Shoulders squared, Don Larnaz faced Tomás. "The deal is done. Her dowry paid. She has no choice except to honor our contract."

"So you can keep the money." Tomás made a dismissive noise. "Or is the problem you have no means to pay the sum back?"

He clenched his fists and teeth. "The dowry is mine, given in good faith."

"Then keep it. The money means nothing. I can settle matters with her father, pay him back what he gave you."

She pulled her hand from Nuncio's. "Tomás, no."

The men ignored her.

Sweat streamed down Don Larnaz's face. "Her papá expects her to wed a marquis, not the son of a count. I know who you are and what you lack."

"As does Beatriz. She can decide her own future." Tomás looked over. "Do you want to wed this man?"

She'd rather die, but couldn't let Don Larnaz or her father use Tomás for what they wanted. "I could never ask you to pay back my dowry."

"I offered. Nothing you say will change my mind. Do you want to wed him?"

"Never."

Don Larnaz stared at her as he would an animal he owned, his ugly smile promising hell on earth. "You have no choice."

"She just made hers," Tomás said. "Leave at once on your own or my guards will see you past the gate.

"Come." Tomás cupped her elbow and led her from the room to the grand stairway.

Don Larnaz rushed after them. "This is not the end."

Tomás squeezed her elbow. "Pay him no heed."

He couldn't be serious.

Don Larnaz followed them, shaking his fist and shouting, "I will have you as my wife." He bellowed through the entryway, "You will never get away from me."

Tomás and Beatriz mounted the stairs. She pressed closer to him. "Where are we going?"

"My bedchamber."

"What?"

"Let me take care of things. All will be well."

She had no idea how.

Nuncio kept flapping his hands and racing after Don Larnaz. "You must leave."

"Get away from me, you old fool." He lifted his face to Beatriz. "Whore."

Tomás stopped and faced him.

Don Larnaz thrust out his belly. "Puto." He spat.

Tomás stomped down the stairs, fists clenched, shoulders bunched. The marquis fled, slamming the door with such force its boom registered in her belly.

Tomás followed him.

"No, wait." She ran after him.

Nuncio grabbed Tomás's arm before he reached the door. "Violence will only make matters worse. You could end up answering charges."

"Well worth it. Let go."

"No." Nuncio panted. "Think of Beatriz."

She gripped Tomás's other arm. "Please listen to us."

He breathed hard. "I want to kill the puto."

"I know." She held fast. "But he ran so quickly he could very well have tripped and broke his neck saving you the trouble."

Tomás laughed. "Let go of me."

Neither she nor Nuncio did.

Tomás sighed. "I promise to behave."

They released him.

"Come." He led Beatriz up the stairs to the landing.

Señora Cisneros ran down the hall. "I heard shouting and the door slam. What happened?"

"Nothing," Tomás took her candle. "Stay here and wait for my return."

Once he and Beatriz were in his bedchamber, he lit several candles. After placing the holder to the side, he pulled her into his arms. "Why did you keep this from me?"

"I had no choice." She pressed her palms against his broad back, and shuddered when she considered Don Larnaz holding her like this. "I was afraid."

"You still are, trembling as though the swine had yet to leave." He hugged her gently. "Did you think I would care what he said or let him take you away?"

"I never wanted to bring you trouble. I tried not to."

"But I kept hounding you until you fell in love with me. Is that it? Are you sorry I behaved so badly?"

Beatriz laughed, surprised she could. "Never. What do we do now? What if he finds a way to fight you?"

"First, you need to take care of yourself. Stay in here until I return."

She gripped his sleeve. "From where?"

"To speak to Señora Cisneros."

"About what?"

"So many questions." He cradled her cheek. "I have a surprise for you."

"What? Where?"

"Take this."

He handed her the miniature portrait her father had commissioned, claiming the practice was popular with elites. At the time, he hadn't told Beatriz he'd planned to use her likeness to seek out a noble son-in-law. "This is your surprise? I want nothing of it."

"I do, you look exquisite." He put the piece on a cabinet. "However, my surprise has nothing to do with the painting. Stay here, please."

He kissed her deeply, took Señora Cisneros's candle, and left.

Beatriz wrung her hands and caught her reflection in a small mirror on the chest. Her eyes were red and swollen from crying, hair pointed in every direction. Dirt smeared her face and clothes. She looked worse than Don Larnaz ever could, and he was a filthy swine.

She snickered, then laughed so hard she couldn't draw a full breath. Her laughter grew to quick tears, then to giggles. What a sorry mess she was. Not wanting to make the bed or chairs dirty, she sank to the floor and propped her back against the cabinet.

A short while ago, losing the orange peel had devastated her. Arguing with Tomás about being his mistress, with him not wanting anything to do with her, had ended Beatriz's world. Then to have Nuncio summon her to the parlor where Don Larnaz had waited had been her worst nightmare. For an instant, she'd believed he'd lead her away from the castle with Tomás closing the door on them, relieved she was gone.

She covered her face, hating that she'd doubted him in the least. He'd repeatedly admitted his love when she'd denied him any response or the truth. Upon learning who she was, he hadn't quit her as any sane man would, but had protected her instead, offering his wealth to keep her free.

If only her mother had known a man like him.

Someone rushed past in the hall. Others followed.

Activity sounded in the next room. Scraping, a clang, and thud, sounds made when someone shifted furniture about. The last person to have slept there was Zita. She'd insisted on the bedchamber closest to Tomás's, with her mamá claiming the one on the other side, trapping the poor man between them.

More footfalls sounded, numerous individuals passing. Servants, she guessed.

Nuncio called out, "Everyone departed. I watched from the parapet. Send for me if you require anything."

Silence. Tomás must have nodded rather than spoken.

The footfalls finally retreated and relative quiet settled in, broken by the door opening. Tomás looked at the chairs and the bed, finally rounded the corner, and spotted her on the floor.

"I need to teach you to sit as a proper lady does."

She giggled. "I warn you, some have called me a poor student."

"Give me their names so I can run them through."

She didn't deserve him. No woman did. He was too good for this earth. "Gracias."

"For threatening to murder putos who dare slander you? What else is a warrior for?"

"You stood by me." No one else had except her mother. Beatriz extended her hand. "I can never repay you."

He wrapped his fingers around hers. "No one said you have to. Come, your surprise awaits."

He brought her to the next room, closing the door behind them. A servant had turned down the bed and lit enough candles to make the large room seem cozy. Someone else had brought in a metal tub. Steam rose from the water. A delicate rose fragrance filled the air from scented oil.

"You want me to take a bath?"

"I want you to relax. I can handle the rest, even washing your back and hair."

She sagged against him, wrapping her arms around his middle. "Can I do nothing for you?"

"Promise to wed me."

"I want to." She hugged him with all her strength. "I always have."

"And here Fernando and Enrique said I had to wear you down."

"What—who?"

"My brothers. I have five in all. Two are twins. I also have one sister, a father, two sisters-in-law, a niece, and a brand new nephew. The family also includes countless uncles, aunts, and cousins. Some we speak to. Others we try to ignore."

She laughed. "What a family you have. Tell me more."

"In time." He leaned back enough to see her face. "I want to hear about you during your bath. Everything."

He wanted the truth and certainly deserved to know what had brought her to this place in life. Tomás didn't push, though, as other men might have. After helping her undress, he eased her into the warm fragrant water, and sank to one knee next to her.

She blew out a sigh. "How I missed this."

"The bath or me tending you?"

"Both." She ran her knuckles down his bristly cheek, loving how his whiskers scraped her skin. "You most, though, even with my aches."

"You hurt? Where?"

"Every part of me." She leaned back, letting water spill over her breasts. "Beating mattresses and draining pools is hard work."

"Forgive me." He turned her hand over and made a pained sound. "You have blisters. This is my fault."

"Shh." She silenced him with her fingertips on his lips. "You wanted me in the harem to remind me of our time there, no?"

"I thought if you recalled our love, you might change your mind about wedding me."

"What a wonderful man you are, making me work until my skin nearly bled."

He seemed torn between laughter and a sigh.

"Not once did I mind." She trailed her fingers over his cheek. "I far preferred work here than my life in the city."

"With your papá?"

She nodded. "He deals in the finest silks, velvets, and wools. Fabrics most nobles purchase from him."

Tomás groaned. "I told you how to handle the harem silk when you already knew how, no?"

She nodded.

"Did you laugh at me afterward?"

"A little, while I was hauling heavy buckets of water to the courtyard."

His cheeks reddened. "I should have been kinder to you."

"No man has ever treated me with as much respect or tenderness, certainly not my father."

"He beat you?"

Worse. "He ruled my life as though I were his property to do with as he willed, not a woman with a mind of my own or even a daughter who wanted his consideration." She shifted slightly in the tub. Water splashed over the side. "Gaining his love was out of the question."

"Why?"

"My mother and I were always tools for him to further his ends. He wants nothing more than to walk among nobles and royals. As a commoner, he had no way except through wealth. He met my mother by working for her father, a prosperous merchant who owned the company my papá now calls his."

"He stole the business from your grandfather?"

"He wed my mother and controlled the business through her. From what my mother told me, my grandfather was a sweet man, wanting naught expect her happiness. He enjoyed the way my father took care of her in the early days, how devoted he seemed. After Grandpapá died, my father had full say in the operations. Until then, my mother had believed he'd married her for love. Mamá soon found out what his intent had been from the start."

Beatriz had found her mother's journal after her death. How eager she'd been to read a portion, hoping the words would ease her sorrow and loneliness. Fear built first, then rage at her father's depravity. What he could do and had done to others.

Tomás searched her face. "He had mistresses?"

"No. Papá has no time or desire for passion. He craves wealth and power. The only way he could get what he wanted was through Mamá. She was quite beautiful."

"Was?"

She cleared her throat, anger and sadness warring within her at what her mother had endured. How much her father had taken from them. "She died when I was fourteen. Everyone thought the fever had killed her, but he had. She couldn't lie with the nobles any longer, humiliating herself to bring him what he wanted."

"Wait." Tomás took her hand. "Your father allowed your mother to couple with other men?"

"He arranged the encounters. As I said, she was quite beautiful. Many men wanted her. Papá encouraged the acts, especially the basest and most demeaning. The kind no woman would agree to willingly unless threatened or she needed money to eat. As long as the nobles did business with his company and allowed him to become a part of their world, letting him use their power for his own ends, he turned her over to them willingly."

Tomás's face paled. "How can that be? She had no chance to refuse?"

The journal entries proved she hadn't. Beatriz would never forget her mother's anguish and finally her losing the will to live. "In the beginning she did tell him no, repelled at the thought of what he'd demanded, even threatening to leave. He promised to impoverish her and take me away. Mamá feared for my safety.

"When she conceived again, she fell and lost the child. As I grew older, I wondered if she did so deliberately to spare the poor soul the life we had, him as a father. The physician said there would be no more children for her. Papá was enraged. I suspect he wanted her to become pregnant with a noble's child so he could secure his hold even more, threatening the man with scandal if he failed to give Papá everything he wanted."

"What of your mamá? How could any man do such a thing?"

"I doubt he thought of her at all. She was nothing more than an instrument to him. Unless he needed her for something, he barely looked her way. If she failed to behave precisely as he expected, he raged at her, threatening to harm me."

Tomás squeezed her hand. "Did he ever follow through?"

"No. I was valuable property in his eyes. Scars from beatings would have lessened my ability to attract a noble husband for him to use for his own ends."

"Larnaz."

"Sadly, yes. I fear Papá has met his match finally. Don Larnaz is as contemptible as he is. A man who beats women to cow them or because he enjoys their pain. A noble without funds given his lifestyle. I heard he likes to wager and uses the most expensive whores. Wedding me would give him access to my father's wealth. My marriage to him would secure Papá's place with the nobility. Not as a mere merchant or a man who handed his beautiful wife over, but as the father-in-law of a marquis."

"How dare he trade you for access."

Beatriz kissed his knuckles, loving his outrage, the same as hers. In many ways, they were similar, not caring about station or wealth, wanting only happiness. "I had no idea he had even promised me to the man until the three of us shared a meal one night. I thought Don Larnaz was simply a business acquaintance until he told me where we would travel after the wedding, what he expected of me as his wife.

"I couldn't comprehend what he said. As you saw tonight, the man is old enough to be my grandfather, fat, ugly, and unpleasant in every way. After he told me my duties, he and my father discussed other matters as if I no longer existed. When I spoke up finally and refused to wed him, Papá said I had no choice in the matter, never had, and would go through with the nuptials whether I wanted to or not."

Beatriz shuddered. "Since Mamá had married him for love, I hoped he would grant me the same grace or some say in the matter. How foolish

I was. For centuries, noble families have forced their children to marry those they neither knew nor loved because of political considerations. Why would a wealthy merchant feel any different when he had a daughter, or rather his property, to trade for a title?"

"Not you. He can have as much access to the nobility as he wants through my brothers and me. I know Enrique will help. Sancha, his wife, is the daughter of a grandee and a duke. Her father had many friends and connections at court before he died. My papá can introduce yours to even more."

She sickened at anyone using Tomás and his family in such a way. "What if your offer doesn't satisfy him? You heard Don Larnaz. My father wants a marquis, and Don Larnaz wants wealth."

Tomás wrapped his arm around her shoulders. "No one can force you to wed the pig."

"Are you certain? Should we run as I had? With you beside me, I should fare better than I had the last time. I nearly starved before I came upon your land. Señora Cisneros only hired me out of pity."

"I intend to reward her greatly for helping you."

Beatriz wasn't certain whether to laugh or cry.

"Neither of us runs." He kissed her cheek. "We wed as quickly as we can. I can ask Enrique and Fernando what to do. They each faced problems before marrying their esposas."

"The same as ours?"

"Different, though equally troubling. Nothing will keep us from each other. Have you forgotten we already consummated our union?" He grinned. "Numerous times, in fact."

She traced his mouth with her thumb. "My papá's money, not my purity, matters most to Don Larnaz. Allowing me to raise your child in order to have the wealth is a small matter for him."

"He has no choice except to give up or battle me, I promise you."

Chapter 11

No one would ever take her from him. Tomás would lie, cheat, or kill, if necessary, to keep her at his side.

He touched his mouth to hers. "Time for you to relax as I tend to you."

Their lips brushed each other's with his words, their breaths blending to become one. He dipped a sponge into the warm water. Its scent reminded him of a spring morning. "Give me your arm."

"Is that all you want of me?"

He smiled at her teasing. "For the moment."

She extended her arm to him, palm up.

Her damaged skin pained him. He cursed himself for having put her through any hardship. From this moment forward, she'd know only leisure and joy at his hands. He squeezed the sponge gently, drizzling water over her blisters.

She held her breath.

He stopped. "Does your skin sting?"

"Only a little."

That was far too much. He blew on her palm to ease the pain.

Beatriz relaxed again, her shoulders drooping.

He ran the sponge over her arm, washing away the day's grime and, he hoped, its bad memories of them arguing, him saying they were finished with each other. What a fool he'd been. If Larnaz hadn't come here tonight, Tomás suspected he would have tried to find another way to convince her to be his.

He drew the sponge over her cheeks, removing dirt and dried tears. He'd never forget Beatriz on her knees in the harem courtyard, head bowed, weeping because she couldn't find an orange peel.

Tomorrow, he'd locate the thing if he had to crawl over the entire yard and chambers inch by inch. Most other women would have wanted pearls, emeralds, rubies, and diamonds. She wanted him. He needed to witness her delight when he returned her lost treasure.

He stepped to the far end of the tub and lifted her foot to wash her toes. Laughing, she tipped back her head, exposing her creamy throat.

He fell more in love with her. "Am I tickling you?"

"Sí. Ah." She exhaled loudly. "Feels good."

He'd run the sponge up her calf to the silky skin behind her knee. Her arms slid over the rim, hands dangling above the floor, lids heavy, lips parted on a prolonged sigh.

Exactly as he wanted her. "Are you falling asleep?"

"Relaxing. In all my days, I have never had a bath like this."

She'd better not. This task belonged to him from here on out. They'd wash each other in the harem pools and make love in the courtyard beneath a heavy sun or star-splashed sky, spending their time cloistered from the world, Beatriz rejecting clothes, her sumptuous nudity tempting him as sultans demanded from their odalisques.

Those men knew how to set a mood.

For the moment, this tub and the candles would have to suffice. The flickering light bathed the room in a rosy glow, wrapping them in intimacy.

He unbraided the rest of her hair, running his fingers through the locks to untangle them. She moaned delicately. The silky mass tested his control. He longed to press his face to her mane, shower her with kisses, touch every part of her, claiming what was now his and would be for all time.

He trembled from desire so intense the feeling was painful yet welcomed.

Using a pitcher, he poured water over her tresses. He eased stray curls from her cheeks and forehead, then rubbed her scalp lightly.

She made a breathy sound.

He leaned over. There was naught but pleasure and peace on her face. Although proud he'd pleased her, he couldn't quell the mischief running so deep within him. "This displeases you?" He rubbed her scalp slowly. "Would you like me to stop?"

"Only if you want me to run you through."

"Aha. You have a mean streak." He grinned. "I like that."

She giggled.

Tomás wanted her moaning in bliss. He kneaded her shoulders, easing away the tightness. She softened further beneath his touch. He cupped her breasts, thumbs grazing her nipples. The tips peaked instantly, the halos grew taut and bumpy.

She pressed her face to his sleeve, her breath warming him through the linen.

With his hand dipping lower, he skimmed her curly bush and waited for her reaction.

She parted her legs to him as much as the narrow tub allowed. He touched her cleft, plump and slippery with her juices, encouraging him to take her.

Heat raced through him, his stiffened shaft pressing against his clothes. Breathing and speech were difficult. "Have you had enough of your bath?"

"I have, though not of you."

Good thing. They had a lifetime to share.

He helped her from the tub. Water streamed over her luscious curves to form puddles on the floor. The small pools reflected the candlelight, orange and gold splashes that resembled a fiery circle at her feet, creating a breathtaking image.

He scrubbed her dry with a towel, leaving her hair in disarray, skin flushed like a woman who'd been loved long and well. Just the beginning.

Tomás swept her into his arms.

She inhaled sharply and held on to him even after he'd lowered her to the mattress. "Stay with me."

He ran his knuckles down her cheek. "Forever. However, you have to let go of me so I can take off my clothes."

"Let me help."

"I can see to the task far more quickly than you."

"Proceed."

He fairly tore off his garments and joined her on the mattress. She stroked his chest.

"No." He cuffed her wrists.

"You need to take something else off before I can touch you?" She craned her neck to see more of him.

"I want you to relax."

She fell back to the mattress. "In a bed with both of us naked? Are you serious, or is this more of your teasing?"

"I want to do all the work."

"Where were you when I nearly killed myself in the harem?"

"I was here being a brute." He rubbed his nose against hers, aroused by her clean scent, the rose trace left from the bathwater, her musk beneath. "Can you ever forgive me?"

"Depends on what you do in the coming moments." She gave him a playful smile. "Proceed."

He positioned her arms above her head and parted her legs.

She bent her knees and lifted her mound to him.

"No. Stay as you are. In fact, remain perfectly still."

"You want me to play dead as most wives do?"

"You will never be most wives." He planted his hands on either side of her and leaned down. "Do you honestly believe you could be with me?" She flicked her gaze at his nudity. Arousal flooded her features. "You have me at a disadvantage."

"Lucky you."

She laughed.

He suckled the inside of her arm.

Moaning, she lifted herself, nipples grazing his chest, the curls between her legs brushing his rigid shaft.

He dug his fingers into the sheets in order to maintain some control. His only purpose tonight was giving her his best. She'd endured so much. Losing her beloved mamá, treated cruelly by her father, terrorized at having no choice except to spend her young life submitting to Larnaz. She deserved what little Tomás could provide. He would have given her the world if he'd had the power.

He kissed her lightly on the shoulder and dipped his tongue in the hollow of her throat.

She pressed closer.

He inched down her, his cheek against her breast, mouth claiming her nipple. The tip hardened, her velvety skin fueling his insatiable hunger for her.

He suppressed a growl, not wanting to alarm her or himself, his lust building to a dangerous level.

Her other breast beckoned him. He cupped the pale globe and feasted on the nipple, tonguing and suckling her scented flesh.

She ran her toes up his calf.

He trembled and rained kisses over her ribs and down her torso, circling her navel with his tongue. She made a contented sound. Still lower, he pressed his face into her dark thatch, pleased at the rose fragrance, entranced by her womanly scent. Musk that spoke of life, love, passion, need.

He slipped two fingers within her hot, tight sheath, imprisoning her with his touch. She stilled. He confined her further with his mouth, holding her nub with care between his teeth, licking her mercilessly.

She cried out, raw desire mingled with tender yearning.

Tomás wanted her breathless with release.

He worked his fingers in and out of her channel. Her moans grew louder. She dug her heels into the mattress and gripped her hair.

Surrendering to passion, he suckled her nub and used her sheath for his pleasure and hers.

Beatriz broke, shouting wildly with her release, seeming not to care if the servants heard. He certainly didn't. This chamber belonged to her and to him. No one would dare come inside.

He slipped his fingers from her pulsing channel and filled her with his shaft instead.

She moaned wantonly.

He smiled at his sex sliding slowly in and out of hers, his rod drenched in her moisture, more proof she desired him. He came alive as he never had, astonishingly sensitive to every touch.

His passion should have made him want to hurry toward pleasure, as he'd desired earlier. Instead, he kept his pace lazy, his gaze locked with hers.

They drank each other in and smiled, deepening their bond.

Too soon, they demanded relief. Beatriz's color was high, eyes glazed. He stroked her nub and thrust faster, pumping his rod into her channel, making the mattress bounce.

She gripped his arms and cried out, her sheath quivering around his sex. He tried to hold off but failed, joining her in a timeless dance of passion, pleasure, and undeniable love.

* * * *

As much as Beatriz would have liked to remain in bed forever with Tomás, she forced herself to wake finally. Light streamed past a gap in the drapes, morning well underway, the staff at their duties.

The servants must have noticed her absence when they woke or had breakfast and surely asked Señora Cisneros what had happened to her.

Someone had to talk to them, though Beatriz had no idea how she and Tomás would handle her going from servant to lady of the house in one night. Even the kindest servant would wonder how any love match could happen so quickly. Their gossip would be endless and possibly hurtful, the same as what happened when Yolanda gained her new job with the chandler.

Oh no. Leonor.

She'd repeatedly rammed into Beatriz over Rufio. Although Tomás would never consider Leonor a love interest, she might feel betrayed because another servant had gotten what she coveted. Her jealousy might truly be dangerous this time. As Yolanda had said, Leonor was good with a knife.

Beatriz rolled over to ask Tomás what he thought. She touched cool sheets rather than him. He wasn't on a chair or the floor, either. She figured he'd gone to his own chamber before the servants had awakened so none would stumble upon him and her naked, limbs entwined.

Beatriz left the bed and frowned at her muddy clothes, reluctant to put them on. She dunked them into the cold bath water for a good scrubbing.

The door opened. She froze.

Tomás strode inside, already shaved and dressed in a fresh linen shirt, dark hose, and his leather belt.

How beautiful he looked.

He leaned against the door, arms crossed. "What are you doing? We have servants to tend the washing, you know."

She dropped her clothes into the tub and sat on her heels. "I have nothing to wear except my dirty clothes. I need you to get my livery from Señora Cisneros."

"So my future wife can dress as a servant? Never."

"Better I walk around naked?"

He glanced at the rumpled bed.

She made a face. "You expect me to wear sheets?"

"What? No. The white tunic from your livery should do."

"Without the red gown? You want me to go about with my arms uncovered?"

"Wear one of my shirts too. They have sleeves." He plucked at his, showing her.

She wasn't certain whether he was teasing or not. "White on white?"

His face brightened. "Like an angel."

He was serious. She scrubbed her clothes. "Until these dry, I have no choice except to wear my livery. What are we going to tell the other servants?"

"About what?"

She gestured to the messy bed, her new status with him.

"Oh." He shrugged. "You want one of the servants to come in here now and tidy the—"

"You *are* teasing me."

He grinned. "I like how easy you are to fool." He joined her on the floor. "I already had a word with Señora Cisneros, asking her to explain our situation to the others, and to hire a servant to replace you. Someone young, nine or ten perhaps, so the new girl has no chance to outshine you for a few months."

Beatriz couldn't share his levity about this. "The staff will gossip about us, you know."

"They do anyway even when absolutely nothing happens. Ignore them from now on."

"After we worked together? I think not. I intend to speak to Yolanda personally. It would be awful if she thought less of me because of our wedding."

Tomás gave her an odd look. "The few times I spoke to Yolanda, she seemed to like me. At least enough to approve of me marrying you."

Beatriz smiled. "No need to feel bad. I was going for another point. Even though Yolanda and I spoke often, I never revealed what was going on between you and me. I told her a tall tale about my past. She has good reason to think I deceived her. Friends tell the truth to each other and share things."

"Put the blame on me then. Tell her I ordered you not to breathe a word. I like the child and want her to keep liking you."

"You are a good man." She hugged him. "Once I get dressed I can help you write missives to your brothers."

"Already finished and sent. One to my papá too. I woke early while you slept." He caressed her buttocks, then explored the separation between her cheeks, tickling her.

She squirmed. "What of my father?"

"You mean writing him a missive? I should see him in person."

"Oh, please, no. Seeing him could make things worse. He schemes constantly and might try something to stop us. A missive would be best."

"Whatever you want. We can work together on what to say to him. Do you know how much he gave Larnaz for your dowry?"

"Are you planning to send money with the letter?"

"The sum will surely make our words easier for him to read."

Although her father craved wealth, what he wanted even more was access to a world he hadn't been born into. "Are you certain you want to go through with our plans?"

He leaned against the tub. "Are you going to give me another hard time? Can I at least have breakfast first?"

She couldn't help smiling, though her amusement didn't last. "My father never gives up."

"Has he ever fought a Moor? I have hundreds of times. Facing an enemy who wants to live as much as you do is a lesson in avoiding defeat. The only one who can fell me is you by turning your back on our love and leaving my side."

"I promise to remain until I see you harmed. Then, I would concede defeat in a moment to spare you."

"Never." He grabbed her shoulders, his gaze locked with hers. "Without you, I have nothing. Promise me we never stop fighting for our future no matter what."

She lowered her face.

"Beatriz, I want to hear the words."

"You ask too much. I could never let you get hurt because of me."

He didn't comment, nor did he release her.

"Very well, I promise this. If my father or Don Larnaz tries to harm you in any way, they will answer to me." She would see them pay.

Tomás regarded her for a long moment, then pushed to his feet. "You can wear livery today but need proper clothes for the future. We can write the woman who used to make your gowns, commissioning dozens in every color and fabric."

"Dozens?"

"Hundreds then. I want you dressed like a queen. No more hiding your hair, either."

"You do know the current style is for a woman to wear a caul or some sort of covering on her head."

"Not you, never in the castle or on the grounds. Please."

He kissed her so tenderly she couldn't deny his request. "My hair will always be down for you."

Tomás grinned. "Let me get your livery."

* * * *

Once dressed, Beatriz had breakfast with him in the dining hall. The servants exchanged glances, their expressions saying the world they'd known would never be the same. The kitchen help peeked around the corner to view the scene, Leonor among them.

The last time Beatriz had felt on display like this was when her father had introduced her to Don Larnaz. Both men treating her as they would a heifer, raised for purchase.

Tomás seemed obvious to anything except his meal and holding her hand.

She forced the last of her milk down.

Antonia rushed up. She'd just turned twenty and had always been friendly but not close. "More, Beatriz?"

The others gasped.

Tomás took another boiled egg from the basket. "Not Beatriz. Señorita Serrano."

"Forgive me." Antonia bowed, apologized again, and departed.

Beatriz's cheeks burned. "Would it be so wrong for them to address me as they always have?"

"Your decision, though it would be best for them to be more formal during gatherings. Otherwise the nobles will talk."

She squeezed his hand in gratitude and looked over. "Everyone, please keep calling me Beatriz."

Rather than returning her smile, they exchanged glances again.

Tomás leaned toward her this time. "Wars are never won in a day. Best you remember that."

After their meal, she made a list of clothes she'd need from her tailoress and other merchants.

Tomás worked on his missive to her father, reading each line to her. At her request, he'd scratched out most of what he'd written and finally sagged in his chair. "No man could be this difficult to win against. Does he breathe fire?"

"He smiles sweetly and is exceedingly kind when speaking with others, making everyone love him so he can learn their weaknesses, which he then uses to destroy them."

Tomás rubbed his forehead. "Clearly you believe my being forthright or firm with him is the wrong approach. What say I use his ploy and use a honeyed tone, giving him a false sense of security in regard to me?"

"Now you have it."

"What if he believes I truly fear him and he strikes even harder, dragging this out for months?"

She pressed her fingers to her forehead. "Write the missive as you think best, though I would mention the dowry at the end, rather than the beginning."

"Why?"

"To make you sound fair rather than paying him off to leave us alone. How right you are about being firm. If he senses weakness, he will pounce, just as he did with my mother when she had me to protect."

He covered Beatriz's hand. "I give you my oath, your papá will never harm you again. He may be fearless against women, children, and nobles gone soft, but he has yet to face a warrior."

"How you make my blood race."

He laughed. "Show me once I finish this missive and my other work."

"I will. While you do, I want to speak with Yolanda. During breakfast, I had a thought concerning her and some of the other servants."

"What kind of thought?"

"I want to speak with Yolanda first, feel her out before I tell you."

"Go on." He waved her away. "Remember to put the blame on me for keeping you from the servant quarters."

After a fast kiss, Beatriz left his study and sought Señora Cisneros, but ran into Nuncio instead.

He actually flushed and had difficulty meeting her gaze.

She took his hand. "Thank you for giving me strength during my darkest time last night."

"Señor Don Larnaz is a beast. Forgive me for saying so, but he is."

"No need for remorse. I agree. I hope you and I can be friends."

His cheeks darkened. "I was so unkind."

"You were protecting Tomás. I trust you to do so in the future. Will you promise me?"

"Of course. I will do so with you too."

"I know." She hugged him soundly and spoke before his shocked expression had faded. "Do you know where Señora Cisneros is?"

"The last I saw she was at the linen closet."

Beatriz found her there.

"Señorita Serrano." The woman bowed her head in deference.

"Beatriz, please. You saved my life. I would have starved if not for you."

"How sad you looked the day you came here. Only a fiend could have said no to your request for work."

Beatriz remembered the encounter differently. "I recall begging you for several minutes to at least give me a chance to prove myself."

The woman grew pensive. "I must have had my mind on other matters to have been so rude. Everything worked out, though. You convinced me what a fine servant you would be. Good for you." She smiled. The hairs on her chin became more obvious, the ones on her upper lip less so. "For the most part you did almost as well as Yolanda."

"I tried my best."

"Of course. What can I do for you now?"

"I want to speak with Yolanda. Will you ask her to come to the bedchamber where I slept last night?"

Señora Cisneros looked uneasy. "Is the girl in trouble?"

"Not at all. I simply want to see how she is. How she likes her work."

"Let me get her for you." She dashed down the hall.

Beatriz returned to the bedchamber. In her absence, a servant had cleaned, tidied, and taken away the tub. Her freshly laundered gown hung in the wardrobe, dried and ready to wear as if by magic. At least that's what a noble or a prosperous merchant and his family would think. Until Beatriz had come here, she'd had no idea the labor needed to run a grand house or a castle. The work was endless and tedious with little reward.

Although Tomás was generous with his servants, giving them a day off, as much food as they wanted, and fair wages, those women and men had little to look forward to other than endless service. Beatriz wanted to give them more, especially Yolanda, who had a spark that needed nurturing.

Light footfalls sounded in the hall. Beatriz expected the door to swing open or for Yolanda to call her name.

Yolanda rapped timidly.

Her heart ached. In the past, Yolanda had vigorously shaken Beatriz to wake her, even pinching if necessary, without worry about consequences. They'd been friends, Yolanda the only one Beatriz had when she'd sorely needed one.

As she did now. "Come in."

Yolanda shuffled inside, cheeks rosy, gaze on the floor.

Beatriz crossed the room and took Yolanda's hands in hers. "How are you?"

She glanced up, then down just as quickly. "I have no complaints."

"Can we have a word?"

"If you want. I can do whatever you say."

"Not as servant and mistress. As friends."

Yolanda stared. "You still want that with me?"

"Of course. Come. Sit." She gestured to a chair.

Yolanda perched on the edge and kept her face down, either uncomfortable in the room's splendor or with this odd relationship. Perhaps both. She'd surely never expected to be here in this manner.

Custom may have frowned upon what Beatriz was doing, but she hardly cared. Yolanda was the little sister she'd never had. She closed the door and took the chair next to her. "Do you know who I really am?"

"Señora Cisneros said you was one of them, those who lead fine lives, not one of us."

"I came from a prosperous family and ran away because I was unhappy. No one loved me."

Yolanda nodded, understanding on her face at being an unloved child. Early on in their friendship, Yolanda had explained how her parents had told her to find work and to send them her wages. If she couldn't get a position, she wasn't to come back. They couldn't feed her any longer as her six brothers needed the food, two of them older than her. She'd been ten at the time and had walked alone from her village to this castle. Not once had she sounded bitter during her tale, saying she understood her parents turning her out. As a female, she had little to offer them.

Beatriz wanted to give Yolanda the world. "My pending marriage changes nothing between us. I would have told you who I was, but I feared my father would find me."

"Is he a cruel man?"

"My mother died because of him."

"Then you did the right thing to leave. Good for you."

Beatriz loved the girl's spirit and sense of justice. "Is your work coming along all right? Do you still enjoy what you do?"

"Has the chandler complained about me?"

"No. I wanted to know if you like what you do or would prefer something else."

"Depends." She grew cautious. "What did you have in mind?"

"A lady needs a personal maid. Would you like to be mine?"

Yolanda's mouth fell open, her eyes brightening, though only for a moment. She calmed quickly and shook her head. "I must say no."

"Why? You seemed excited."

"I am, but being a maid to a lady is for someone much finer than me. Look at my hands." She stuck them out, knuckles red, skin rough. She was only twelve.

At that age, Beatriz had ridden the finest Arabians, read countless books, learned how to paint, and play the harp, her father grooming her for marriage to a noble without her knowledge.

Yolanda drew in her shoulders. "If I was to touch your fine silk and other things, I could hurt them."

"What if I show you how to make your hands soft and tend to velvets and silks so nothing bad happens?"

"You can do that?"

"I can teach you everything you need to know. All you have to do is say yes."

"I will. I mean I do. Wait." She bit her lip.

"No need to worry about the chandler. Señora Cisneros can find someone else to help the man."

"I know she can. Ever since I started the work, everyone else wants to take my place. My wages concern me. My parents and brothers need the money."

Of course. "Your pay would be what others in the same position make. Twice what you earn now."

Yolanda gasped. "Truly?"

Beatriz had offered her more than the normal amount, knowing Tomás worried about people, not money. "Truly."

"Can I begin today?"

"Whenever you want."

"Today it is. Can I embrace you?"

"Of course."

They hugged like sisters, friendship and love flowing between them.

Yolanda pulled away first and jumped to her feet. "Should I look for you here after I tell the chandler?"

"I may be elsewhere. You can come in and wait for me. Before you leave, though, I have something else to ask."

"Ask and I will answer as best I can."

Beatriz smiled. "Would you like to learn to read and write?"

* * * *

Tomás thought he'd never finish his missive to Beatriz's papá, but at last he had. Eager to show her, he hurried from his study and nearly collided with her in the hall.

He jumped back.

She grabbed his sleeve and pulled him into the room. "I have news."

He hoped it was good. Specifically, her father having already sent a missive stating he had no objections to the union.

Not likely, though. Too little time had elapsed for Larnaz to tell the man what had happened last night and for the message to reach here.

Once she'd closed the door, she bounced on her heels. "Yolanda agreed to be my personal maid."

Tomás wasn't sure how to respond. "I know little of these things. Is that good for you?"

"Both of us. The work is easy, the wages excellent." Beatriz told him what she'd offered the girl.

"A fine wage."

"Twice what she made with the chandler. I offered her more than the usual rate. Do you mind?"

He had no idea what anyone earned here. Perhaps he should pay more attention. "As long as you two are happy."

"We are. Yolanda will need to have a room next to mine."

"Why?"

"To be at the ready should I need her."

"Wait. A room next to yours? No. Once we wed, we share the same bedchamber. I insist."

"As do I. We can settle Yolanda in a room next to ours." Beatriz frowned suddenly. "We may have to put a lock on the door."

"Hers or ours?"

"Hers."

"To keep her from barging in on us?"

"No." She made a face saying he'd lost all sense. "The other servants may be jealous and could ruin her things."

"What things?"

"That list I gave you." Beatriz glanced around his study. "Where did I leave…"

"Why?"

"We need to get her proper clothes as my personal maid."

Ah. "And the other servants may destroy those garments if we fail to put a lock on the door to her room."

"Best to be cautious. I also offered to teach her to read and write. She agreed."

"What?"

"She should learn. Everyone should. Only makes sense. Rather than having to speak to the servants when you want something done, you could write out your instructions as you did with me for the harem. With the written word, there would be no excuses for work done incorrectly or forgotten."

"You want to teach all the servants now?"

"During their free time."

Did they have any?

"Is that my list?" She gestured to the missive he held.

"No. What I wrote your father. I was coming to show you."

She slumped.

Tomás wished their wedding were already a done deal with their second or third child on the way. He needed to see her smile. "Would you like me to read what I wrote?"

"Can we do so together?"

"Certainly." Once he was in his chair with her on his lap, he held out the missive, reading as she did.

Dear Señor Serrano,

As Don Larnaz has most likely told you, your daughter, Beatriz, has been staying at my estate. She came to us during a time of great need for her, arriving with nothing, not having eaten for days. My housekeeper was kind enough to offer assistance and a place for Beatriz to live and work.

In the months she was here, I grew to know and admire

Beatriz for her kindness to others, her unfailing honesty, and her determination to finish her tasks no matter how difficult. Respect grew to love and my offer of marriage. She refused me at first. I now know she did so because of her betrothal to Don Larnaz. A matter that cannot stand.

She fears him. Such a marriage would destroy her. As a noble, I can give Beatriz whatever she needs and introduce her to those at court. To be fair to Don Larnaz, I willingly pay you the dowry he received to keep him from having to return the sum. I have included the money in this correspondence, expecting no dowry from you.

Beatriz wants nothing more than to be happy. I will move heaven and earth to see she has the best life possible and that no one ever harms her. I will fight to the death for her. I trust you want her best interests and will rejoice as she does for the new life she has.

Señor Don Tomás de Zayas

Chapter 12

Beatriz agreed with Tomás that Nuncio should deliver the missive, and called him into the parlor to deliver the news.

Nuncio bowed slightly. "Serving both of you is an honor."

She hugged him.

He stiffened as he had the last time.

She hardly cared. He'd turned out to be a good man and a friend. Such devotion deserved a reward.

Tomás raised his eyebrows, then addressed Nuncio. "Two guards will accompany you."

"Should I ask to speak with Señor Serrano, making certain he, not anyone else, receives the money? Or do I simply deliver the missive and sum to one of his servants and take my leave?"

Tomás looked at Beatriz. "Having him meet with your father would be best."

She spoke to Nuncio. "If my father weeps during your visit, take no heed, the tears are for show. No matter how gracious he appears, be on your guard. If he asks anything about Tomás or me, say you have no knowledge of what he wants to know. You are merely the messenger. Tell him nothing. Reveal nothing. He will use whatever you say, no matter how innocent, to destroy us."

Nuncio seemed surprised, then squared his shoulders and stood more erect than he usually did. "I would never allow him to deceive me into saying something I should not."

Tomás put down his goblet. "Perhaps I should go as I first intended."

Panic gripped her. "Absolutely not. He may have you waylaid on the journey home."

"Is that why you begged me not to meet with him? Do you honestly believe your papá would stoop to murder?"

She didn't want to think so badly of any man. However, she'd seen her father's icy determination. People were obstacles or pawns, dealt with as he chose in order to reach his goal. "He wants a marquis for his son-in-law, no matter how indebted Don Larnaz may be to his creditors. If Papá could have interested a duke in wedding me, he would have." She squeezed Tomás's hand. "You may be of noble birth, but you will never be the first-born son or have the title he desires. Remember what you told me about Isabella and Sancha's uncle, Don Rodrigo?"

To get his hands on his brother's wealth, Don Rodrigo had murdered him and his wife, who were Isabella and Sancha's parents, making one death look like an accident, the other an illness, then arranged Sancha's kidnapping. As first-born, she inherited everything and stood in the way of riches he sought to use. Luckily, his plan failed.

Tomás pushed away from the mantel. "Perhaps we should wait to deliver the missive until after we wed. What can your father do then?"

Make her a widow. She gripped a chair.

He crossed the room to her. "You do believe he would have me killed."

"I put nothing past him. Are you certain you want to go through with this?"

"You know I do. Never ask again.

"Nuncio, you leave at first light. If necessary, stay in the city at the home of one of my friends should Señor Serrano delay you unduly. You can—"

"Forgive me for interrupting. How would the man delay me?" Frowning, Nuncio glanced at Beatriz.

She smiled softly. "Take heart. He has another target in mind, not you. His delay would most likely be in putting on an act for you, inviting you to dine with him, trying to make you his friend."

"Never."

Craftier men had said the same thing. "Always keep up your guard around him."

Tomás gestured for Nuncio's attention. "Before you depart, I can pen a missive to my friends. Show the letter to any of them if you need to stay the night. Each will welcome you. No matter how long this takes, do not travel in the dark."

"Which guards should accompany me?"

"The sturdiest and bravest ones." She touched Tomás's arm. "Please."

He offered the names to Nuncio. "Inform them of the journey."

"At once." He left the study.

Tomás patted her hand. "You need to watch your tongue. You nearly scared poor Nuncio to death and even gave me pause."

She wrapped her arms around his middle, her head on his shoulder. "I fear for you."

"I can take care of myself."

"With a Moor. You have yet to meet my father. He makes the conspiracies among nobles look like child's play, even those committed by Don Rodrigo."

"I promise to take care. We should hear from Fernando and Enrique shortly. Surely, each of them can offer advice on the best way to approach this."

* * * *

Shortly after Nuncio left for the city, Enrique's missive arrived. Beatriz prayed it held good news.

In the study, Tomás pulled her onto his lap and opened the letter for both of them to read.

My dearest little brother,

Sancha and I offer our best wishes on your love and impending nuptials. Beatriz sounds like a wonderful woman.
How lucky you are.
As far as Beatriz's good fortune, we pray the poor girl can put up with you for longer than a day.

She slapped the missive. "Put up with you? Is he serious?"

"My brother likes to jest. With his life settled and serene, he intends to get back at me for the times I teased him about Sancha. I was merciless."

"I know how you are, my love." She ran her fingers over his bottom lip. "Enrique may have a point about me needing prayers."

Tomás cuffed her wrist, licked her finger, then bit the tip gently. "Read."

I agree you should wed Beatriz as quickly as possible.
Alas, Dominico is not available for your nuptials. He joined with the King and soldiers in the Crown's newest effort against the Moors. Dominico is finally getting his wish to be a warrior.

Beatriz shook her head. "Dominico?"

"Enrique's childhood friend. Mine too. A sacerdote now. Dominico wed Enrique and Sancha in secret, without banns, when they needed to fight the witchcraft rumors against her."

Beatriz had known about Sancha saving Tomás's life, and that she pursued medicine in secret, fearing the Inquisition. However, he'd never mentioned her fighting talk about being a witch. "I want to hear the full tale someday, please. First, though, I thought no one could wed in secret or without banns."

"Our monarchs did. They knew each other no more than a few days before wedding, and kept their union from the Queen's father for years. Quite the scandal. See what you find out when you live with a noble?"

She'd learned far more from him than monarchs' missteps. "Especially one who has a harem at his castle."

He laughed.

"About Dominico, is he the only sacerdote who can wed us without our publishing banns first?"

"I know of no others. I have little use for priests. Remember when I told you I fell ill at the fortaleza and my men sent for the sacerdote? He refused to come anywhere near me, not even to anoint me before death. He feared catching what I had and told my men to send for him after they put me into the ground."

"And he calls himself a man of God?"

"He never loved me as you do." Tomás lifted the letter. "We should read the rest of this. Could be Enrique offered a suggestion we can use."

The only other sacerdote I know is the one who was at the fortaleza for Fernando and Isabella. You remember him. I advise you not to seek him out.

"Why?" Beatriz asked.

"He discovered Isabella had lied, claiming to be Fernando's betrothed when her sister Sancha actually was. Before he could do anything about the matter, we learned Don Rodrigo was pursuing Sancha to kill her so he could control the estate. Of course, Isabella was next in line for the inheritance, then her two younger sisters. Don Rodrigo would have had to murder them all and probably would have if given the chance."

"And here I thought my father was good at plots. He could learn much from the family your brothers married into."

"Best we not tell your papá and give him any ideas. Shall we resume reading?"

"Of course."

Sancha can think of no one, either. If not for Bartolomé

being newly born, we would visit to help you and Beatriz in this time of need. Perhaps Fernando has an answer for you.

My best, along with Sancha's.

Your brother, Enrique

* * * *

During Beatriz and Tomás's evening meal, a guard strode into the dining hall. She searched his face to see if anything was amiss. His eyes and features gave away nothing. He bowed slightly. "A visitor requests entrance."

She leaned toward Tomás. "Don Larnaz?"

"He had better not." He frowned. "Your papá?"

She hoped not.

Tomás turned to the guard. "Who?"

"Señor Don Fernando."

Tomás pushed away from the table so quickly his chair nearly tipped over. "My brother? Invite him onto the estate. Never keep him waiting."

"No, Patrón." The guard rushed from the dining hall.

Tomás took Beatriz's hand. "Come."

They ran through the castle to the front entrance and outside to wait. Tomás craned his neck, looking for Fernando.

Beatriz smoothed the sole gown she owned, the one she'd stolen from her papá's housekeeper the day she'd fled his house. She'd feared traveling in silk or velvet lest someone recognized who she was and dragged her back to her father and Don Larnaz.

If only Fernando had waited a few weeks until she had her gowns. She didn't want to embarrass Tomás with her poor clothes and wild hair. Wind pushed the locks into her cheeks and forehead.

"There." He pointed at torchlight on the dark path. "He—wait. Fernando arrived in a carriage? Could he be ill? Why else would he be riding in that thing rather than on his Arabian?"

She shrugged.

The conveyance pulled close and stopped near the guards, each man holding a torch.

Tomás ran to the carriage. "Fernando!"

The door popped open. A man nearly as handsome as Tomás stepped out, hair dark, skin bronze, his doublet and robe a rich brown in the torchlight. He grinned. "How are you little brother?" He hugged Tomás, then tried to swing him around as one would a child.

Tomás punched Fernando's shoulder.

Fernando laughed.

Tomás glowered. "How are you, besides trying to prove your waning strength? Are you so feeble now you have to ride in a carriage like a woman?"

From inside the conveyance, a woman asked, "What did you say?"

Fernando elbowed Tomás. "Watch your tongue around my wife and daughter."

Oh no, he'd brought his entire family.

With Fernando's assistance, Isabella left the carriage next, her skin milky and flawless, features exquisite, clothing worthy of a queen. Her gown was the finest blue silk trimmed with gold embroidery and beads. A large sapphire hung from a silver chain about her neck.

Isabella hugged Tomás. Spotting Beatriz, she grinned, her eyes sparkling, their color too pale to be brown. "Release me at once." She slapped his shoulder. "I want to meet the woman who finally tamed you."

Fernando smiled at Beatriz. Tomás held out his hand for her to join them.

Her legs weakened, her stomach even more unsettled at meeting anyone when she looked so dreadful.

Fierce pride and love filled Tomás's smile. After taking her hand, he presented her. "Fernando, Isabella, this is Beatriz González y Serrano. She is lovelier than a summer's day, fresher than a morning breeze, more passionate than—"

"You are exquisite." Fernando kissed Beatriz's knuckles. "How could a woman as perfect as you have given my brother a glance? Look at him."

Tomás's hair wiggled in the wind, the same as his linen shirt. His dark hose revealed his powerful build.

Beatriz's legs weakened even more. "I have never seen a more splendid man. Look at me." She gestured to her poor clothes.

Isabella fingered the lace-trimmed kirtle that reached her throat. "You should have seen how I used to dress. When Fernando escorted me across the countryside from Granada, where I was held prisoner for sale to the harem, before he rescued me, of course, he had me—"

"Rescue? Harem?"

Isabella nodded. Auburn tresses bobbed against her cheeks. "My uncle, the puto, had—"

"Wife." Fernando pinched his nose. "We have spoken repeatedly about that word."

"Forgive me." She bent her head to Beatriz. "My uncle wanted Sancha kidnapped, not me. The fiends who carried out my uncle's orders had no idea they took the wrong woman. I ended up in Granada, with the Sultan's eunuch about to purchase me, when Fernando came to my rescue. Do you know about fakirs? I have never seen anything more incredible. Juggling hot coals, breathing fire. Fernando stunned the crowd. Me too. But I had to keep my wits about me to escape with him to Spain." She paused to breathe. "Once we were back in our beloved country, he had me dress as a boy to avoid notice. Of course, there were thieves and brutes everywhere. At one point, I took his sword and had to save his life."

Stunned, Beatriz looked at Fernando.

He gazed at his wife with boundless love. "Isabella was magnificent."

She beamed. "If I can dress as a boy, you can surely wear whatever you want."

"At the moment, she has what she wears now and livery." Tomás shrugged. "We ordered dozens of gowns. I wanted a hundred or more, but Beatriz declined so many. The garments have yet to arrive."

Isabella smiled at her. "I have several with me. You can have whichever you want."

"Oh no. You offer too much."

"I insist. We can go through them while Fernando and Tomás discuss Spain's latest battle with the Moors and Pedro's role in the conflict."

Tomás leaned toward Beatriz. "Another brother you must meet. He took over my command." He glanced at Fernando. "Have you heard from him?"

"He sent a missive the other day saying all is well. The one he wrote to you will probably come shortly."

"Good."

A thin wail sounded followed by mewling and then a piercing cry.

"Juana." Isabella frowned at Fernando and Tomás. "You men were speaking too loudly and woke her." She smiled at Beatriz. "Would you care to see our daughter?"

She nodded.

Fernando helped a servant from the carriage, an older woman with a kind face. Juana shrieked. The gold blanket covering her flapped from her flailing limbs.

With the infant safely in her arms, Isabella presented her daughter.

Beatriz pressed her hands to her chest. The little girl was exquisite. She had her father's dark hair, her mother's light eyes. Her scrunched face and reddened skin spoke of her unhappiness, how helpless she was.

No different than Beatriz had been growing up, though Juana's future would be far different.

Isabella bounced the infant lightly. Juana refused to settle. "She must be hungry. Is there a place where I can feed my daughter in private?"

Tomás stroked the babe's cheek. "Beatriz will take you to our finest bedchamber."

She brought Isabella to the one Señora Cisneros had always cleaned in case an important guest arrived. More than one servant had said the housekeeper hoped the monarchs would drop in since they'd moved the court to Jaen.

The bedchamber was larger than the one Tomás had chosen for his own, wall hangings and carpets sumptuous, furniture heavy and dark with breathtaking designs carved into the wood. Three windows, rather than two, faced the lawn leading to the harem. After lighting numerous candles, Beatriz opened the wooden screens to air the room.

"How beautiful." Isabella turned a slow circle, taking everything in. "When Fernando and I were on our journey to my papá's castle, after we escaped Granada, we would have enjoyed such a chamber. The places where we stayed were loathsome but fun." She grinned.

Beatriz liked her already. "Someday, I want you to tell me the whole story."

"I will." She sank into a box chair near the bed and undid her top. Juana cried piteously until she latched on to her mother's breast.

"Ah." Isabella sighed. "Peace at last."

Beatriz leaned closer. "Your eyes are blue-green." The color unbelievable in the candlelight. "How amazing."

"Fernando likes them. What of you and Tomás? Have you decided when to wed?"

She sat on the mattress. "Do you know about my papá and Don Larnaz?"

"Tomás told us everything in his missive. Is there no way your father can soften his position in this? Clearly, Don Larnaz is a puto. Say nothing to Fernando about me using the word. He forbids me to do so constantly. I do anyway and beg his forgiveness, after which, he grants me his grace. We go in circles constantly."

Beatriz laughed. "Whatever you say in here is our secret."

"I knew I would like you. About you wedding Tomás, surely your union would put a stop to Don Larnaz's claim."

"If we post banns, he or Papá could voice their objections. They may be able to stop us. What we need is to wed without notice and in secret the same as Sancha and Enrique. The monarchs too."

"You can include me and Fernando. Another tale I must tell you someday. Do you know a sacerdote who will wed you in secret?"

"No." Beatriz hid her disappointment. "We were going to ask you and Fernando. Enrique already wrote saying his friend Dominico was away with the soldiers in the newest conflict."

Isabella chewed her lip. "I know of no others. Are you lying with Tomás? Forgive me for being bold, but are you?"

Beatriz's face stung with heat. She wanted to lie but nodded.

"Well then. When you conceive, Don Larnaz and your papá will have to leave you alone."

"I fear not." Beatriz explained the situation to Isabella.

Juana stirred and grew fussy. Isabella stroked her daughter's cheek, cooing until the infant had settled. "Don Larnaz is worse than a puto. He would raise another man's child to have your father's wealth? Tomás would never allow anyone to take his son or daughter from him."

"I know. I worry for his safety."

"The marquis reminds me of my uncle, Don Rodrigo. Soft, yet cunning. I kept telling Fernando the man would strike and he did, nearly killing Fernando."

The room spun. Beatriz gripped the counterpane. "I worry Don Larnaz will try to waylay Tomás somehow. I would rather he forget me than be in danger."

"I saw how he looks at you. Giving up that kind of love would never be possible for him."

A gentle knock sounded on the door.

"Most likely a servant with my trunk." Isabella adjusted herself in the chair. "Juana will finish her meal in a moment. Once my things are in here, we can work on a plan to fix your and Tomás's problem while you choose one of my gowns."

* * * *

Tomás was on his second goblet of wine, ready for his third.

Fernando shook his head. "No matter how many times you ask, I know of no sacerdote other than Dominico and the fool who came to the fortaleza."

"There must be one priest in Spain I can bribe to wed Beatriz and me as quickly as possible without banns. When did money stop talking in Spain?"

"Never, as far as I know. Why not wait to see what happens when Nuncio returns from speaking with her father? He may have good news. When do you expect him?"

"I hoped for today before dusk. Señor Serrano must have delayed him to the point Nuncio and the guards had to spend the night. Given what Beatriz says, only harm comes from her father."

Fernando sat back in his chair, legs crossed at the ankles. "Isabella said the same about her uncle."

"You failed to heed her advice and nearly died."

Fernando frowned. "Would her papá actually do bodily harm to have you out of the way? Once you wed her—"

"A widow is always free to marry again, no?"

"Are you serious? If the man is mad enough to try to kill you for marrying his daughter, why are you racing to the altar?"

"For the same reason you did with Isabella. I love Beatriz."

"I know, but why not settle this with him first? Persuade her father to see things your way. You have noble blood running through your veins, the same as Larnaz. Our family has connections at court. Sancha does too. Everything he could want is his for the asking."

"Except the title of marquis for his son-in-law, the one thing Larnaz can give him that I never can. Although being a prince may seem nice, not all will become king."

Fernando finished his wine and filled his goblet again. "Perhaps you should think this out before you make a hasty decision."

"If you mean in wedding Beatriz, I have no time to waste."

"Why?"

"If I delay my union with her, I may lose her forever. Beatriz already fears what her papá may do if we stay together. She ran from him. She would run from this castle too in order to keep me safe. She might even go back to her father and agree to wed Larnaz to protect me. I have to find a way to make our marriage happen quickly or it may not happen at all."

* * * *

The gowns in Isabella's trunk were plentiful, beautiful, and in a rainbow of colors with beads, pearls, or intricate embroidery embellishing each.

Isabella gestured Beatriz over. "Help me unpack these so you can try them on."

"Do you mind if Yolanda takes the gowns out? I just hired her as my personal maid. Seeing these would thrill her."

"Is this her first time assisting a lady?"

Beatriz nearly laughed. "She began here as a scullery maid, hoping to gut animals next."

"A curious path to take in becoming a personal maid."

"Yolanda came from the village. She never complains or stops working. Keeping up with her is impossible, even though she has yet to turn thirteen. She has a fine mind too. I promised to teach her to read and write."

Affection flooded Isabella's face. "Your love for her shines through. I feel the same about my sisters, especially Sancha. Of course, Yolanda should handle my gowns. She sounds delightful."

Beatriz called her in.

Yolanda gaped at the lovely clothes and Isabella. "You want me to touch these?"

"And lay them on the bed, please. That way, Beatriz can see which one she likes best."

As quick as Yolanda had been with every task in the past, she took a painfully long time putting the first gown on the mattress. The dress might have been made of glass, capable of shattering into a million pieces.

"Well done." Isabella leaned toward Beatriz. "What an adorable child. I like her."

"I knew you would." She wrapped her arm around Isabella's waist. "Help me keep Tomás safe."

"Nothing else will do. That and you wedding him. We will find a way, I promise."

Chapter 13

With Isabella and Yolanda's help, Beatriz chose a plum-colored gown. Silver embroidery and tiny pearls adorned the silk.

Yolanda clapped. "Even the queen would envy you in this."

"That she would." Isabella handed her sleeping daughter to the servant, waiting until she left before motioning Beatriz over. "Wait until you get to court and see what the other women wear."

Only if life with Tomás allowed them to leave the safety here and enjoy each other as a married couple. A simple notion so seemingly out of reach.

Isabella took her hands. "How sad you look. Once you have the gown on and I fix your hair, your mood will improve."

"Not until I have the answers I need about Tomás's and my situation."

"You remind me of myself when I tried to keep Fernando from my uncle before the puto could…oh my." She glanced at Yolanda.

She was all eyes, expression rapt.

Isabella smiled. "Can you bring us water, a cloth, and scented oil?"

"At once." She ran from the room.

Isabella closed the door. "Fernando is right. I need to watch my tongue." She joined Beatriz by the bed. "Have you thought of fleeing to another land with Tomás until your papá gives up?"

"He never will. He sees naught except what he wants."

"My uncle was the same. I begged Fernando to take us to Portugal to protect himself. He refused, wanting to stay and fight for what he thought was mine, not Sancha's. Even after he knew who I was, he insisted on going after Don Rodrigo."

"Tomás boasts of his time in battle as though those days will keep him from harm forever."

"Men are far too obstinate, thinking they know everything. Will you speak to your papá if he requests an audience?"

She cringed. "I dread reading a missive from him." She told Isabella about Nuncio's trip to the city. "I hoped for his quick return to know what Tomás and I are going to face. Not that my father is one to give his plans away." She wrung her hands. "I worry for Nuncio."

"Is he easily swayed? Will he help your papá?"

"Never. He would die for Tomás. I worry my father will take him hostage, threatening to harm the poor man unless I return. Something must have happened to keep him past dusk."

Isabella wrapped her arm around Beatriz's shoulders. "I know how you worry. Even so, only a madman would risk his reputation and the authorities coming down on him to get what he wants."

"No one has ever opposed my father before, especially a woman. He destroyed my mother and meant to cow me as he had her. I have no idea what his plans are, or what he may have talked Don Larnaz into doing."

"Unless the marquis plans to storm the castle, he has little hope of doing anything. Until Nuncio returns with your father's response, your only choice is to wait and make your plans based on what he says."

Or flee and disappear forever, giving Tomás a more peaceful future.

"Are you thinking about leaving?" Isabella asked. "If you do, Tomás will follow and try to bring you back."

"Not if he believes I fear Papá beyond anything else. What woman wants a life constantly looking over her shoulder or dreads becoming a widow, forced into a second marriage with a brute? All I have to do is convince Tomás I want an end to this madness by never seeing him or my father again."

"Although women have succeeded in deceiving men since time began, you will never fool Tomás. The man would have to be blind not to see how you feel about him even if you say otherwise. Best you stay here with us and face this."

Light footsteps sounded in the hall.

"You may want to smile too." Isabella cupped Beatriz's chin. "No need to alarm Yolanda with your mood. The child may take off to slay your papá and the marquis on her own. Then where would you be with your personal maid having to face the *alguacil*?"

Beatriz laughed at the prospect of dear Yolanda facing the sheriff, so eager to please she'd undoubtedly confess without pause, offer to launder the man's clothes, clean his house, prepare a meal, and finish the day by making candles for him.

"There now." Isabella smiled. "Until Nuncio returns, what say we have some fun?"

Despite her concerns, Beatriz did relax, hope pulsing through her for an end to problems and the beginning of a new life.

Isabella ran the damp cloth over Beatriz's face and neck, leaving a faint rose scent. She brushed Beatriz's hair until the tresses shone. After braiding a portion, Isabella selected a caul to match the gown.

"No, please. Tomás wants my hair loose."

"Loose it shall be." She tossed the caul back into the wooden box. "We should give our men precisely what they want, but only when we feel inclined to do so, never before."

Yolanda drank in the converse. If she paid this much attention to reading and writing, she'd master the skills within days.

Beatriz caught Isabella's eye and inclined her head to the girl.

"Right. My tongue again." Isabella spoke to Yolanda. "Pay no attention to what I say in here. Promise to forget every word immediately."

"Can I keep listening?"

Beatriz crossed her arms. "As long as you repeat nothing."

"I would never."

Isabella grinned at Beatriz. "We have an ally."

Once she'd finished with Beatriz's hair, Isabella laced her into the gown. Yolanda saw to the buttons. Together, they adjusted or smoothed hair and silk, the way one would when preparing a woman for a meeting with the queen or her own wedding. Beatriz allowed herself to dream of marrying Tomás. If given the choice, she'd have the ceremony on the lawn, the grass cool and damp beneath their feet, a soft breeze chasing fluffy clouds across the sky.

Isabella, Fernando, Enrique, Sancha, Yolanda, and Nuncio would attend as Beatriz's new family, each one protecting her happiness as she would theirs.

Isabella offered a mirror. "Want to see what you look like now?"

Yolanda bounced on her heels. "She must."

Her complexion was radiant, hair tamed, the gown shimmering in the candlelight, fabric light as a cloud unlike the heavy material she wore for livery. "I look nearly as good as you, Isabella."

"Far better, no?" She elbowed Yolanda.

She nodded vigorously. "An angel would envy you."

Isabella sped to the door. "Beatriz, wait here."

"For what?"

"Something I just thought of. Yolanda, come with me." With their fingers laced, they left the chamber.

Beatriz wasn't certain what to think or how to feel. Although she enjoyed looking like a lady again, the effort seemed such a waste when she and Isabella should have made plans to win against her father and Don Larnaz. Perhaps Isabella realized how hopeless the situation was and didn't know what else to do except make the best of things.

The laughter Beatriz had shared earlier seemed a distant memory already. Doom clung to her, tightening her chest, moistening her palms. She paced like a caged animal, knowing she should leave the castle to give Tomás a chance at happiness with another woman.

Her legs went watery, not allowing her to flee. Dizzy, she leaned against the cabinet and breathed hard, trying to think of a solution.

She kept failing.

"Señorita Beatriz," Yolanda called out.

Beatriz raised her face. "What?"

"Señora Doña Isabella has something she needs you to see."

Hopefully not another trunk the servants had left in the hall with more gowns and other jewels. She didn't want to try on anything else but couldn't stomach being rude, given Isabella's dear support. Beatriz pinched her cheeks and bit her lips to give herself color. Looking like a corpse wouldn't solve anything.

Outside the chamber, she reminded herself to smile. What she produced felt more like a grimace.

Yolanda stood on the far side of the landing, gesturing for Beatriz to join her.

Isabella wasn't around. Juana must have needed her again. Whatever Yolanda was doing on her own was a mystery, unless the girl wanted to show off the gown to the other servants.

Fearing Leonor's foul attitude and knife, Beatriz touched the gown protectively.

The moment she reached the landing, Yolanda motioned for Beatriz to stop, then pointed to the stairs.

She looked down.

The world faded away, tension draining from her shoulders, warmth replacing worry.

Tomás stood at the bottom of the staircase, his arm on the railing, face lifted to hers. Candlelight turned his hair to gold. Respect, friendship, love sparkled in his eyes.

She ran down the steps. Tomás took them two at a time to reach her. They met in the middle and held each other, their embrace more powerful than any spoken vow. Whatever happened in the future, he would always have her love.

Tomás kissed her neck and cheek. "No words are sufficient to describe your beauty. The heat of the sun could never be greater, not even Spain will last as long, the finest rose pales in comparison. You are a marvel."

Beatriz laughed softly. "Then you like Isabella's gown?"

"On you, no one else." He pressed his mouth to her ear. "Though I do prefer you naked. Say nothing to her, of course."

"Of course."

They descended the stairs, arms wrapped around each other's waists. Fernando and Isabella stood to the side, smiling.

Beatriz stopped. "Wait." She looked over. "Gracias, Yolanda. You helped me just as a personal maid should."

She smiled widely.

"You can go to bed now. Take the chamber next to Don Tomás's." Beatriz had Señora Cisneros prepare the room.

Yolanda gaped. "Truly?"

"Truly." Tomás shooed her away. "Go."

"At once." She bolted down the hall.

"What a delight she is." Isabella beamed. "When you and Tomás visit us in the future, you must bring Yolanda along."

Beatriz pressed against him, hoping they'd have a chance to share more days.

He embraced her gently. "What say we go to the parlor, have a sip of wine, and talk?"

* * * *

They discussed Beatriz's father and Don Larnaz well into the night with each suggestion falling short of what Beatriz sensed would work.

Fernando and Isabella listened patiently to each objection, finally suggesting they should wait for Nuncio's return before making any plans.

"He should be back tomorrow, that is, today, no?" Fernando asked.

Beatriz hoped.

She awoke early, more restless than tired, missing Tomás's warmth. He'd left the chamber for his own bed hours before, shortly after they'd made love.

Dressed in her simple gown, Beatriz climbed to the highest parapet. The sun tipped over the horizon, its rays pouring across the land. A thin mist hovered over fields, groves, and vineyards in the valley. The crisp morning breeze bore the earth's fragrance, its bounty.

The road below was deserted.

Spotting Nuncio and the guards at such an early hour was too much to hope for, but she still searched. The last of the sun had cleared the horizon before she gave up and retreated inside.

Yolanda was waiting in Beatriz's chamber, perched on a box chair, hands folded in her lap. She jumped to her feet. *"Buenas días."*

Returning the greeting, Beatriz glanced around the room. "You tidied up already?"

"Did you want me to turn down the bed again?" Yolanda raced to do so.

"No. Everything looks wonderful. But the other servants will see to my room."

"Not with me around. After I help you dress, I can scrub the floor, take the wall hangings down to beat the dust from them, do the rugs next, then finish whatever else needs doing."

"I would prefer you have your first lesson today, the basis of all reading and writing, the alphabet. You need to know the letters from memory and practice how to draw them. Much like you did the map you made for me. You already know one letter. X. Once I teach you to read and write, we can move on to mathematics and other subjects, even painting and learning to play the harp."

Yolanda's eyebrows kept inching up, her mouth going slack.

Beatriz cradled her cheek. "I want you to learn. No more scrubbing or dusting for you. Taking care of my silks and velvets is your work now. Have you forgotten you need to keep your hands soft?"

"You forgot last night when I helped you with the gowns." She looked embarrassed. "The silks were so lovely, I forgot too."

"Today we remember and start making your hands the way they should be. Give me a moment."

Beatriz crossed the hall to Isabella and Fernando's chamber. Uncertain how long they usually slept, she knocked lightly on the door. "Isabella?"

"Beatriz?"

"Sí. Have I awakened you?"

"Not at all." She opened the door. Her hair was mussed, a sheet to her breasts, shoulders bare. "Has Nuncio returned?"

Beatriz made certain not to look past Isabella to the bed, not wanting to see Fernando sprawled over the mattress, possibly nude. "Not yet. Did you pack lotion? I told Yolanda I could make her hands soft."

"Of course. Give me a moment." She darted away and returned quickly with a squat jar. "What are your plans for today? Have you had breakfast yet?"

"No. I planned to teach Yolanda the alphabet."

"May I join you for both?" She pushed her fiery hair back. "Tomás slipped a note under the door saying he wanted to spend the day with Fernando."

"Doing what?"

"Hunting, fishing, riding, talking about war, the things men usually do. Fernando left minutes ago. He and Tomás are probably eating breakfast now. As soon as I dress, we can do the same."

"Would you like Yolanda to help you with your gown?"

"Good idea. See both of you in a moment."

Back in her room, Beatriz smeared the fragrant lotion on Yolanda's hands, working in the thick cream. The same mixture of olive oil, beeswax, and rose water she'd used when living with her father. "Rub your hands together until the last of the cream is gone."

"Feels strange."

"Wait until you finish."

Once Yolanda had, she ran her hand against her cheek and smiled. "As soft as a chick. Smells good too."

"I can order several jars when I commission your new clothes."

"New clothes?"

"A personal maid must look the part."

"I have no complaints."

Beatriz smiled. "Isabella asked for your expert assistance. As soon as you help her dress, we can breakfast in the dining hall."

During the meal, the other servants frowned at Yolanda, the same as they had when she'd gone from scrubbing pots to making candles. The child tensed whenever they came near. Too many had pinched, shoved, or burned her in the past.

No longer, though. Not with Beatriz around.

Isabella tapped her chin. "Are your servants always this surly?"

"Only with me." Yolanda lowered her face. "Every time I get new work or do something special, like eating in here, they get angry."

Isabella clucked her tongue. "Never let what they think hurt you."

Beatriz nodded. "Or keep you from improving your life."

"Little chance of that. If they was in my place, each one would be grinning from ear to ear, happy for themselves, not caring a whit about me."

Isabella winked at Beatriz.

After their meal, they gathered in the parlor to begin Yolanda's lesson.

Outside, Tomás and Fernando strode from the castle. With Tomás's study free, she ushered Isabella and Yolanda in there.

"The perfect place to work." Beatriz gestured. "We have books and writing materials."

Yolanda bit her lip.

Beatriz patted her shoulder. "Nothing to worry about."

"What if I fail?"

"We keep trying until you succeed."

* * * *

Yolanda had taken Beatriz seriously, toiling for hours.

Head down, tongue sticking out, she repeatedly tried to draw the first three letters of the alphabet. She wouldn't let Beatriz move to the others until she'd mastered these.

Discarded papers littered Tomás's study, each filled with Yolanda's failures. She'd gone from writing the letters as big as each paper to gradually reducing the size until she could get several letters on a sheet.

She puffed out a breath. "This is harder than carrying a dead pig."

Isabella pressed her hand over her mouth to hold back a laugh. Although her shoulders and torso jiggled, Juana slept peacefully on her mamá's chest.

Beatriz wagged her finger at Isabella only because Yolanda had her back to them. She patted the girl's shoulder. "Practice makes writing and reading easier. Everything else too."

"How long must I do this?"

"Several hours each day for years."

"Years? This is like scrubbing pots and pans. They never end."

"This will once you master the task. Then, you only have to read and write when you want to."

Yolanda rested her head in her palm and resumed writing the letters.

"Beatriz," Tomás called.

"In your study." She hurried into the hall, nearly running into him and Fernando. Dirt stained their hose and boots. Their hands weren't too clean, either. She made a face. "Were the two of you crawling around in mud?"

Fernando pressed his lips together, trying not to laugh.

Tomás elbowed him, but his snickers were getting the best of him too. Someone had imbibed too much wine.

She asked, "Has Nuncio returned?"

"No. Can we have a word?"

"Of course. Give me a moment." She returned to the study. "Yolanda, please keep working until I get back."

Tomás came up behind Beatriz and pressed his mouth to her ear. "What is she doing?"

"Learning the alphabet." She'd spoken as quietly as he had. "Praise her. Yolanda. Show Don Tomás what you did."

She lifted her papers. The letters were too large, lines wobbly. The way a feeble, old woman with an unsteady hand would write, rather than a healthy twelve-year-old.

Tomás applauded. "Well done."

Yolanda grinned.

After he and Beatriz left, he leaned into her. "Will she get better?"

"We all do. Where are we going?"

"Our bedchamber." With Beatriz in tow, he raced up the stairs and rushed down the hall.

Once inside, she leaned against the door, panting. "If you mean to have me, you may have to wait until I can catch my breath."

"I have something for you." He pulled a square of linen from his pouch, the cloth smeared with dirt and folded to hide whatever was inside. "Go on, take it."

"Do you have something alive in there?" He did like to tease. "Will it bite?"

"Hard to tell. If it does, I can kill it."

She shrank away.

He laughed. "I give you my word, this will never harm you."

Beatriz finally took the cloth and unfolded the ends cautiously. "My orange peel?" Tears filled her eyes.

"Took me and Fernando most of the morning, on our hands and knees, to find the thing."

Beatriz threw her arms around him. He staggered slightly, breath puffing out.

She cried. "You did this for me?"

"Who else?"

"Because you fear this is all I may have left of you?"

"No." He pulled her arms from him and cupped her face. "You cried as though your heart had broken when you lost the rind. I wanted to get it back for you. As a memento of our first time, nothing more."

Beatriz hugged him again. "I want the trouble with my father and Don Larnaz to be over. Where is Nuncio? Why hasn't he returned? When will he be back?"

"Today, before twilight. We have to be patient and wait."

Nuncio didn't return. Not by twilight or the hours well beyond dark.

* * * *

Come morning, Beatriz could barely keep still, dread over Nuncio's absence consuming her.

Tomás paced the parlor.

Isabella and Fernando kept out of his way, exchanging glances.

She wanted answers, an end to this. "Where is Nuncio? He should have been back by now or sent a missive telling us why he was delayed, unless he and the guards can do neither."

Tomás stopped. "I refuse to believe your father killed all of them or even one. The man may be cruel, scheming, and—"

"May be? He is."

"And a murderer too?"

Isabella took everyone in. "Perhaps we should send for the alguacil."

"Not yet," Fernando said. "One of the group may have had an accident that delayed all three. Tomás and I can ride out to look for them."

"No. Absolutely not." Beatriz couldn't stomach that. "You may be riding into a trap. Send more guards."

"I agree with Beatriz." Isabella grabbed Fernando's hand. "We have no idea what Señor Serrano or Don Larnaz is capable of. Look at what my uncle's agents did to me. If Beatriz's papá and the marquis planned something to draw Tomás out of the castle, the agents who attacked Nuncio and the others would search for Tomás, not more guards. The men can wear their own clothes, rather than their uniforms. That way, no one will be looking to waylay them."

Tomás waved away the comment. "Fernando and I know how to take care of ourselves. Neither of us had an easy life like Enrique, studying rather than learning how to avoid death. We can survive a short ride without pulling the men from their duty, which is to protect the castle."

"Perhaps I need to be clearer." Isabella pressed Fernando's hand to her cheek. "You nearly left me once. Remember those dark days? I could never survive moments like those again."

Beatriz spoke to Tomás. "If I lost you, my spirit would die, leaving only my body, which my father would gladly deliver to Don Larnaz. Is that what you want?"

"Of course not." His face was red, shoulders tensed. "But you seem to forget that Fernando and I are warriors, not fools."

"I have an idea." Isabella tapped Beatriz's arm. "Since my husband and Tomás are such skilled soldiers, able to meet any challenge without fear of injury or worse, braver than the—"

"Prepare yourself," Fernando said to Tomás. "Whenever my wife starts talking like you, I know trouble is at hand."

Beatriz leaned toward Isabella. "Go on. I want to hear what you have to say."

"Since neither of the men feel there will be any danger on this ride, you and I can accompany them."

"No," both brothers said at once.

Beatriz crossed the room to Tomás. "If you insist on your plan, I will leave here immediately and go to my papá without delay."

"You will not put yourself in danger."

"What danger? He may be able to murder everyone else in the world, but he has to keep me alive, no? What value would there be in a dead daughter? Even a brute as greedy as Don Larnaz would hesitate to accept a corpse."

Isabella leaned back in her chair. "She has a point."

"Fine," Tomás said. "The guards can search for Nuncio and the others. This time. If they fail to return at dusk, I go." He looked at his brother. "Stay with the women if you want."

Fernando frowned. "When did I say I was afraid to join you?"

"My love." Isabella smiled gently. "If you want to keep in my good graces, you had better take care with your safety."

Fernando threw up his hands.

Tomás left the room grumbling.

Fernando followed, swearing beneath his breath.

"Well done." Isabella hugged Beatriz. "You kept both from unnecessary risk. I will love you forever. At times, I think Fernando chases death deliberately."

"What do you think happened to Nuncio and the other men?"

"I have no idea. All we can do is wait to find out."

* * * *

When the sun was low in the sky, Beatriz held a solitary vigil on the parapet, searching for Nuncio and the men. "Please return. Let all be well."

The road remained empty.

Panic swept through her. If Tomás made good on his promise to leave tonight and never came back, she'd find whoever harmed him and would kill the man without guilt or regret. Then, she'd destroy her father as he'd done to so many others. Hell didn't frighten her. A lifetime without Tomás was the greater punishment.

Something moved in the distance. She craned her neck, blood thundering in her ears.

Riders carried torches, mere pinpoints in the darkness. As they neared, she leaned over the stone, trying to see more.

"Beatriz." Tomás ran to her. "What are you doing?" He wound his arm around her waist and pulled her back. "Are you trying to kill yourself?" She pointed. "Riders approach."

"I know. Fernando and I spotted them from the other parapet. Come." They raced to the castle entrance. Fernando and Isabella were already there. The second set of men arrived before the others, followed closely by Nuncio and the guards he'd left with.

Before Nuncio had a chance to dismount, Beatriz ran to him. "Where were you? Why did you take so long? You never thought to send a missive to let us know what happened. Why not? Did you think we knew or could guess what was going on?"

"Beatriz." Tomás pulled her back. "Give Nuncio a chance to answer."

"Go on." She gestured to the man. "Good or bad, I want to hear what my father said."

With his shoulders drawn in, Nuncio glanced at the crowd. "In front of the others?"

Tomás gestured to the guards. "Everyone leave."

Nuncio dismounted.

Beatriz rushed him.

He took several steps back.

Didn't matter. She needed to know what her father had done or said. "Talk."

"I should have sent a missive, but I feared having only one guard to fight against robbers or other brutes on the journey back. Forgive me for being old and a coward."

Beatriz wasn't certain whether to rail or hug him. "What took so long?"

"Señor Serrano was unable to see me at first."

"Why? Was he playing more of his games, pretending he had no idea who you were or why you had come? Ha. Don Larnaz surely had told him about his visit and Tomás agreeing to return my dowry. When he read Tomás's missive, did he demand more money from him?"

"Señorita Beatriz, you may want to take care with what you say."

She couldn't believe this. Nuncio was worried about her conduct when her future was at stake. "Fernando and Isabella know about my father. You can speak freely in front of them."

He sighed deeply, his expression pained rather than relieved. "Your father refused the money."

He handed the satchel to Tomás.

Beatriz had feared as much. Still, her heart sank. "He demanded my return, no? And my marriage to Don Larnaz. Did you tell him I would never wed the man?"

"He said he understood your feelings for Don Tomás. He declined the money, saying you would have his estate soon enough."

Beatriz shook her head, not understanding, and then she did. "He was playing you for a fool. He has something planned."

"No. Your father is gravely ill."

Chapter 14

Beatriz stared, too shocked to speak. Guilt came next, barreling through her for thinking so poorly of her father, never wanting to see him again. Death would certainly accomplish her goal. Deep down, she'd never wished him dead. She'd wanted him to care for her safety and happiness.

Tomás took her arm. "We should go inside and allow Nuncio to rest, quench his thirst before we ask him anything."

In the parlor, Nuncio finished his beaker of water before color returned to his sunken cheeks. He smoothed his hair and sat straight as an iron pole.

Beatriz edged closer. "Tell us everything from the moment you arrived."

Tomás joined her. Isabella and Fernando also drew near. Nuncio's face grew white again.

Tomás leaned into Beatriz. "We should ask about your papá's illness first, no?"

No. Her initial shock and guilt had already passed. She couldn't bring herself to trust any change in her father. "I need to handle this in my own way."

"Of course." He pulled a box chair over.

She sat on the edge as Nuncio did on the bench. Horrible memories of her mother's suffering fueled her doubt. "Who greeted you at the door?"

"His housekeeper."

Pascuala. The day Beatriz's mother had died, her father, having already arranged for their sale, had ordered Pascuala to pack his wife's clothes and jewels.

Beatriz had raced ahead to her mamá's chamber and threw open the wardrobe doors. She'd pressed her face to her mother's gowns and chemises, inhaling deeply of her scent, desperate to have whatever remained of her. Within the day, her mother's possessions were gone. She might never have existed. She had certainly never mattered to him.

Pascuala's loyalty had always been to Beatriz's father. She'd longed suspected they'd been intimate even before her mamá had passed. "What did she say?"

"After I introduced myself and the guards"—he glanced at Tomás—"I had them come in with me as I had no idea what to expect. I know I should have told them to wait outside, but I was afraid."

Beatriz patted Nuncio's hand. "You did the right thing."

Tomás nodded. "We understand."

"Did the housekeeper seem surprised by your visit?" Beatriz asked.

"Not that I could tell. She behaved as all servants do, hiding whatever feelings she had."

Beatriz suspected Pascuala and her father had discussed a possible visit after Don Larnaz had told them what happened here. "When you asked to see my father, what were her first words to you?"

"She said he was unable to speak to anyone at the time. If I wanted to wait, I was free to do so. However, hours could pass before he might be able to see me."

"Might? Did you ask her why such a delay?"

Nuncio straightened even more, looking appalled. "Not my place. I thanked her and waited with the guards."

Fernando pulled chairs close for himself and Isabella.

Nuncio turned to Beatriz. "When night fell without your father giving us a chance to visit, his housekeeper asked us to leave, saying we could return on the morrow if we wanted. The guards and I spent the first evening at Señor Don Martin's home." He glanced at Tomás. "He was gracious enough to have his cook put out a feast. None of us had eaten since morning. He wants you to visit him soon to hunt and ride."

Beatriz asked, "What happened the second day?"

"More of the same. The housekeeper said we would have to wait. We did, and spent the night at Señor Don Luys's home."

Isabella gestured impatiently. "And the third day?"

"Upon our arrival, the housekeeper said I could finally see Señor Serrano, though he and I would speak in his bedchamber. She explained he was quite ill, had been for weeks, and I should—"

"Wait." Beatriz's suspicions increased. "Weeks? No. Impossible. Don Larnaz made no mention of illness when he was here. Why keep such a thing secret when he could have used the information to sway me?"

Tomás squeezed her shoulder. "He might not have been aware of your father's declining health. Once Rufio told him where you were, Don Larnaz may have come here immediately without telling your papá first."

Reasonable, yet she couldn't shake her doubt. "Given what they both had to lose with me remaining out of reach, one would think they would have met at regular intervals."

"Don Larnaz may have deliberately stayed away from your father," Fernando said. "Afraid he might have wanted the dowry back."

Isabella nodded. "The pu—ah, the beast may have already spent the money."

Beatriz wasn't certain what to think. She gestured to Nuncio. "Go on."

"The housekeeper said if I pressed Señor Serrano in any way, I would have to leave." His face flushed suddenly. "I must confess I did ask her what was wrong with him. Coward that I am, I feared catching something, though I would have still marched into his bedchamber."

Tomás clamped him on the shoulder. "Good man."

Beatriz nodded. "Did she say what afflicts him?"

"The physician told her mortal weakness. He had no other name for what ails your father. He has no strength. Even a few steps cause him to gasp for breath. At times, he had pains here." Nuncio pointed to his chest. "And here." He grasped his left arm near the top.

She'd never heard of such a thing. "Have any of you seen this illness?"

Tomás and Fernando shook their heads.

So did Isabella. "If only my sister were here. Sancha could—" She glanced at Nuncio.

"We can trust him," Beatriz said.

"Sancha's books tell of every disorder known to man. All she has to do is look up symptoms."

Beatriz considered that. "If there are none in her volumes, then the disease is a ruse."

"Why not write her and know for sure?" Tomás asked.

"I will. Nuncio, how did my father look and sound?"

"Forgive me for offering my opinion, but his distress seemed real to me."

"So did his tears at my mother's deathbed. The moment the physician left, he was fine, looking at her cold body with annoyance, eager to get back to his business. A good man like you would never do what my father has, making you blind to the person he is."

"That may be, but I saw him." Nuncio glanced from one to the other. "Even though I have many years on the man, he looked worse than I do, his complexion gray, lips pale. He struggled for breath, saying only a few words before he had to rest. His hands shook so badly when he held the missive, I ended up reading the letter. At times, he gritted his teeth and his face turned red. Not from anger. Pain. I thought he was going to die before my eyes. I begged him to tell me how to help or if his housekeeper should send for the physician. He held up his hand and shook his head.

"My heart kept pounding. I held my breath and waited for the worst. The pain finally passed. He slumped against his pillows and told me to continue reading. I could barely see the words my hands were trembling so much."

Beatriz wasn't certain what to think.

Tomás leaned over to Fernando. "When you spied for Spain, would you have been able to look and act as Beatriz's father had to fool anyone?"

"Of course," Isabella said before Fernando could. "When I first saw him, he seemed older than Nuncio, speaking and tottering like a frail old man, until he bolted through the marketplace, pulling me with him." She smiled. "He was magnificent."

Fernando's cheeks darkened slightly. He and Isabella shared a private glance and bumped shoulders.

"I could have easily pulled off such an act," Fernando said to Tomás. "If this is one." He looked around Isabella to Beatriz. "Your father is far older than I am. His illness may be real."

Nuncio nodded. "What I saw was no act."

Beatriz took Tomás's hand. "What do you think?"

"Has your father ever been ill before?"

"Not a day in his life."

Nuncio sighed. "What would he gain from such an act?"

"My guilt for having caused him to fall ill by running away, followed by my agreement to finally wed Don Larnaz so he recovers."

Nuncio wrinkled his nose. "No man could be that loathsome."

"My uncle was." Hatred filled Isabella's beautiful face. "He resorted to murder, killing my parents."

Beatriz patted Nuncio's hand. "See how easily Papá swayed you?"

He reddened. "I thought—your father seemed—I would never want any harm to come to you or Don Tomás. Nor would I want to influence you with my perception of what I saw and heard. Please excuse me for saying this, but if the man were my father, I would want to know for certain whether his illness is real or not before I decided to let him die without ever seeing him again."

Beatriz sagged in her chair.

"I can write Sancha immediately." Isabella stroked Beatriz's arm. "Once she answers my missive, we have our answer."

Unless something else came up, confusing the matter further. "Did he ask about me at all?"

"He wanted to know if you were happy now. I told him never have I seen anyone more in love. Your father grew thoughtful, then said he understood your feelings for Don Tomás."

Hard to believe unless he was truly ill and wanted to make amends for what he'd done before facing God. She tried to imagine such a thing but still couldn't. Her father wasn't a pious man. "He knows nothing about Tomás. Did he ask about him or mention Don Larnaz? Wait. Was he surprised I was living here?"

"He was or seemed to be. I wish I could be sure, but he appeared surprised to me."

"Why would he agree to speak with you if he had no idea who you were or that I was here?"

"I told the housekeeper I was there concerning you and Don Tomás."

"Did my father ask who Tomás was? Where he hailed from? His family connections?"

"No." Nuncio leaned up. "Every word he spoke tired him, or seemed to. I sensed he wanted to say more but lacked strength. After I read the missive to him, he had all the information he needed."

Tomás squeezed her shoulder. "You, Isabella, and Nuncio should go to my study and get started on the letter. I can send two guards out tonight. They can easily reach Enrique's castle by dawn. The faster Sancha knows what we need, the sooner we have answers. Possibly by tomorrow evening."

Isabella shook her head. "Not likely. She has dozens of volumes. Finding the illness may take some time." She stood and took Beatriz's hand. "Best we not delay. Nuncio." She gestured to him. They left the parlor.

* * * *

"Out with it," Fernando said the moment he and Tomás were alone. "Do you think this is a ruse by her father?"

Given what Beatriz had said about the man, and what Isabella's uncle had done to her and Sancha, Tomás supposed anything was possible. How to know for certain, though? "I should have gone rather than sending Nuncio."

"Why did you send him?"

"If I had left to speak to her father, Beatriz might not have been here when I returned."

"Or if you returned, considering what she said about him. Where would she have gone?"

"Anywhere in the world except here in order to protect me from her father."

"I suspect she would have headed for the next estate within walking distance."

"Exactly, with Beatriz meeting the noble there, him falling in love with her, convincing her they should wed and have children. What chance would I have then?"

"As many as you have now. Even if she somehow reached a farther estate, a three or five-day ride would get you there from here. Who could fall in love, wed, and have children in that time?"

Tomás leaned against the mantel. "I know Beatriz. Her first thought would be hiding out to keep me from finding her and putting myself in danger. Enough of this. I should go to the city now and see what he might be up to."

"And possibly put yourself in danger exactly as she fears. Are you hoping Isabella and I could keep Beatriz in this castle once she knows you left? Trust me, Isabella would side with her, forcing me to go along with whatever they wanted. Welcome to falling in love and considering a woman's feelings rather than your own. Why not wait for Sancha's answer?"

"What if Beatriz's father dies while I do and she misses her last chance to see him? No matter what went on between them, the man will always be her papá."

"Clearly not in the way she needed or wanted. Are you worried about her feeling guilty?"

"What else? His death would always hang over our marriage if I failed to act. What if she and I went to his house together?"

"How? With her shackled and gagged in the carriage? You know her better than I do, but she strikes me as not wanting to be anywhere near the man."

"There must be some way to settle this."

Isabella entered the room.

Tomás pushed away from the mantel. "Has something happened?"

"I need to speak to my husband." She stopped at Fernando's side, cupped her hand over his ear, and whispered.

After she stepped back, he sighed but nodded.

"Gracias." She kissed him lightly on his mouth and flicked her hand at Tomás. "Go on." She left the room.

Tomás asked, "Want to tell me what that was about?"

Fernando lifted his finger until Isabella's footfalls had faded. "She said not to let you talk me into visiting Beatriz's father with you, nor to let you go alone. Beatriz wants you safe. If either of us leaves, she promises to go to Don Larnaz and offer herself to him to settle this once and for all."

* * * *

The guards departed with Isabella's missive, leaving Beatriz to wait for Sancha's answer and to listen to Tomás rail at her in his study.

"How dare you threaten to go to that pig, that swine, that puto to keep me from leaving here and going to your father."

"I love you."

He pressed the heel of his hand to his forehead. "This is how you show your devotion by promising to offer yourself to that beast, that monster."

"Only to stop you from behaving recklessly, as you well know."

"Now you claim I have no sense. How nice. Is that why you sought to humiliate me in front of my brother?"

"Humiliate you? Have you forgotten Fernando learned from a servant, not Isabella, that he wed the wrong sister? She told me any number of soldiers and several of his brothers, including you, surrounded him at the time, and that you thought little of how terrible Fernando felt. You even told Isabella he would get over her deception. From what I can see, he did, surviving quite nicely because he finally realized she acted out of love, not malice. The same as I have with you."

"Isabella and Fernando's situation was different. She never threatened to deliver herself to another man."

"I had to let you know how serious I am about this, since you refuse to consider my feelings. I understand you need to act as you deem necessary, but so do I. You rail at me for behaving like you."

Tomás frowned. "As a man I have the right."

"Not with me."

He gestured wildly. "How can you say such a thing? Honor demands I protect you first and at all cost."

"Love requires we protect and cherish each other so neither of us dies needlessly. Why would you want our lives to be any other way?"

On a loud groan, he dropped to a bench and held his head.

Oh, Tomás. Beatriz sank to the floor in front of him. "Are we through arguing?" She kissed his knee. "Please say we are."

He groaned, then sighed. "How can I stay angry with you?"

"Do you really want to?"

He wrapped his arm around her shoulders and pulled her closer. "I worry what might happen if your father is ill and passes before you can see each other again to make things right."

Beatriz wasn't certain she could ever forgive her father for what he'd done. However, to grant the man a small measure of peace before his death would be the right thing to do, even if she did so for her conscience rather than his soul. "I wish no one harm. But my loyalty is to you over everyone, including my papá. Whatever happens, I want us to wait for Sancha's answer."

* * * *

Beatriz didn't bring up the subject again, nor did Tomás. The following morning, he and Fernando visited the fields, groves, and vineyards, then discussed agriculture methods during the midday meal. They tried to outdo each other with what they knew, despite claiming they hated being landowners.

They were still competing during their chess game after the last meal of the day.

On the parapet, Beatriz and Isabella leaned against the stone columns, their hair pulled by the cool wind. They searched the darkness for torches in the distance. Even though Isabella had said too little time had passed for the men to return, she kept Beatriz company rather than telling her how foolish she was.

"If you want to go inside to Juana, I understand."

"With her asleep finally?" Moonlight sparkled in Isabella's eyes, making the color ethereal. "Up here I have no chance of waking her."

"Yolanda would be more than happy to rock her back to sleep."

The girl couldn't stop cooing over the infant or letting Juana curl her tiny fingers over Yolanda's thumb.

Even Nuncio made funny faces at the baby, coaxing her to laugh.

"What a treasure you have in Yolanda." Isabella pulled her cloak tightly around herself. "Have you thought what you might say to your father if he is ill?"

Since Nuncio's return, she'd troubled over visiting her father, especially for the last time, having his full attention for once, with him unable to turn his back on her. She pushed windblown tresses from her face. "Do you really want to hear this?"

"Rage away."

Beatriz loved Isabella's spirit and acceptance. "Hardly rage. More like confusion. As I looked at him for the last time, I'd ask, 'Why, papá? Was what you did to mamá and me, and so many others, worth losing your soul? Did you ever love us, even for a moment? When you saw me on the day I was born, were you proud or indifferent? If I had been a boy, would you have wanted me more? Would you have listened and cared?'"

Tears sparkled in Isabella's eyes. She hugged Beatriz. "If matters do come to a last visit, I hope he gives you the answers you want."

Not likely. "My fantasies of those last moments are probably far different from what I would end up saying. To borrow Nuncio's comment, forgive me for being a coward. Most likely, my final words would be about what a fine business he had and wealth everyone envied. That would make him happy."

"What a good daughter you are."

"Not if this is a ruse and he tries to harm Tomás."

"We shall see."

* * * *

On the second day, Beatriz strove for normalcy and busied herself with Yolanda's lessons. She'd finally advanced to D, E, and F in the alphabet, her progress painfully slow, determination remarkably dogged.

After the afternoon siesta, Beatriz found Yolanda outside, drawing letters in the dirt with a twig.

"I can hide my mistakes this way." She grinned slyly. "And keep using the same spot, unlike paper."

Beatriz clapped in approval. "How right you are. We should move our lessons outside."

"I have no complaints."

She, Yolanda, and Isabella spent a pleasant afternoon on the grounds, returning to the castle at the same time Fernando and Tomás did from the pastures.

"Did you see this?" Tomás gestured to the cabinet near the front entrance. A letter rested on a silver tray.

From Sancha? "A servant must have brought the missive in when we were outside. Isabella, you should open it."

Fernando shook his head. "Not Enrique's seal. Must be for you, Tomás. Or Beatriz?"

"No. Not my father's."

Tomás looked. "Don Larnaz?"

"I have no idea." Beatriz gestured to the letter. "Please open the thing and find out. I have no desire to touch anything that he has."

Tomás broke the seal and read. "For me. A merchant I spoke to last month finally has four Arabians for sale, each black, just as I asked for."

Fernando chuckled. "As a child, Tomás refused to ride any other color. What say we have a look at them?"

"What else? Wait." Tomás took Beatriz's hand. "The merchant's stable is right at the edge of Don Guzman's estate that begins at the southern border of my land. No more than two hours ride from here. I can make the purchase and return quickly. Faster than when Fernando and I toured the pastures and fields to the east."

The city lay in that direction with a route that held myriad dangers. All land from here to Don Guzman's estate had either his guards or Tomás's protecting property and inhabitants. The same as Tomás's castle that had men at the gate and walls, keeping her from harm.

Was this what their life was to be like? Tomás hesitant to move freely beyond these confines because of her endless worry.

She wouldn't have that, especially for him and particularly when his stated direction was so safe. "Go, my love, and enjoy yourself. But can you put off leaving until morning?"

"For you, anything."

* * * *

That night, Beatriz needed to store each moment to sustain herself for their brief separation and sensed Tomás felt the same. Their kisses were long and deep. They made noises that would shame them if anyone else could hear.

They were in the harem, the space lit by oil lamps as a sultan might demand, Beatriz bared, though not fully tamed. Wearing a wicked smile, she ran her fingers down Tomás's torso, making his muscles jump. "Lie down."

"I will, after I have you."

"No, now."

He touched his nose to hers. "I rescued your orange peel, I gave you a bath, I even let you take over my study for Yolanda's lessons, and still you deny me?"

"Only if you keep talking. Once you lie down, I can serve you, while you serve me in the most wanton way."

Tomás leaned back. "What did you have in mind?"

"Do as I ask so I can show you."

He fell to the mattress. Purple silk puffed up with his weight and floated back down. "What now?"

Beatriz faced his feet and straddled his hips.

Tomás stilled. "What are you doing?"

"Watch." She positioned herself so her face was above his stiffened rod and sac, her soft folds near his mouth.

He gripped her hips. "I like this."

Isabella had told her about the position. Best to keep that secret to herself.

Beatriz licked his member and swirled her tongue around the plump crown. His toes curled. He pulled her down to him, his mouth on her sex. Heavenly pleasure tore through her, but she saw to his enjoyment too and eased the right side of his sac into her mouth.

Tomas growled, the sound raw and virile, filling the chamber.

Her blood raced. She licked his hair-roughened sac, adoring his sex, its heat, musky fragrance, and faint salty taste. He breathed hard and forgot to see to her pleasure. Beatriz didn't care. In here, she was his carnal slave, required to submit and bring him boundless satisfaction.

With great care, she suckled, tending to him as he did with her, finally remembering to lick her nub and spear his tongue into her opening, claiming what was his.

She showered her attention on the other side of his sac.

He groaned.

They filled the chamber with love sounds, worshipping each other's sex in a strikingly intimate act that left them panting.

* * * *

The following morning, Beatriz was tired but still wanted more of Tomás.

He gave her a hearty goodbye kiss and ordered several guards to accompany him and Fernando. Hardly necessary, considering where they were going, but the added protection pleased Beatriz.

She waved until he could no longer see her.

Isabella pressed her hand to her chest. "Whatever did we do before we met our men?"

"I cried a lot, thinking of the beast I was supposed to wed. What about you?"

"No time for tears. I was worried about Sancha. I hope her missive comes today."

So did Beatriz, wanting an end to this.

She busied herself with Yolanda's lesson held beneath a cork tree. Yolanda sat cross-legged, drawing in the dirt near the trunk. Isabella reclined on the blanket, dangling her sapphire above Juana. The sparkling gem mesmerized the infant. Several times, she batted her tiny hands trying to catch it.

After Juana had her meal, the rest of them paused to refresh themselves with bread and cheese, oranges, olives, and roasted pork, washed down with milk. Isabella yawned. Yolanda returned to her alphabet.

"Señorita Beatriz." Nuncio hurried across the lawn holding two papers. Panting, he handed one letter to her and the other to Isabella.

Isabella turned hers over. "From Sancha."

Beatriz had no idea who hers was from. Hoping Don Larnaz hadn't written, she broke the seal and read.

Dear Señorita Serrano,

Forgive my words written in haste. As your father's physician, I must inform you that his health grows increasingly worse. He may not last much longer.
His future is in God's hands now. The only thing left for me to do is to make him as comfortable as possible. Those few times he can sleep, he keeps calling for you.

Your servant,
Señor Cristóbal Yniguis, Médico

Numb, she lowered the letter. Isabella took the missive from her and handed Beatriz the one from Sancha. Beatriz forced herself to read.

My dearest sister, Isabella,

How sorry I am for Beatriz and all her troubles. May God grant her and Tomás naught but happiness here forward.
I raced through my volumes, the symptoms you provided in hand. At length, I found a passage matching what you wrote me. The illness is real.

Your loving sister,
Sancha

Chapter 15

Needing to move, think, do something, Beatriz crossed the lawn to the castle. Nuncio and Yolanda caught up with her.

Yolanda touched Beatriz's sleeve. "What happened?"

Isabella joined them, Juana in her arms. "Her papá is sick."

"The illness is real?" Nuncio asked.

Beatriz nodded. Her father was a monster who deserved to burn in Hell, but he was also helpless now and most likely frightened. To ignore or hurt him, as he'd done to her and her mother, was unthinkable. Beatriz couldn't manage that much hatred. She entered the castle.

Isabella followed close behind. "Are you going to him?"

"What other choice is there? I have to do the right thing."

"Do you want me to go with you?"

"No." She crossed the kitchen. Servants paused in their work, staring at her and the others. Beatriz raced down the hall to the grand stairway.

Nuncio caught up again. "Would you like me to accompany you?"

She stopped and threw her arms around him for his kind gesture. This time, Nuncio hugged her in return. Tears stung her eyes. "I need to do this on my own. Please arrange for a carriage. I need to leave at once."

"Of course." Nuncio hurried down the hall.

Isabella rushed to the stairs. "Yolanda, help me pack what Beatriz needs for her journey."

"At once." The girl bounded up the steps.

Isabella spoke to Beatriz. "Please wear the gown I gave you."

"What I have on is fine." She wore the simple dress she'd taken from Pascuala, relished seeing her expression when she realized Beatriz had donned a servant's clothes to escape.

Beatriz guessed she had malice in her after all. Suddenly, she was a fourteen-year-old girl again, clinging to her mother's things, with Pascuala pushing her aside in order to dispose of them calmly and coldly.

"Forgive me for being so bold," Isabella said. "But do you want your father's last view of you to be in servant's clothes rather than dressed as a noble, looking beautiful and happy for having made the right choice in running away? Whatever you may be feeling now, this is your final chance to prove you survived his cruelty, unlike your mother. You can make her proud."

Beatriz stopped on the landing. "How wise you are." She pressed her cheek to Isabella's.

Juana gurgled.

"I can take her." Yolanda reached for the infant. "You two can talk."

"No time for converse." Isabella delivered her child to Yolanda, then tugged Beatriz down the hall. "We have to prepare you and pack. How long will you be gone?"

Beatriz had no idea. "I know this sounds terrible, but should I wait for him to pass?"

"Could be days, possibly weeks if the physician is wrong. They often are." She steered Beatriz into her and Fernando's chamber. "I learned as much from Sancha, especially when Tomás fell ill. The fool surgeon bled Tomás twice, even though he was already too weak to stand on his own. When Fernando lost so much blood trying to protect me, he nearly…" Tears welled in her eyes. She cleared her throat. "Although your father's condition is grave, he may last awhile."

She pulled a leather satchel from the wardrobe. "This is large enough to hold items for several days. If you need to stay longer, Tomás can bring what you need…unless you want to use what you left behind when you fled."

"Never. I want nothing of that life."

"Very well, you shall have what I give you." She opened a cabinet drawer and pulled out several chemises, the undergarments as white as the finest pearl, lighter than the morning mist. "These should do. I can also give you some of my gems and shoes and—"

"The plum-colored gown is enough." Too much to Beatriz's way of thinking. "Could be all my father wants is for me to show up, proving I care, so his physician can tell others what a good man he is and how much his daughter loves him. Once I serve my purpose, he may tell me to quit annoying him as usual."

Isabella lowered the chemises to the bed. Yolanda sat in a box chair, rocking Juana. Both looked sad for her.

What grand friends they were. "Never fear. What my father thinks of me is in the past. I have Tomás now."

"That you do." Isabella pulled out a pair of low shoes in black leather, the toes pointy. She put them on the satchel. "Stay with your father or leave as soon as you make an appearance. Do what you feel you must. But I still want you prepared."

* * * *

When Isabella had finished packing and Beatriz was dressed like a noble, Nuncio had the carriage waiting. Tomás's most able guard drove the conveyance. Several guards would also accompany them on horseback for protection against robbers.

Beatriz hugged Nuncio. "When Tomás returns, please tell him not to worry about me."

"I will, but he will."

She laughed and released him.

Yolanda lifted the snowy napkin on the basket Cook had prepared for the journey. "Everything you like." She wiped a tear. "Especially olives and oranges. I picked the very best for you."

Isabella smiled. "She is such a treasure."

Beatriz embraced Yolanda. "No need to cry. In no time at all, I will return. You can watch for me from the parapet."

"Take care, please."

With her father near death and Tomás's love sheltering her, Beatriz was safer than she'd been her entire life. She cupped Yolanda's chin. "No slacking off on your lessons. Practice your letters every day."

"I promise to learn all of them before you return."

"Half will do." She brushed away Yolanda's tears and kissed her cheek.

Once Isabella had handed Juana to Yolanda, she embraced Beatriz. "I need to thank Tomás for finding you and giving me another sister to love."

Beatriz laughed and cried.

With the carriage packed and the guards ready to leave, there was no more delay. Nuncio helped Beatriz into the transport. The horses started forward, the wheels creaking. Missing everyone already, she leaned out the window and waved farewell. Yolanda ran down the path, but couldn't keep up. Soon she and everyone else became mere specks in the distance before disappearing completely.

Beatriz still looked, finally slumping against the cloth seat embroidered with Tomás's coat of arms. Already, she longed for a return to the castle, the only place she'd ever been welcomed fully and could call home.

All too soon, the carriage passed through the gate and clattered down the road. Fields streamed past, followed by vineyards and groves. Peasants toiled on the land, wearing tunics in yellow, red, purple, and green more vivid than new grass. Women walked down the road, holding young children's hands, unmindful of dust stirred by horse hooves and wheels.

One mother carried an infant in a sling wrapped tight to her breasts. She didn't seem happy or unhappy, simply resigned to doing what she must. With never-ending work, these people hadn't time to consider anything except survival. A hopefully full belly, enough clean water to drink, a place to sleep undisturbed, children who survived past the first years and thrived to adulthood.

Beatriz recalled Yolanda, tongue peeking from her mouth as she drew in the dirt, learning what she should have at a much earlier age. Juana would have the best tutors, Isabella and Fernando educating their daughter so she had every chance to succeed.

The same as Beatriz's papá had done for her, though hardly out of pride or love. She closed the velvet curtains over the windows, blocking out dust, light, and her farewell to a place she adored. She considered her first moments alone with her father after so many months. For those images, she needed darkness.

A knot formed in her chest, aching dully. Similar to what Nuncio had said about her father's pain, though hers was different. Dread, not mortal weakness, crowded out her guilt. If her father railed at her for having taken Pascuala's gown and fleeing, rather than wedding Don Larnaz as a dutiful daughter should, Beatriz wasn't certain she could keep her tongue.

She feared losing control of years of pent-up hurt and anger. She might enrage her father to the point where he wouldn't be able to breathe any longer and she would be responsible for his death.

Although the physician had written how her father called for Beatriz in his sleep, the man hadn't said whether her papá's voice was loving or filled with contempt. Maybe her father wanted her to kill him so her guilt would never end.

She covered her eyes, certain she was losing her mind. After collecting herself, she drew back the velvet curtain on the right. The guard on that side scanned the area, ever watchful.

She leaned out. "How long until we reach the city?"

"Three hours at best. If you need us to stop, say the word."

She nodded and let the velvet swing back into place, hoping a nap would make the trip seem shorter and silence her uncomfortable thoughts. After propping a pillow behind her head, she leaned against the transport and closed her eyes.

* * * *

The carriage jolted, nearly sending Beatriz to the floor. She grabbed the window ledge to steady herself. The horses squealed.

She shoved aside the velvet. "What is it?"

"A cork tree in the road." The guard pushed up on his horse, craning his neck to see more. "The wind must have pushed—"

Air poured from him. He fell from his horse.

In front of the carriage, men fought, fists hitting flesh with sickening thuds, muttered words spoken, fierce howls released, steel blades clanging. Robbers. The tree in the road had been a ploy.

She tore through her things for something to protect herself, not having thought to bring a dagger or sword as Tomás had once warned. Thankfully, Cook or Yolanda had packed a knife with her meal. With the weapon hidden within her skirt folds, Beatriz waited. A pulse beat hard in her temples, her palms sweaty. She might not fell more than one man, but she would have blood for this horror.

The horses' squeals finally quieted to snorts and sniffs, the way they would when someone had calmed them. Seconds passed with nothing else happening. Birds chirped, the wind whistled through trees, leaves rustled.

Footfalls struck softly on the packed dirt, someone rounding the transport. Sun shone on the curtain, making the scarlet cloth a lighter red. A shadow fell across the fabric, the dark outline showing a man's shoulders and head.

She gripped her knife.

The half-door flew open. Rufio smiled. "Now, you pay."

Beatriz's shock delayed her reaction, though not by much. She slashed his forearm.

He stared at his injury, disbelief on his face. "Whore!" He grabbed her skirt and yanked her to the carriage floor.

She stabbed air rather than him.

Two men ran up, burly and young like Rufio, each wearing livery, marking them as a noble's servants. Don Larnaz.

Beatriz screamed.

Rufio slapped his hand over her mouth.

She wrenched her head back and forth to loosen his hold, succeeding enough to part her lips and bite his finger.

Howling, he jerked away.

Beatriz kicked the next man, hitting him squarely between his legs. On an agonized gasp, he staggered away and fell to his knees.

The third man punched her calf. White-hot pain pumped through her, snatching her breath. He pulled her from the carriage, one arm around her waist, the other clamped on her mouth.

Tomás's guards lay to the side. None moved or seemed to breathe.

She fought, but the man was too strong. He dragged her to another conveyance.

Rufio caught up, clutching his bloody sleeve. "I wish he would have let us kill you."

"Quiet." The man holding her breathed hard. "Help me."

Dark blue velvet covered the window. Rufio opened the door.

Don Larnaz sat on one side, her father on the other, healthy, powerful, and smug.

He'd fooled her as he had her mother, the physician's missive a lie. He'd had to trick her into visiting him after he'd gotten rid of Tomás, that letter surely a ruse.

Beatriz screamed her outrage and fought as she never had.

* * * *

The merchant shook his head. "I have yet to acquire any black Arabians since we last spoke. Who told you I had more? Never mind. I have three white ones for you. Never have you seen such exquisite creatures."

Tomás thought the man daft not to recall writing only a short while ago. "No one told us anything. You sent me a missive."

He pulled the letter from his pouch.

As the merchant read, he mouthed the words and finally shook his head. "Someone must be playing a trick on you. This is my seal, but I never wrote this."

Understanding and fear hit Tomás hard. "Don Larnaz sent the missive."

He ran from the merchant's stable, Fernando following him.

"I have brown Arabians too," the man called out.

Tomás raced to the guards, who stopped speaking.

"Wait." Fernando grabbed Tomás's arm. "Where are we running off to?"

He wasn't certain. "Do you think Don Larnaz went to the castle to force Beatriz to go with him?"

"How would he get that far with your men guarding the gate and walls? The only way inside would be if he mounted an attack. Would he be that foolish or skilled?"

Never. Soft and unused to battle, the coward won by scheming and finding out about his enemies. As he'd said that night at the castle, telling Tomás he knew about him. Tomás's friends were well aware how much he loved black Arabians. "He sent the missive to get me away in order to have a clear path to Beatriz if she left the castle. But nothing would make her do so."

"News of her father would. What if Don Larnaz knew of the man's condition and sent her a missive claiming he was near death, hoping Beatriz would visit him so Don Larnaz could intercept her?"

Tomás turned to the guard on his right. "Ride to Don Enrique's castle. Tell my brother I need him and the guards he can spare at..." He paused and spoke to Fernando. "Where first? The road to the city or Don Larnaz's estate?"

"We should cover both at the same time."

Tomás directed the first guard. "Tell Don Enrique to take the road to the city past my castle."

"Sí, Patrón." The man rode off.

"Go to Don Gabriello and Don Alfonso's homes," Tomás said to the other guard. "Tell my brothers I need them and any men they can gather, including the alguacil. They should look for me near Don Larnaz's castle."

The man nodded.

"Wait. We don't know where Don Larnaz's estate is."

"I do." The guard stepped closer. "My cousin works in the fields nearby." He provided directions.

Tomás committed them to memory. "Go."

"Where do we ride?" Fernando asked.

"Between the city and the puto's castle." Tomás mounted his gelding.

Fernando wheeled his horse around. "What if Larnaz has Beatriz in his castle?"

"We storm the gate and I kill him."

* * * *

The men forced Beatriz into the carriage next to Don Larnaz.

She squirmed away.

He gripped her wrist, pulling her back.

She punched him wherever she could, yanked their hands up, and sank her teeth into his thumb.

Yelping, he wrenched free.

She drove her elbow into his gut and turned to the door.

Her father slammed his walking cane on the seat.

She reared back.

"Sit down and stay down." He glared. "If you refuse, I will beat you until you can no longer stand."

She cried, "How could you even think of doing such a thing?"

"You mean securing a noble for you and a title for your children?"

"For yourself. I want none of this. I love Tomás and intend to wed him."

"How touching and misguided. The man will never see you again, except at gatherings with the marquis, your husband."

"That marriage will never happen."

The carriage jerked forward.

Beatriz tried to see past the velvet curtains on both sides but couldn't. Her father leaned back in his seat. "You think you can stop this?"

"I would die before I wed that puto."

Don Larnaz gasped and raised his hand.

"Go on, strike me." She gave him a mean smile. "Tomás will gladly run you through while I cheer him on."

Larnaz stilled, dark spots staining his cheeks. At last, he lowered his hand, looking as cowed as he had at the castle when Tomás had gone down the steps, ready to kill him.

She turned her wrath on her father. "I would die before going through with this marriage."

"We shall see. Your mother clung to life far longer than I wanted her to."

Beatriz seethed. "How dare you."

"What? Speak the truth? Kill yourself if you must, but do so after the ceremony and bearing a male heir. I have no intention of losing access to what Don Larnaz's title can do for me."

"What kind of a man are you? What kind of a father?"

He regarded her with indifference. "I have no brats. Not even you."

He'd gone mad, evil corrupting his mind to the point of lunacy. Beatriz pushed into her seat to get away from him. "To think I felt guilty about your failing health as a daughter should with her papá."

A smile tugged at his lips. His eyes remained cold. "Quite a performance I put on. My physician likes to talk and told me about a noble patient of his who has difficulty breathing and feels pain here." He pressed his fist against his chest. "And here." He touched his left arm near the top. "How easy to pretend I had that rather than the fever. White powder on my face made me look ghastly. I suspected either Tomás or one of his servants would show up to pay back your dowry, as he told Don Larnaz. The manservant Tomás sent seemed close to swooning every time I pretended I was in pain. I knew after that my missive, written as the good doctor Cristóbal Yniguis, would bring you to my side just as though you were my daughter."

"What are you talking about? I am your daughter."

"No. Your father died shortly after you were born. Sorry fool killed himself. Seems you inherited his taste for putting on a show."

The ground beneath Beatriz seemed to have opened up, trying to suck her inside. "What?"

"No need to look so shocked. It is what it is, or rather what society has made of us all. Your father never understood how lucky he was, having wealth and power from birth simply for being born to noble parents when I had to earn everything." His scowl grew even uglier. "Hardly fair, but I was smarter than those around me, especially your mother. She fell in love with me so easily. Her papá welcomed me into his home as he would a son. All I had to do was wait until the old fool died to do what I wanted."

Beatriz shook her head, refusing to hear anymore.

Eyes glittering, faced flushed, he leaned forward. "She resisted what I wanted in the beginning. I tried to explain how my plan would benefit both of us. During her liaisons, she could learn the most intimate secrets of the nobles she was with. Men in the throes of passion always talk, offering a wealth of information simply begging for use." He shook his head. "Sadly, there was no reasoning with the woman. What do you do with an animal that refuses to obey? You beat them until they submit to your will, as they should." He smiled.

Beatriz wanted to be sick. She hadn't been able to finish the journal, not wanting to know how her mother had suffered. To have him boast about what he'd done... "Enough."

"I think not. You need to know everything to put your resistance in the past where it belongs. Your father was one of the first nobles to have her. They fell in love quite readily and he wanted to spirit her away to his castle, especially after she became pregnant with you. A grand romance." Jaw tightened, he tapped his cane hard. "I warned him how foolish his plans were. His father had numerous secrets I made certain to learn about in order to exploit his weaknesses. Exposure would have destroyed the family name. For a set fee every month, I was willing to keep silent on the matter of his dear papá. I told your father if he changed his mind, I would hurt your mother, the love of his life. If he tried to harm me, I had everything written down, the document held by my lawyer who would seek justice after my death. In the end, he chose family, position, power, and wealth over her but never recovered from the loss. After his death, I found other nobles for your mother to entertain, ordering her to learn their secrets.

"Of course, my main hope was to have her bear a son by one of them. Your birth was so disappointing. No noble wants a female. Only a male heir would work to my advantage. I wanted to kill your mother after she lost a duke's child and the physician said she could never conceive again. She was as frustrating to me as you were, but I made her pay every day of her life for failing me."

Her mother had warned her. *He is not what you think.*

Beatriz wished she could kill him.

He rested his hands on his cane and studied her. "Now you know how determined I am to reach my goal, as Don Larnaz found out."

No longer pompous and assured, Don Larnaz pressed against the carriage, the same as a beaten dog eyeing its tormentor.

"I expect you to still call me papá." He leaned back. "But know this. No fatherly love lives in me for you. I would murder you in a moment if doing so served my purpose. If you defy me in the least, including killing yourself before at least one male heir arrives, I will see Tomás dead."

She gripped the seat to keep from lunging. "Leave Tomás out of this."

"As long as you obey, nothing untoward will happen to him. The man will meet another woman, fall in love, have no end of children, and forget you existed."

Tears clouded her eyes. "Harm him and I will see you dead."

"Empty words. You have no power against me so keep your tongue and use these moments to rest. Our ride to the sacerdote is long. The wedding night that follows will be the beginning of your new life, being a wife to Don Larnaz, bearing many children for him. I intend to make good matches for them when the time comes, with those unions giving me what should have been mine all along."

Beatriz wished he were dead. She struggled for a way to stop this and send him to the Devil.

* * * *

Tomás rode to the crest of the highest hill overlooking the valley, Fernando behind him. The city was to the east, Larnaz's castle to the north. Tomás searched forested areas leading to the marquis's land.

"There." Fernando pointed.

Riders streamed from their brother's estate, surely Enrique and his guards.

"Look." Tomás swung his arm to the right. Riders raced from where Gabriello and Alfonso lived. They'd gathered men as numerous as

Enrique's. "Check the road to the city while I watch the one leading to Larnaz's land."

They searched for what seemed an eternity. Tomás wiped sweat from his eyes and strained to see more.

Fernando shook his head. "No riders or carriages here."

In an opening in the trees, metal glinted in the sun. Blue flashed. A horse's white mane appeared. "To the right." Tomás pointed at the carriage, surely Larnaz's. "Alert Enrique and his men where to go. I can tell Alfonso, Gabriello, and the others. We meet together down there."

He and Fernando clasped arms, then rode hard.

* * * *

Never again would Beatriz think of Serrano as her father. Relief rather than sadness filled her. Now, she could hate him without guilt and plot against him as he'd done with others.

She wanted his cane. She'd have to be strong and fast, taking him by surprise, pummeling him until he lay still. With him felled, gaining Don Larnaz's sword and dagger would be an easy matter. The man had proved he was naught but bluster, hardly the fiend Beatriz had heard about.

Of course, there were still the servants to consider. And Rufio.

Beating him with the cane, forcing him back until he fled into a field or a copse would be a pleasure. The other men might be easier or more difficult to manage. A sword and dagger in her hands should gain their cooperation. What man would want to die to protect Don Larnaz or the puto Serrano?

The carriage jolted as Tomás's had earlier.

She grabbed the seat.

A thunderous sound rolled toward them, dozens of hooves striking the ground. Don Larnaz's horses squealed, hurting her ears.

She pulled the velvet curtain back.

Serrano slapped her hand.

Beatriz kicked his shin three times. Before he could recover from his shock, she lunged toward him and rammed her fist into his jaw. His head snapped back.

The carriage lurched again.

Whimpering, Don Larnaz held on to the seat.

Men shouted.

Rufio begged for mercy.

The carriage teetered to a stop.

She pushed the door open.

Serrano grabbed her skirt, ripping the silk, losing his hold. Swearing, he clutched her hair.

Beatriz shouted and rammed her elbow into his chest.

His hand dropped away, and she scrambled out of the coach.

Fernando and countless other men were at the rear of the carriage. She screamed, "Tomás!"

He rode from the front, dismounted, and ran to her.

Serrano jumped from the carriage and grabbed her cloak.

She punched his hands, kicked his shins, clawed his face, and screamed, "Kill him! He is not my father!"

* * * *

Men quieted. Animals settled too.

Relieved Beatriz wasn't harmed, Tomás drew his sword.

She twisted away from Serrano.

Tomás motioned to her. "In back of me."

She scooted behind him.

Serrano tried to follow, but Tomás lifted his blade to the puto's heart. Killing him would be easy. All he needed to do was finish the job Beatriz had started. Serrano's mouth was bloodied, doublet and robe askew, face scratched. He was at least twenty years older than Tomás with much of his body gone soft.

Tomás looked over at Beatriz. "Are you all right?"

"I am now. Kill him. Please."

"For you, anything. May I ask who is he?"

The man growled. "I *am* her father."

"Liar." She grabbed Tomás's arm. "He told me everything in the carriage. How he wed my mother, but was never my papá. He beat mamá and drove her to the grave. He threatened to kill me if I refused to wed Don Larnaz. He said he would murder you if I resisted what he wanted. Ask the marquis."

Fernando glanced around. "Where is he?"

A guard pointed. "Trying to escape into the forest."

Several men hauled Don Larnaz to Beatriz.

The marquis cowered like a frightened child. He pointed at a man in the group. "What is the alguacil doing here?"

"He means to arrest you for kidnapping my betrothed." Tomás glared. "And for harming my guards."

"No, no, no." Don Larnaz waved his hands in front of himself. "Señor Serrano forced me into this."

"Quiet, fool." Serrano stepped toward him.

Don Larnaz ran to the alguacil. "I beg of you, protect me from him. I never wanted any part of this."

Serrano bared his teeth. "Quiet."

Don Larnaz bounced on his feet. "He threatened me, Beatriz, and Don Tomás too."

"So." Tomás stalked toward Serrano, blade raised. "You think you can harm me?"

"No. Never." Serrano tried out a smile. "You misunderstand."

"Do I?" Tomás sliced Serrano's dark green doublet, not yet reaching skin. "Come now, tell me what I misunderstand."

"Beatriz *is* my daughter. I was only trying to frighten her so she would—"

"Frighten her?" Tomás lifted his eyebrows. "Like this?" He slashed the man's sleeve.

Serrano backed away.

Enrique pushed him back toward Tomás.

"The truth." Tomás rested the tip of his blade on the man's throat. "Or I will run you through where you stand. The last thing you see on this earth will be my smile."

"And mine," Beatriz said.

Tomás loved her more than he believed possible. He winked. She did too. He focused on Serrano. "Talk."

Serrano turned to the alguacil. "Stop him from harming me."

The man frowned. "Stop who?"

"Him." Serrano flung his hand at Tomás.

The alguacil lifted his shoulders. "Why?"

"Are you mad in addition to being deaf?" Serrano gritted his teeth. "He threatened me."

"I heard no threat." He regarded the others. "Has anyone else?"

A chorus of "No" rose through the crowd.

Rufio kept his tongue, docile as a lamb between the two guards gripping his arms.

"Talk." Tomás drew blood from Serrano's throat. "Or die. Your choice." Killing him would be a privilege for what he'd put Beatriz and her mamá through.

As the sun dipped below the trees and hills, the puto told his hideous tale of greed. Every time he tried to make himself sound like a victim, Beatriz stopped him. "Again, he lies."

Repeatedly, Tomás flicked his blade on the swine's throat for not telling the truth. Soon there were enough nicks to bleed him as the surgeon had done to Tomás when he'd fallen ill.

The lies finally stopped, naught but truth came out. The alguacil led Serrano away.

Beatriz slumped against Tomás.

He sheathed his blade and took her into his arms. "Did he hurt you?"

"A few bruises."

"Swine. I should run him through."

"No." She tightened her arms around him. "Stay with me."

"Always."

"Take me home," she cried.

Gladly.

Epilogue

A month later…

Beatriz crossed her bedchamber, a room she'd grown to love. After today, she'd never sleep here again.

Yolanda leaned out the window, face raised to the sky. "Not a cloud anywhere, just the sun. No one could ask for better." She pushed back inside and bounced on her heels. "Lovely afternoon for a wedding."

Indeed. With people Beatriz loved in attendance. Besides Yolanda, Isabella was here. Sancha had arrived days before. She was as beautiful as her sister, her auburn tresses threaded with gold, eyes a rich brown rather than blue-green. Both women took Beatriz's bright yellow gown from the wardrobe, the silk adorned with pearls and glittery beads. She and Tomás had chosen the dress as their favorite among those he'd commissioned for her. Today, she'd wear their choice as they finally joined as man and wife forever.

"I just thought of something." Isabella draped a chemise over her arm. "Beatriz is the first to wed a de Zayas brother after posting banns."

With Serrano held by the authorities for his crimes, and Don Larnaz eagerly bowing out, there wasn't any need to hide the impending union.

"True," Sancha said. "At last, one of us did this the right way."

Isabella nodded. "None too soon, either. How many sacerdotes are there, especially ones willing to wed a couple in secret because of friendship, like what happened with you and Enrique? Not a lot I would wager. Which only leaves holy men susceptible to bribes or those easily fooled like the one who wed Fernando and me when I—"

Beatriz cleared her throat loudly and inclined her head to Yolanda. The girl was all eyes and ears.

"Right." Isabella looked sternly at the child. "Tell me the rule about what you hear within these walls."

"Never repeat a word to another soul and forget everything promptly."

"Such a treasure. Turning into quite the beauty too."

Yolanda blushed. Her new clothes had arrived. The child's gowns were in silk or velvet, simply designed yet elegant. Today, she wore the light blue frock, her favorite. With her dark hair in a braid adorned with flowers, she hinted at the exquisite woman she'd be someday. Bright too.

"May I show everyone what you gave me earlier?" Beatriz asked.

Yolanda's rosy cheeks bloomed red. "Long as no one laughs."

"Never," Isabella said.

Sancha smiled gently. "You can trust us to be kind."

"Go on then." Yolanda still wrapped her arms around herself, bracing for cruel judgment.

Not a chance. Beatriz adored the child. She gave her a tender look and unfolded the paper Yolanda had offered as a wedding gift. At the top was the alphabet, drawn much smaller now than during her first lesson, though her hand was still unsteady. Beneath the letters, she'd printed *Good Wishes*.

Happy tears rolled down Beatriz's cheeks.

Yolanda slumped. "Is it so awful?"

"Beautiful. The most wondrous thing I have ever seen." She hugged the girl.

Sancha looked next and applauded the effort.

Isabella winked at Yolanda. "Well done."

She blushed hotly. "Don Tomás helped me over several days, until I got the words right."

Such a good man. Beatriz marveled at her luck in finding him. "I intend to have this framed to hang on the wall."

"Oh no." Yolanda laughed self-consciously but looked pleased too, proud of what she'd accomplished.

Isabella shook out the chemise. "Best we get Beatriz ready before Tomás and the other men storm this room, asking when, or if, the ceremony will start."

They were getting married on the lawn just as Beatriz had fantasized. Tomás's papá had traveled from the north to attend. He was outside now with his sons, except for Pedro, who was still fighting for the Crown. Their sister, Catarina, was on her way with husband and son.

Yolanda leaned out the window again. "Looks to me like the men are having a grand time. Some of them are playing dice on a blanket. My guess is they have wine in their goblets, not milk."

Beatriz joined her.

Fernando, Gabriello, and Enrique played dice, Enrique's white forelock a startling contrast to his dark hair. Back from battle he'd found distasteful, Dominico stood nearby to officiate. Alfonso and the brothers' papá each held a goblet, sipping their drinks and conversing.

Tomás stood apart from the others, face tipped to Beatriz. He smiled. She sagged against the window frame, warmth gliding through her. The tenderness and heat in his gaze promised a future she never believed existed and couldn't resist. Grinning, Beatriz held up her forefinger, asking for a moment.

He mouthed, "Hurry," or "harem." Either way, she wasn't about to keep him waiting.

She ducked back into the room. "Ladies, we have no time to waste."

Juana and Bartolomé gurgled, both infants on the bed.

With three sets of hands helping her, Beatriz was soon ready, her gown buttoned and laced, hair free, except for two long braids to hold a garland on her head. Long yellow ribbons dangled from the back of the flowers.

Hardly a proper style for a Spanish noblewoman, but Beatriz didn't care. Pleasing Tomás and herself mattered most.

Yolanda clapped. Isabella grinned. Sancha pressed her hands to her chest, her eyes glittering.

Laughing, Beatriz ran outside.

Nuncio smiled at her before she passed.

She grinned in return and quickly reached Tomás's side. The breeze stirred his blond locks, his deep purple doublet, and robe. The right leg of his hose was gold, the left leg brown.

Dazzling.

Despite the others here, Beatriz leaned into him, savoring his clean scent, her hand on his chest. "How handsome you are."

"I have to be. You are beyond compare."

She beamed, waiting for more praise. He offered naught but silence. She pushed out her bottom lip. "Is that all you have to say about me?"

"You want more?" He seemed surprised. "Very well. You make the finest jewel weep with envy, the breeze dance with delight, the sun shine on you alone, forgetting everyone else."

She never tired of how he went on. "Tonight, I have a surprise for you."

Tomás looked intrigued and amused. "You had better."

"Not that."

He regarded her belly.

"I think…that is, I hope… I need a few more weeks to be certain." She pressed her mouth to his ear. "Will we go to the harem for our first evening as husband and wife?"

"Where else?"

"I like how you think."

"Is that your surprise, agreeing with me?"

Better. Over these last weeks, Beatriz had written an epic poem about him as they'd discussed when first becoming friends. She told of his bravery in rescuing her from Serrano and Don Larnaz, Tomás's skill with a blade, his honor, and good heart.

El Cid had nothing on this man.

Tonight, she'd read the poem to him while he rested before taking her again.

She stroked his chest. "Perhaps my newly docile manner is my surprise. Then again, perhaps not. To find out, you need to wed me first."

"I like how you think." He offered his arm, prepared to give Beatriz his future.

As she would with him, offering Tomás her heart for eternity.

Their passionate pursuit of each other had only begun.

Be sure not to miss Book 2 in Tina's erotic historical
Dangerous Desires series.

WICKED WHISPERS

Follow the heart through darkness…

As the Inquisition gains force, even the faintest rumor can brand one a
heretic. In this world it is Sancha's gift—or curse—to be blessed with the
gift of healing. But the villagers are in need of her arts more than ever,
and she feels it is her duty to help them at the risk of losing her life. And
at the sacrifice of her heart…

Enrique has never wanted a woman as he does Sancha. Determined to
have her love, he woos her with exquisite passion, giving her refuge to
pursue her healing in secret. But their very desire and escape from the
ruthless forces of the world may be their undoing. And together, they
must pit themselves against a jealous rival and archaic tradition to secure
their place in a hopeful new world…

A Lyrical Originals novel on sale now!

Learn more about Tina at
http://www.kensingtonbooks.com/author.aspx/24772

Chapter 1

Andalucía, Spain—1488
The castle of Don Fernando de Zayas

Of all the perils a man might face, Enrique de Zayas figured the worst was unending desire for a woman. Especially one whose heart he hadn't yet claimed, because the lady in question was being remarkably difficult. Heat had burned in Sancha's eyes the few times she'd deigned to meet his gaze. Of course, she had been busy tending to his brother Fernando's grave injuries, sparing him death and life as a cripple.

Isabella would never have forgiven her sister if Sancha had chopped off Fernando's arm and leg to save his life. He was a warrior knight and had proved his bravery by falling in love with and wedding Isabella, one of the Lopéz de Lara sisters, who appeared to be delicate Spanish flowers but were as hard as any man.

Steeling himself for whatever happened tonight, Enrique joined the other nobles in his brother's grand dining hall. Exotic spices, garlic, and onions scented the cavernous space. Rich tapestries depicting country life hung on the walls below ornate Moorish designs in gold and silver. The metal glinted from the flickering candlelight and oil lamps. A harpist, flutist, and a man playing a lute sat in the center area on red chairs. The musicians' vibrant Spanish melody was scarcely audible beneath too much converse and loud laughter from hundreds of guests, all dressed in their finest.

He spotted Isabella, regally attired in a gold silk gown that complemented her auburn hair and milky complexion. She saw him too and threaded through the crowd, heading his way. Numerous *señoritas* also edged close, eyeing him as the main fare for this evening's feast. Being a rich man in need of a wife was the second greatest peril a man could face. Isabella stood only as close as etiquette allowed to quell wagging tongues. Spaniards loved intrigue whether it involved the Crown or one of Spain's wealthy subjects. Her earlier abduction and near sale as a concubine for the Sultan's harem had certainly fueled enough gossip.

She turned into him, the top of her head reaching his shoulder. "Take heart. Sancha is here tonight."

His pulse pounded. Warmth rushed to his groin.

Isabella glanced around the opulent, red-walled room. "This time she promised not to take too long with the servant."

"Too long doing what?"

Isabella paled then shrugged. "Whatever one does with servants. Trust me, she will not keep you waiting."

She already had, repeatedly, in the few weeks since they'd met. To him the time seemed longer than most of his life. He wasn't a man who needed decades to determine his feelings for a woman. With Sancha, he'd fallen in an instant. Each day without her added to his torment.

He frowned.

"Oh no." Isabella regarded him closely. "Have you lost interest in her already?"

She'd made him sound like the worst sort of beast when he was the one in pain. "It would appear your sister has never shared my passion."

She flicked her hand dismissively. "You need to woo her as Fernando wooed me."

"When he believed you were Sancha, his betrothed, or after he learned your true identity?"

"Both." She grinned despite the hell she'd put him, Fernando, and two of their other brothers through. "Everything worked out as it should."

Indeed. Sancha had never wanted to wed Fernando. With Isabella taking her place, she remained blissfully unattached in order to torture Enrique with his endless yearning. "Where is my brother?"

"Resting before the meal. I insisted he do so until his strength returns."

"Fernando allows you to order him about?"

Her slender eyebrows lifted slightly. "You believe I or anyone could make demands of a warrior-knight? Never. I request and woo. Something for you to keep in mind with my sister." She searched the crowd and inclined her head. "There she is."

God help him, Enrique couldn't resist staring.

Bathed in the light of candles and oil lamps, she seemed unearthly, an angel sent to visit mere mortals, her complexion creamy and flawless, streaks of gold highlighting her auburn hair, a shimmering mass of temptation.

He locked his knees to steady himself, lost in her allure.

She stepped deeper into the room, emerald skirt swaying, her gown cut modestly, though still providing a hint of her ripe breasts and narrow waist. Unlike the other women here, she wore no jewels to prove her wealth, which was considerable. She was sole heir to her late parents' estate, her holdings as vast as his.

Caballeros watched as she passed.

She didn't glance at any of them.

Enrique wasn't about to suffer such treatment for himself any longer. Tonight he would change everything between them. First though, she had to look at him. To see him.

She stared into the distance, lost in her own world. A server passed too close and brushed her arm. Despite his heavy tray, he stopped and inclined his head in apology. She offered a gentle smile and stepped back to give him more room, her gaze touching Enrique.

He stilled, unable to draw a full breath. Pleasure registered on her lovely face, followed by the same longing he'd seen during their previous encounters, her dark eyes luminous with unmasked desire.

They wouldn't satisfy their craving for each other easily. She may have believed she was independent and even enjoyed playing a role more suited to a male. However, she still had a woman's need for a man to thrill and protect her within his strong embrace.

He fully intended to be that man. His inertia broke. He stepped toward her.

Her passion instantly turned to caution.

Fearing she might bolt, he prepared to give chase.

Isabella dug her fingers into his sleeve. "Give me a moment with her. My sister is shy."

Sancha's impassioned expression upon seeing him had said otherwise. Hunger had burned deep within her, simply waiting to be free.

"Stay here." Isabella patted his sleeve and brushed past the others.

Enrique waited a moment, lost patience, and followed. Another hand clamped on his arm. He gritted his teeth and turned.

Luscinda de Cortés held onto him, her strength surprising, her expression too eager. He would have expected such desperation from a homely woman, not her. She was remarkably beautiful, her snowy skin, long black hair, and dark eyes enhancing her sultry features. Her full lips had surely given many caballeros pleasant dreams. The scandalous cut of her red silk gown barely covered her ample breasts, quivering with each breath she took. Numerous pearl necklaces studded with diamonds graced her long throat.

From the rumors he'd heard, her clothing and gems represented the full sum of her family's wealth. A matter her *mamá*, Señora de Cortés, seemed determined to change, allowing her daughter to dress as she had tonight to catch a rich husband. The older woman stood to the side, watching closely. He regarded Luscinda's hand on his arm.

A painfully long moment passed before she finally released him. "So good to see you here, Enrique."

Where else would he be with Fernando celebrating his and Isabella's union? Given how their wedding had come about, he'd suspected his brother might need help defending against any unkind comments or gossip.

He, on the other hand, needed to keep Luscinda and her grasping family away from himself. Rather than address him as Don Enrique, as good manners required, she'd addressed him as a betrothed or a man who was already her husband. He'd willingly face death before wedding her or anyone other than Sancha. Rather than explain the obvious, he bowed his head slightly. "Doña Luscinda."

Señora de Cortés snapped her fan and beat the air with the thing. He pretended not to notice the woman's outrage at his failure to add señorita to his greeting, affording her daughter even greater respect.

Luscinda's expression remained inviting and seductive. Color stained her cheeks, her pupils dilating unnaturally, possibly the result of using belladonna in her eyes and on her face. The poison was supposed to enhance a woman's beauty, if it didn't kill her first.

He hardly wished her harm, wanting only to have her bother someone else. Perhaps if he simply ignored her, she'd drift away. He glanced at Sancha. She neared one of the tables, speaking to Isabella as if no one else in the room existed, not even him.

He huffed.

"Poor Sancha." Luscinda looked to where he had and inched closer to him, her fragrance heavy and cloyingly sweet. "We must understand what she goes through and pity her."

His chest tightened with indignation, fury heating his face. "What did you say?"

She stepped back, her smile faltering. "I meant no harm. Everyone feels quite badly for her. Any woman would be shamed at having lost her betrothed to a younger sister, leaving her alone and unwanted at such an advanced age. Fernando surely had his reasons for spurning her and the great wealth she could have brought to their union. However, she has no recourse now except to enter the order and remain at the convent. As soon as she returns there, of course. Perhaps she prefers such a sad fate rather than fulfilling her duty as a wife and mother as the rest of us long for."

Señora de Cortés stopped working her fan despite perspiration dotting her fleshy cheeks and stout throat. "Our women have always carried out their duty in birthing the finest heirs. Nothing has stopped them."

Not even a man's disinterest. Poor Luscinda. She might have been a nice girl if not for her greedy mamá.

"Excuse me." He turned on his heel and left before her mother suggested he offer his future to Luscinda or threatened him if he refused to comply.

Sancha sat at a long table laden with tonight's feast. Isabella stood behind her sister, motioning frantically for him to fill the empty chair next to hers.

Was there any doubt?

He reached the spot. Another man put his hand on the back of the chair to make his claim. Isabella scowled, warning him away. Good thing. Enrique was ready to push the fool aside. He offered a slight bow to Isabella, acknowledging her assistance.

She grinned.

Once seated, he warned himself to give Sancha a chance to meet him halfway. He considered clearing his throat to capture her attention or asking her to pass the olives and boiled eggs, both slightly out of his reach. Of course, the servants who stood behind the chairs were well prepared to see to every need, except what he wanted most. Her in his arms.

She wore the same fragrance he'd come to identify with her. Her delicate rose scent brought to mind soft, heated breezes, a night sky in summer, threads of moonlight piercing the velvety dark, the silvery glow glittering off countless stars.

Perhaps a simple greeting would encourage her to look at him.

Before he could open his mouth, Luscinda took the seat to his other side with her mamá directly across from them. Both women regarded him intently. No different from beasts in the wild before those animals pounced on their prey.

He ignored them and filled himself with Sancha. No one else mattered. "*Buenas noches.*"

She looked at him without pause, her expression guileless and wanting.

He smiled helplessly. Her eyes were more beautiful than he recalled, lushly lashed and expressive, the dark brown color unbearably warm. His brother had always boasted about Isabella's blue-green eyes as the most beautiful on earth.

Unique, yes, but more exquisite than Sancha's? Never.

Her cheeks grew rosy as they always did whenever he was near. If that wasn't proof of her attraction, what was?

He had much he wanted to teach her. The delights of their carnal play, the pleasure of wedding him, bearing their many children, their future filled with enough joy to last a lifetime. She only had to agree to his plan.

She inclined her head. "Buenas noches, Señor Don Enrique."

His stomach sank. Such formality when she'd already claimed his heart. She should take lessons from Luscinda, whose leg brushed his. He shifted in his seat to get away from her. She controlled herself for a moment, then slid her foot toward his. Their shoes touched.

Enough of this. He leaned toward Sancha to keep the others from hearing. "We must have a word after we eat. I insist."

Rather than acquiesce or demurely turn away, she studied him without reserve, her inner strength and resolve showing through. "Why must we?"

Expressing himself when they were alone would prove difficult enough. Doing so in front of this crowd would be impossible. He lifted one eyebrow. "The matter is not one I intend to speak of here."

Her cheeks darkened, but she didn't draw back, apologize, or try to change the subject as another woman might have. He liked her bravery in facing him even though her spirit rankled at times. Like now.

She straightened even more. "You know a chaperone has to accompany us if we speak alone."

If there were anyone else around, they would hardly be alone.

Isabella leaned down between them. "I will chaperone willingly."

Enrique had forgotten she was behind them. He gave her a hard stare, wanting her to go to her husband.

Fernando had arrived finally, thinner than he'd been before his brush with death, but his complexion matched Enrique's healthy bronze shade. They resembled each other closely, both tall with hazel eyes and dark brown hair. Only Enrique's white forelock set them apart.

Fernando waved away his guests' cheers and a servant's assistance, but he did take Isabella's arm. She led him to his chair at the head of the longest table. Rather than sitting at the other end, as custom dictated, she took the seat at his side, her full attention on her husband, father to the child she'd recently conceived.

Enrique wanted Sancha to treat him the same way and let him fill her with their babes.

After eating a bite of roasted pork, she peeked at him. A pearl of juice clung to the corner of her mouth. He longed to lick it away, then run his tongue over the seam of her lips, coaxing them to part.

"Dear Sancha." Luscinda leaned over. "How wonderful to see you out and about despite what occurred. Are you feeling all right?"

He turned to Luscinda and pulled back quickly at how close she was. "If you mean her health, as you must, she was never ill."

"Señor Don Enrique is correct." Sancha remained composed as always. "I am quite well."

Luscinda gave him a sweet smile, then looked around him and spoke to Sancha. "When do you return to the convent?"

"Tonight, surely." Señora de Cortés heaped more mutton on her plate and took the last of the white bread near them. "Prayers are important and should never be put off."

He drummed his fingers against the table. "Can she finish her meal first?"

"Of course." Luscinda grew as serious as he had. "We want her to be happy." She leaned past him again, her arm touching his, her breasts nearly falling out of her gown. "Eat, please. You have no reason to deny yourself now with your betrothal in the past. You can fatten up as widows do when they no longer have to worry about pleasing men."

Enrique shot Luscinda and her mother a warning look to say no more.

Both women kept their tongues. Once they'd stuffed their mouths with food, not words, he ate a small portion of bread and cheese, his hunger hardly for tonight's fare. He wanted what his brother had.

Fernando and Isabella held hands during their meal, sharing comments and quiet laughter, shutting out the rest of the world. Having witnessed what they'd gone through to come this far, including rogues intent on their destruction, Isabella's unfortunate deception, and a murderous uncle, Enrique was happy for them and sad for himself.

Sighing, he reached for an orange. So did Sancha. Their hands touched.

Bursts of heat raced up his arm, his skin tingling, throat constricting with desire. Before she could pull her hand from his, he folded his fingers around hers. Their softness and warmth stole his breath.

Others laughed boisterously, leaned back in their chairs, or indulged in the food and drink. She stroked his thumb.

His blood thickened with hard lust and aching tenderness. She wasn't like Luscinda and the other young women who flirted shamelessly, pursuing a man until they ran him down. A touch from her meant something.

He inclined closer to ensure no one heard them speak. "Will you join me after you sup? Please."

Meet the Author

Tina Donahue is an Amazon and international bestselling novelist in erotic, paranormal, contemporary and historical romance for Kensington, Ellora's Cave, Samhain Publishing, Siren Publishing, Decadant, Luminosity, Booktrope, and indie. Booklist, Publisher's Weekly, Romantic Times and numerous online sites have praised her work. Three of her erotic novels (Adored; Deep, Dark, Delicious; Lush Velvet Nights) were named finalists in the 2011 EPIC competition. Sensual Stranger, her erotic romance, was chosen Book of the Year 2010 (erotic category) at the French review site, Blue Moon reviews. The Golden Nib Award at Miz Love Loves Books was created specifically for her erotic romance Lush Velvet Nights. Deep, Dark, Delicious received an Award of Merit in the RWA Holt Medallion competition. Take Me Away captured second place in the NEC-RWA contest. And The Yearning was honored with an Award of Merit in the RWA Holt Medallion competition. She's featured in the 2012 Novel and Writer's Market. Before penning romances, she worked in Story Direction for a Hollywood production company. You can find her online at www.tinadonahue.com, twitter.com/tinadonahue and facebook.com/tina.donahue.75.